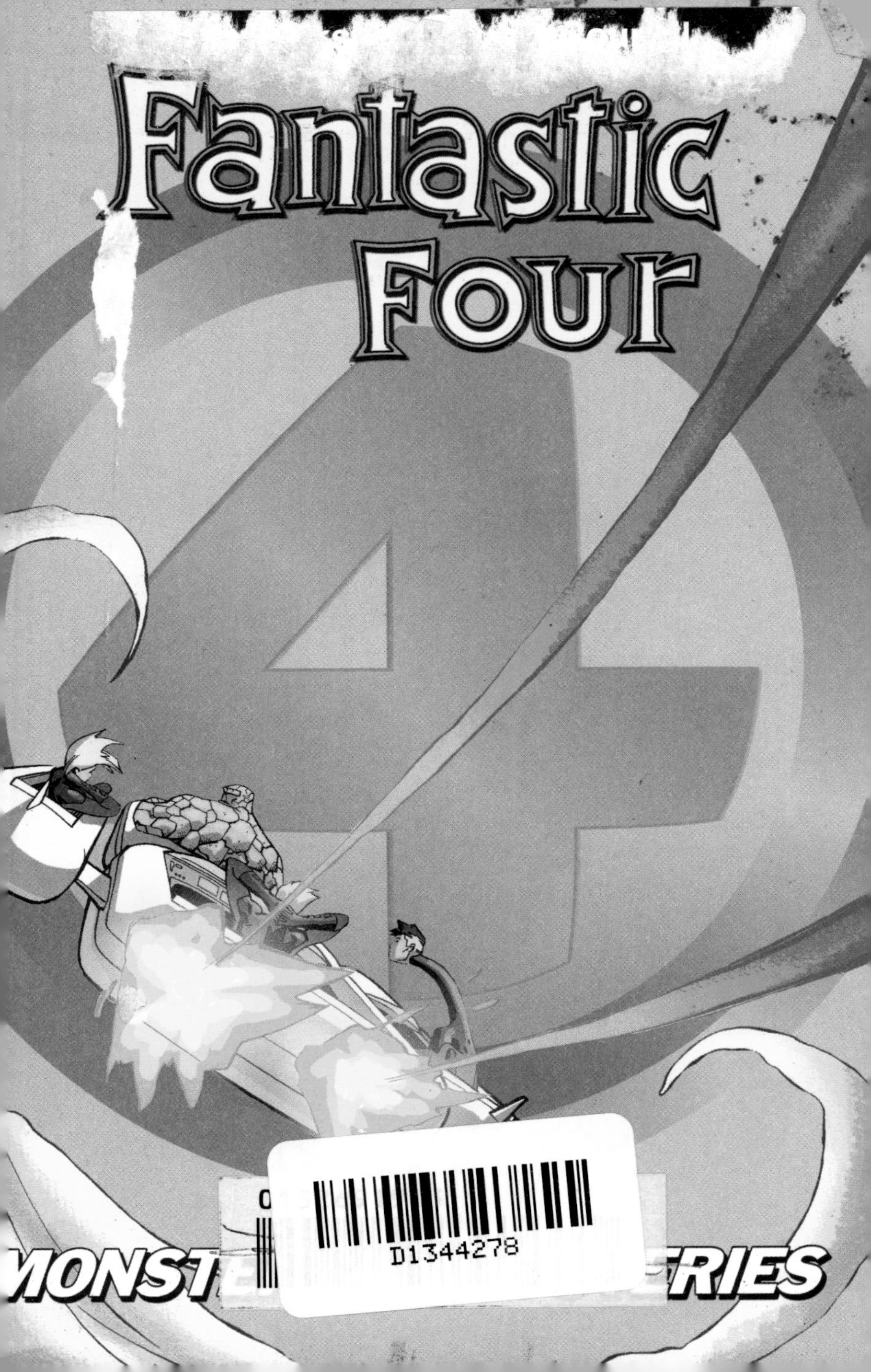
Fantastic Four

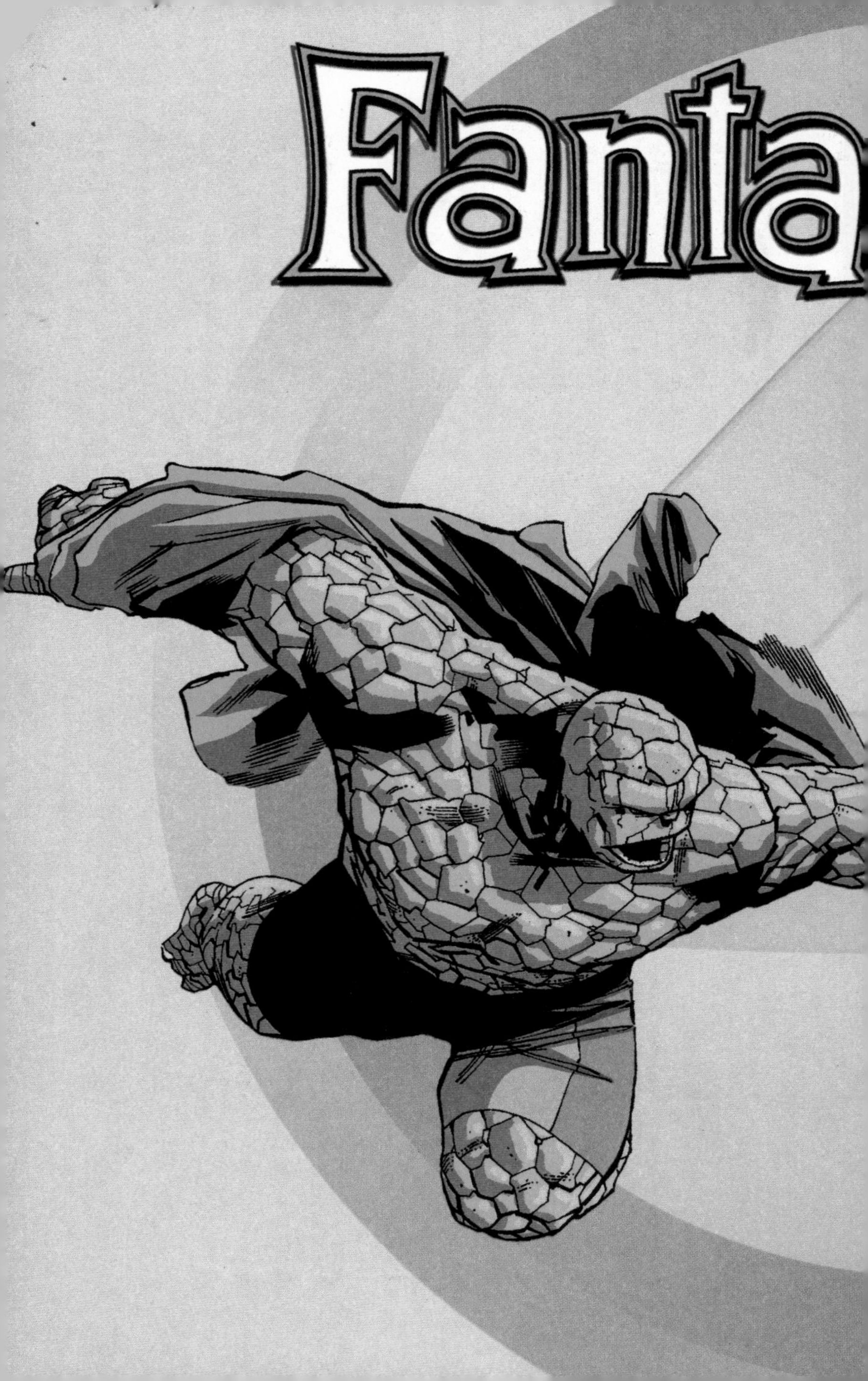
Fanta

tic Four

MONSTERS & MYSTERIES

Writer:
Fred Van Lente
Penciler:
Clay Mann
Inker:
Terry Pallot

Colorist: **Lee Loughridge**
Letterer: **Dave Sharpe**
Cover Artists: **Carlo Pagulayan,
Jeffrey Huet & Chris Sotomayor**

Assistant Editor: **Nathan Cosby**
Editor: **Mark Paniccia**

Collection Editor: **Jennifer Grünwald**
Assistant Editors: **Cory Levine & Michael Short**
Associate Editor: **Mark D. Beazley**
Senior Editor, Special Projects: **Jeff Youngquist**
Senior Vice President of Sales: **David Gabriel**
Production: **Jerron Quality Color**
Vice President of Creative: **Tom Marvelli**

Editor in Chief: **Joe Quesada**
Publisher: **Dan Buckley**

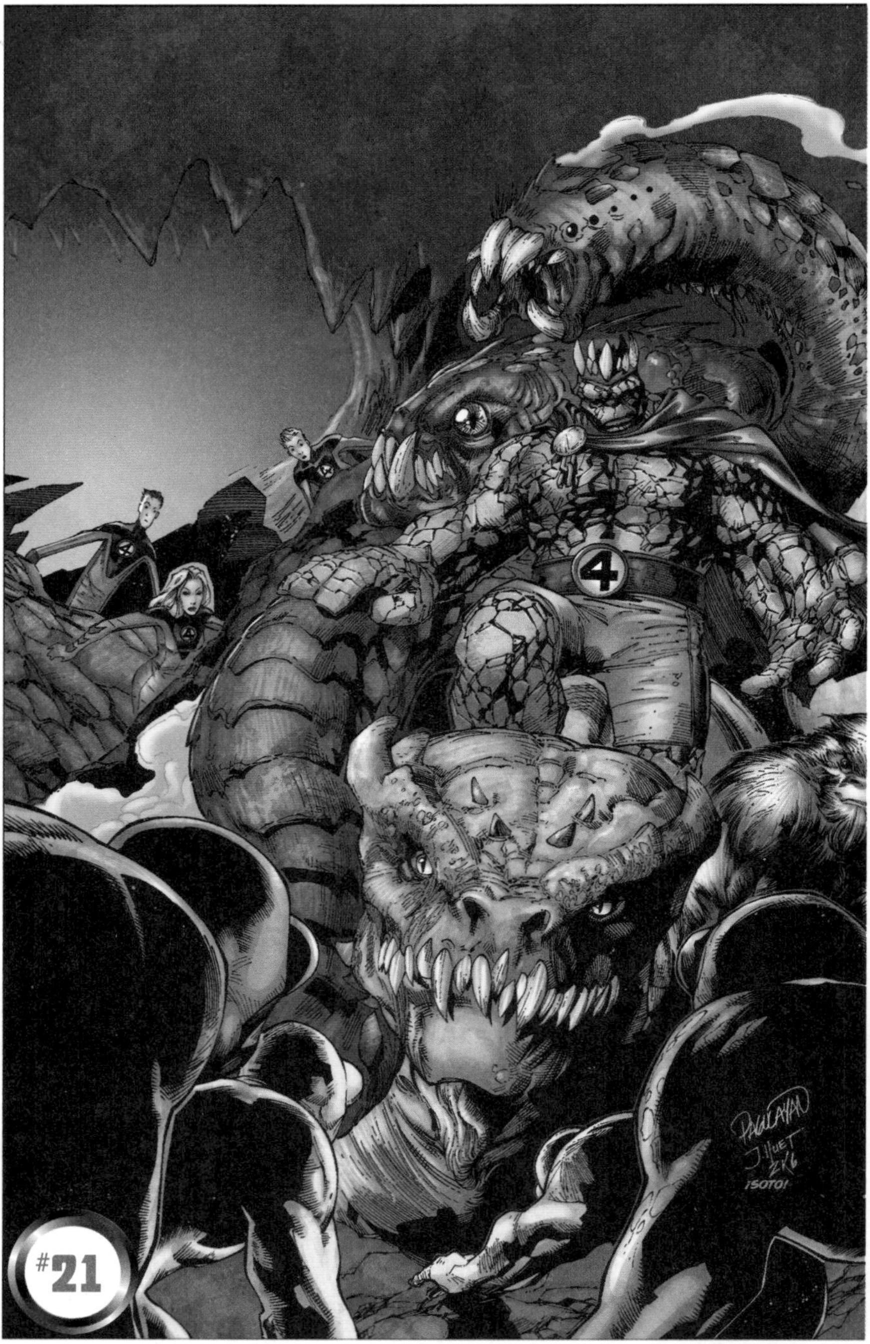
#21

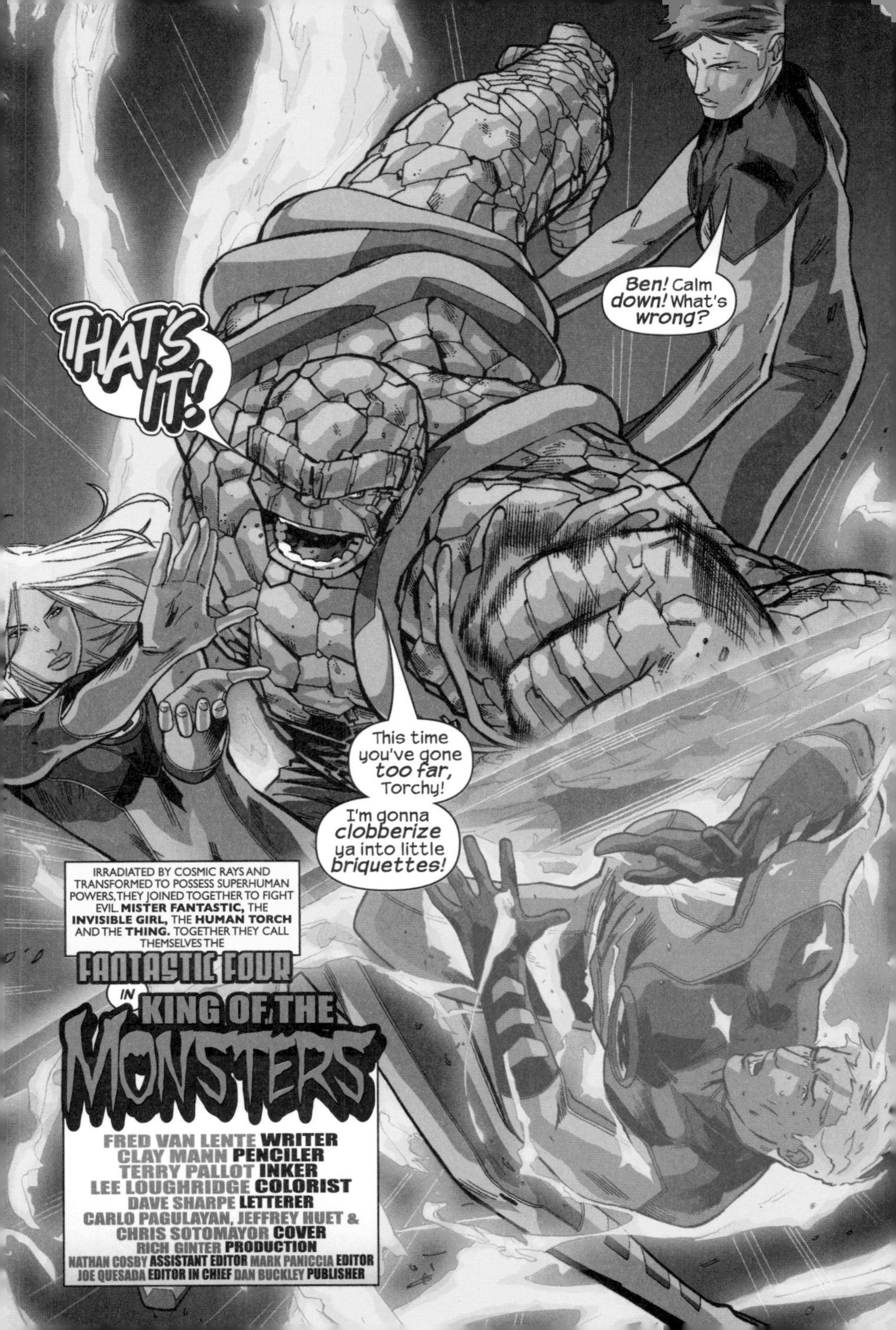
THAT'S IT!
Ben! Calm down! What's wrong?
This time you've gone too far, Torchy!
I'm gonna clobberize ya into little briquettes!
IRRADIATED BY COSMIC RAYS AND TRANSFORMED TO POSSESS SUPERHUMAN POWERS, THEY JOINED TOGETHER TO FIGHT EVIL. MISTER FANTASTIC, THE INVISIBLE GIRL, THE HUMAN TORCH AND THE THING. TOGETHER THEY CALL THEMSELVES THE
FANTASTIC FOUR
IN
KING OF THE MONSTERS
FRED VAN LENTE WRITER
CLAY MANN PENCILER
TERRY PALLOT INKER
LEE LOUGHRIDGE COLORIST
DAVE SHARPE LETTERER
CARLO PAGULAYAN, JEFFREY HUET & CHRIS SOTOMAYOR COVER
RICH GINTER PRODUCTION
NATHAN COSBY ASSISTANT EDITOR MARK PANICCIA EDITOR
JOE QUESADA EDITOR IN CHIEF DAN BUCKLEY PUBLISHER

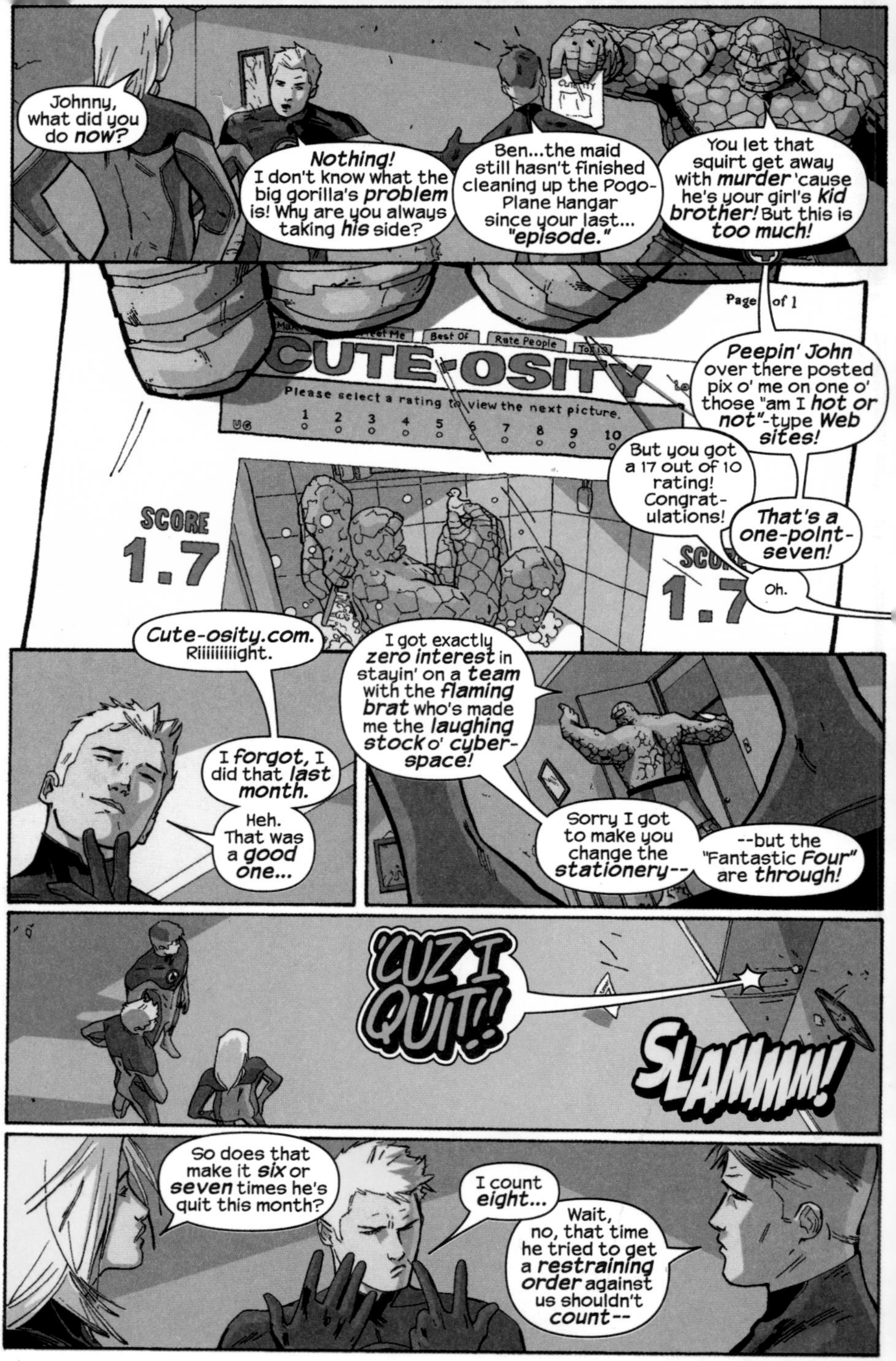
Johnny, what did you do *now?*
Nothing! I don't know what the big gorilla's *problem* is! Why are you always taking *his* side?
Ben...the maid still hasn't finished cleaning up the Pogo-Plane Hangar since your last... *"episode."*
You let that squirt get away with *murder* 'cause he's your girl's *kid brother!* But this is *too much!*
Page of 1
Best Of
Rate People
CUTE-OSITY
Please select a rating to view the next picture.
UG
1 2 3 4 5 6 7 8 9 10
SCORE
1.7
Peepin' John over there posted pix o' me on one o' those "am I *hot or not*"-type *Web sites!*
But you got a 17 out of 10 rating! Congrat-ulations!
That's a one-point-seven!
Oh.
Cute-osity.com. Riiiiiiiiight.
I *forgot,* I did that *last month.*
Heh. That was a *good one...*
I got exactly *zero interest* in stayin' on a *team* with the *flaming brat* who's made me the *laughing stock* o' *cyber-space!*
Sorry I got to make you change the *stationery--*
--but the "Fantastic *Four*" are *through!*
'CUZ I QUIT!!
SLAMMM!
So does that make it *six* or *seven* times he's quit this month?
I count *eight...*
Wait, no, that time he tried to get a *restraining order* against us shouldn't *count--*

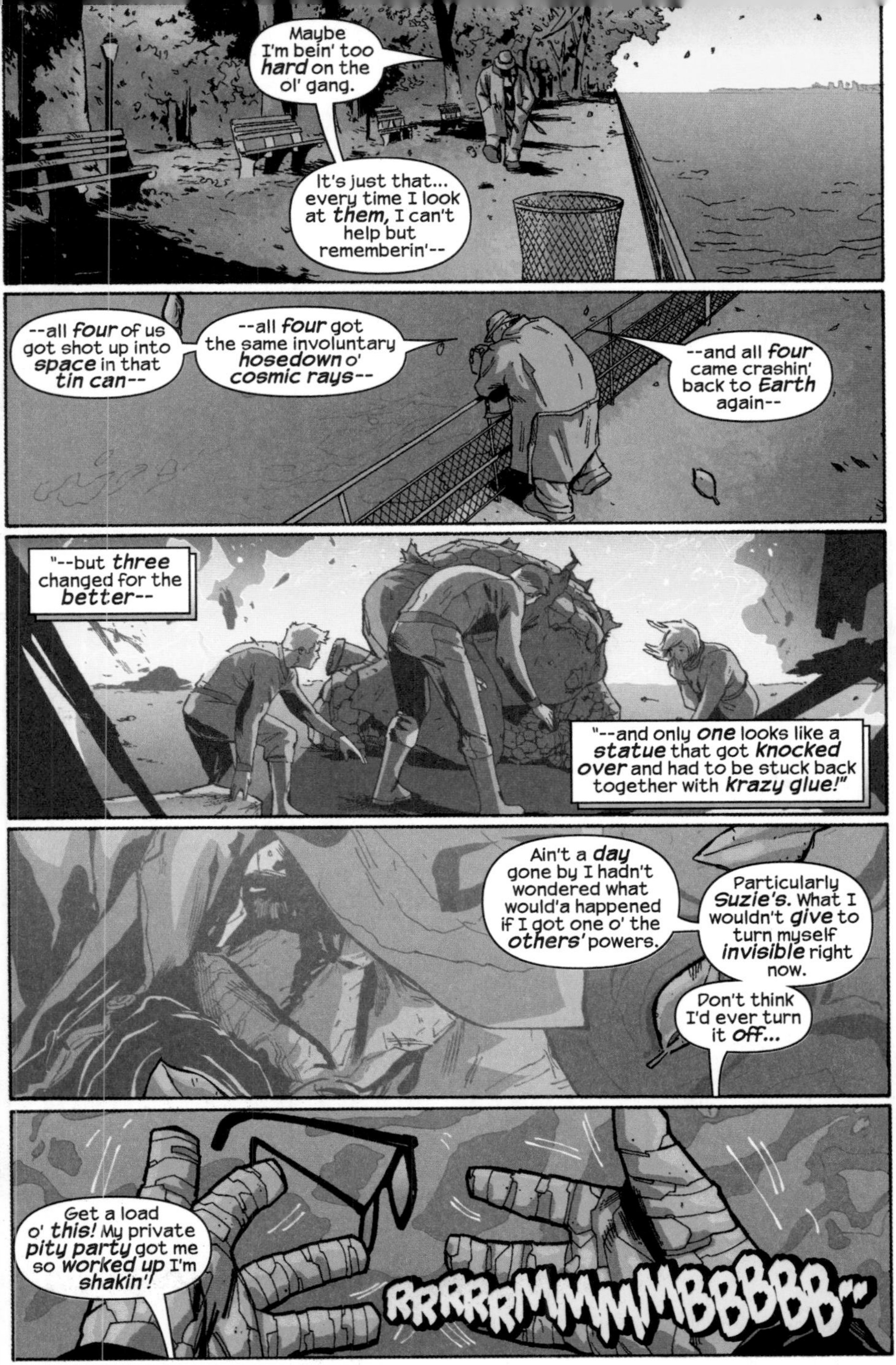
Maybe I'm bein' too hard on the ol' gang.
It's just that... every time I look at them, I can't help but rememberin'--
--all four of us got shot up into space in that tin can--
--all four got the same involuntary hosedown o' cosmic rays--
--and all four came crashin' back to Earth again--
"--but three changed for the better--
"--and only one looks like a statue that got knocked over and had to be stuck back together with krazy glue!"
Ain't a day gone by I hadn't wondered what would'a happened if I got one o' the others' powers.
Particularly Suzie's. What I wouldn't give to turn myself invisible right now.
Don't think I'd ever turn it off...
Get a load o' this! My private pity party got me so worked up I'm shakin'!
RRRRRMMMMMBBBBB--

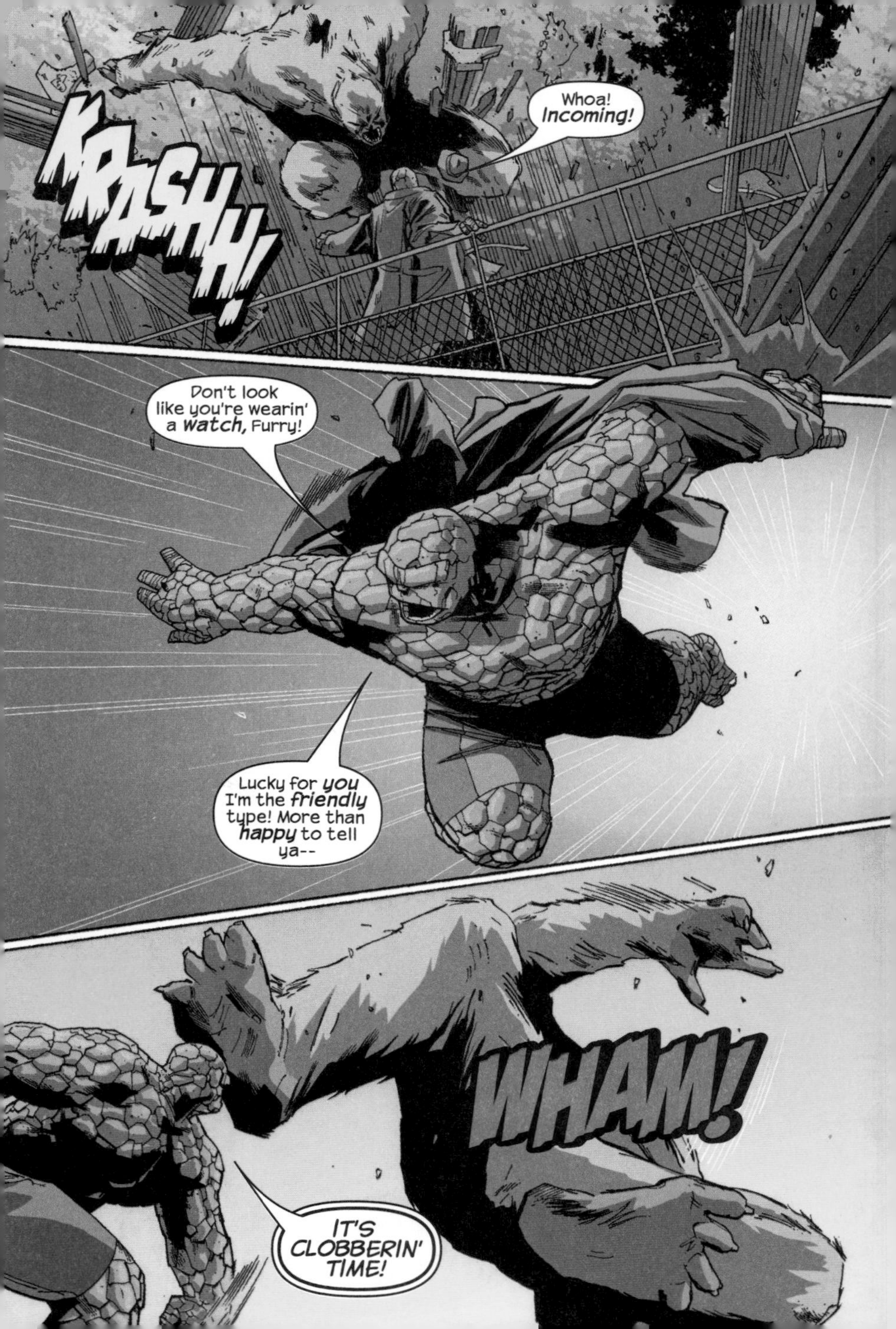
KRASHH!
Whoa! Incoming!
Don't look like you're wearin' a watch, Furry!
Lucky for you I'm the friendly type! More than happy to tell ya--
WHAM!
IT'S CLOBBERIN' TIME!

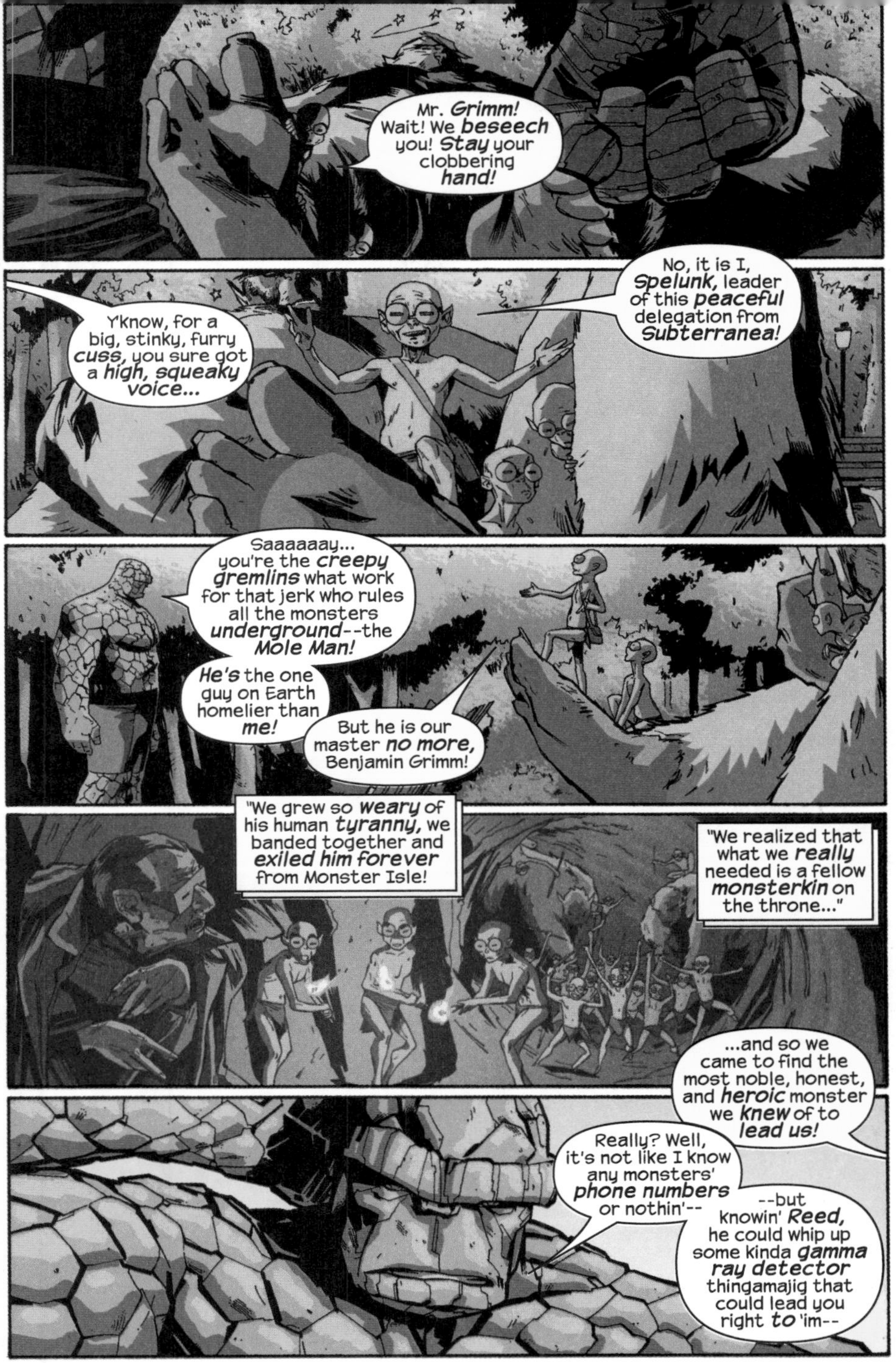
Mr. Grimm! Wait! We beseech you! Stay your clobbering hand!
Y'know, for a big, stinky, furry cuss, you sure got a high, squeaky voice...
No, it is I, Spelunk, leader of this peaceful delegation from Subterranea!
Saaaaaay... you're the creepy gremlins what work for that jerk who rules all the monsters underground--the Mole Man!
He's the one guy on Earth homelier than me!
But he is our master no more, Benjamin Grimm!
"We grew so weary of his human tyranny, we banded together and exiled him forever from Monster Isle!
"We realized that what we really needed is a fellow monsterkin on the throne..."
...and so we came to find the most noble, honest, and heroic monster we knew of to lead us!
Really? Well, it's not like I know any monsters' phone numbers or nothin'--
--but knowin' Reed, he could whip up some kinda gamma ray detector thingamajig that could lead you right to 'im--

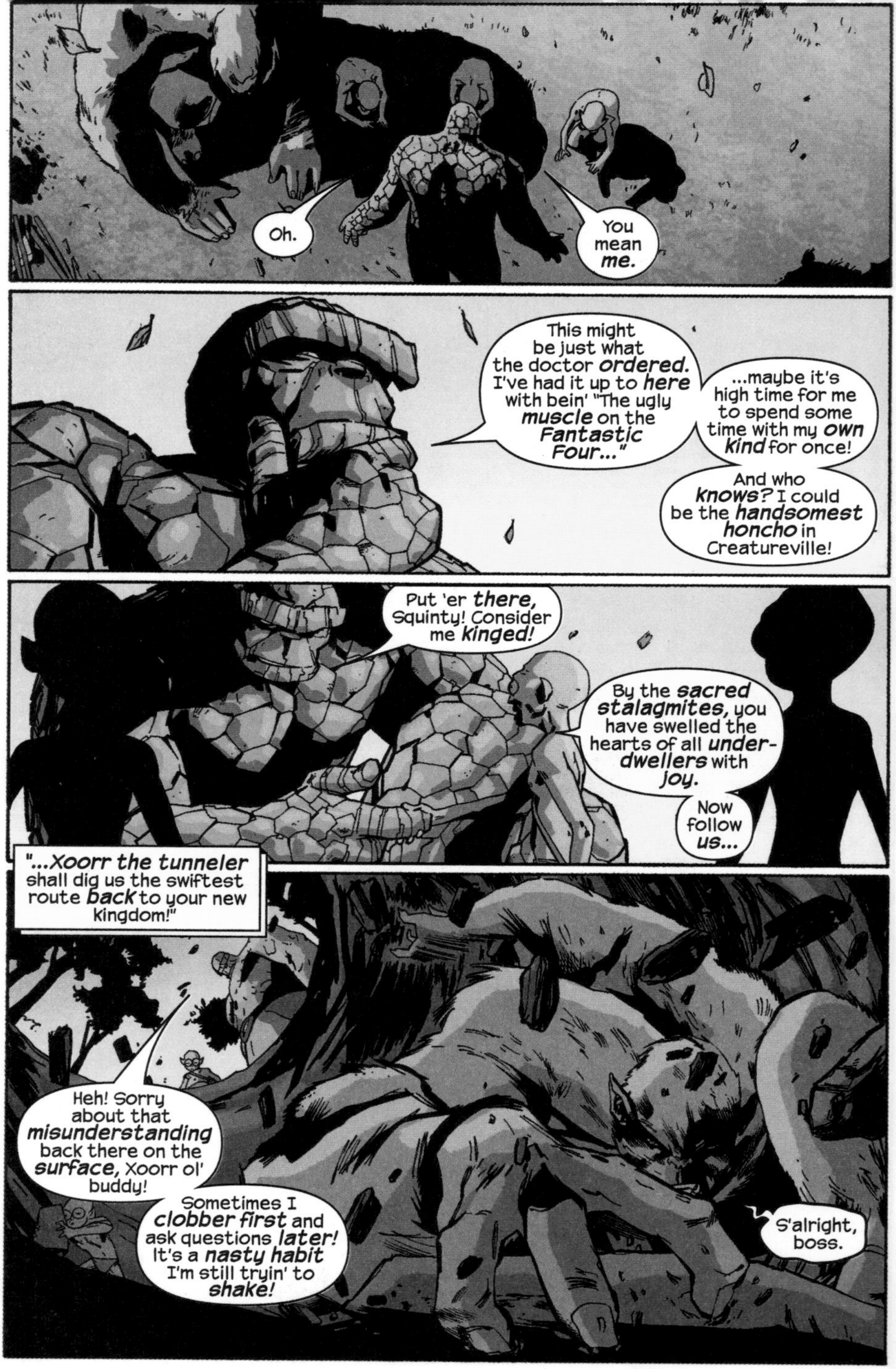

Oh.
You mean me.
This might be just what the doctor ordered. I've had it up to here with bein' "The ugly muscle on the Fantastic Four..."
...maybe it's high time for me to spend some time with my own kind for once!
And who knows? I could be the handsomest honcho in Creatureville!
Put 'er there, Squinty! Consider me kinged!
By the sacred stalagmites, you have swelled the hearts of all under-dwellers with joy.
Now follow us...
"...Xoorr the tunneler shall dig us the swiftest route back to your new kingdom!"
Heh! Sorry about that misunderstanding back there on the surface, Xoorr ol' buddy!
Sometimes I clobber first and ask questions later! It's a nasty habit I'm still tryin' to shake!
S'alright, boss.

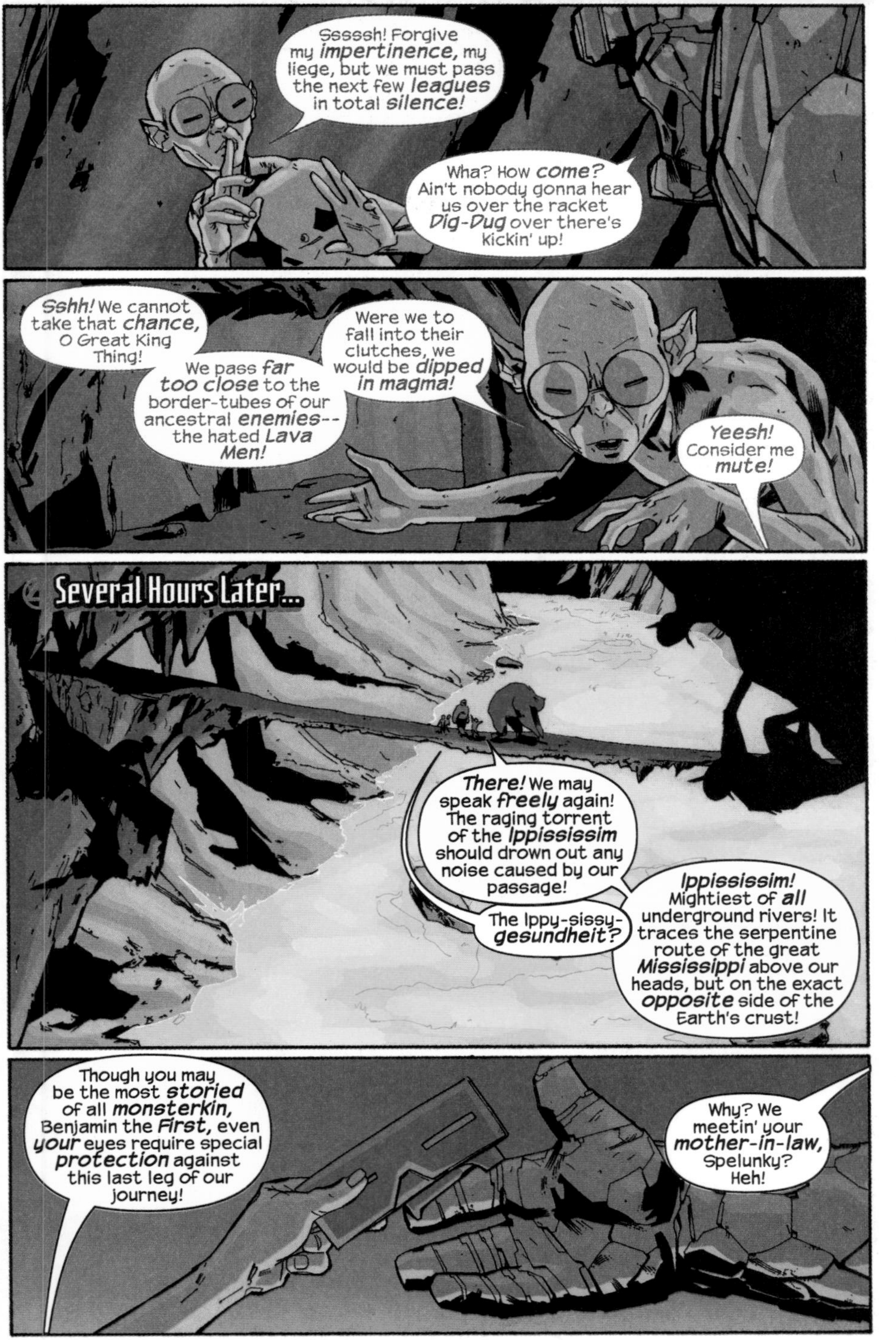
Sssssh! Forgive my impertinence, my liege, but we must pass the next few leagues in total silence!
Wha? How come? Ain't nobody gonna hear us over the racket Dig-Dug over there's kickin' up!
Sshh! We cannot take that chance, O Great King Thing!
We pass far too close to the border-tubes of our ancestral enemies-- the hated Lava Men!
Were we to fall into their clutches, we would be dipped in magma!
Yeesh! Consider me mute!
Several Hours Later...
There! We may speak freely again! The raging torrent of the Ippississim should drown out any noise caused by our passage!
The Ippy-sissy-gesundheit?
Ippississim! Mightiest of all underground rivers! It traces the serpentine route of the great Mississippi above our heads, but on the exact opposite side of the Earth's crust!
Though you may be the most storied of all monsterkin, Benjamin the First, even your eyes require special protection against this last leg of our journey!
Why? We meetin' your mother-in-law, Spelunky? Heh!

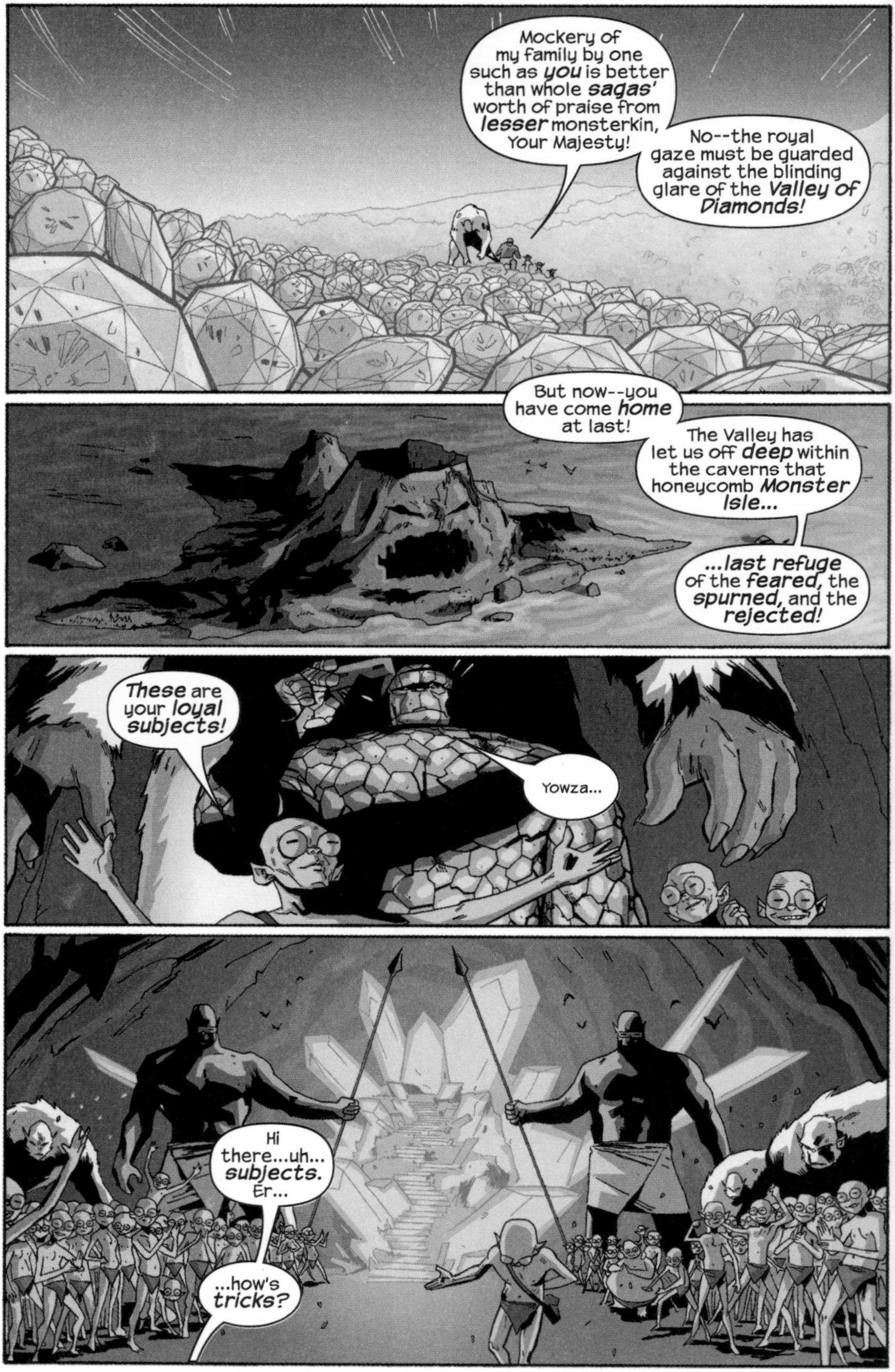
Mockery of my family by one such as *you* is better than whole *sagas'* worth of praise from *lesser* monsterkin, Your Majesty!
No--the royal gaze must be guarded against the blinding glare of the *Valley of Diamonds!*
But now--you have come *home* at last!
The Valley has let us off *deep* within the caverns that honeycomb *Monster Isle...*
...last refuge of the *feared,* the *spurned,* and the *rejected!*
These are your *loyal subjects!*
Yowza...
Hi there...uh... *subjects.* Er...
...how's *tricks?*

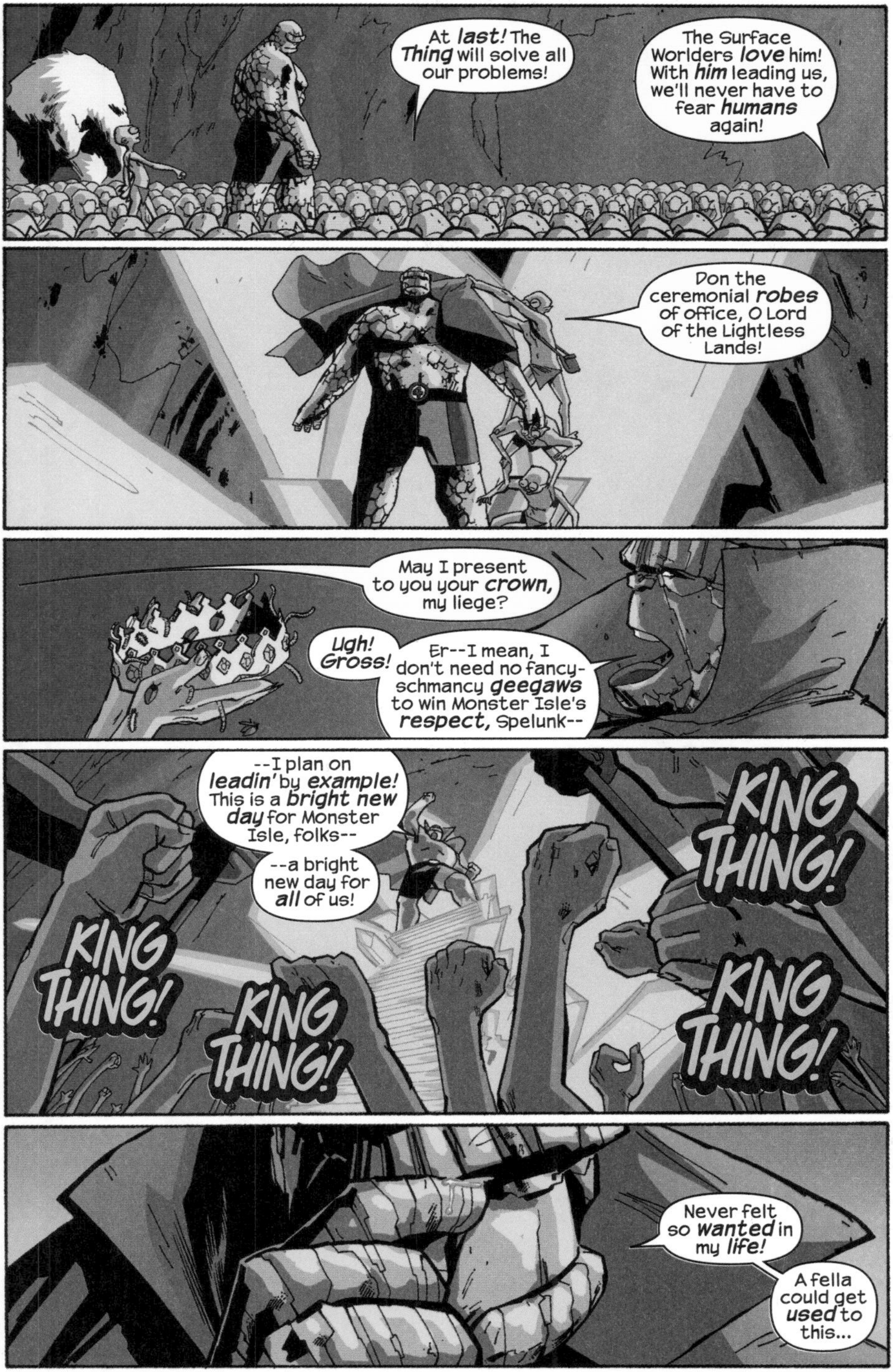
At last! The Thing will solve all our problems!
The Surface Worlders love him! With him leading us, we'll never have to fear humans again!
Don the ceremonial robes of office, O Lord of the Lightless Lands!
May I present to you your crown, my liege?
Ugh! Gross!
Er--I mean, I don't need no fancy-schmancy geegaws to win Monster Isle's respect, Spelunk--
--I plan on leadin' by example! This is a bright new day for Monster Isle, folks--
--a bright new day for all of us!
KING THING!
KING THING!
KING THING!
KING THING!
Never felt so wanted in my life!
A fella could get used to this...

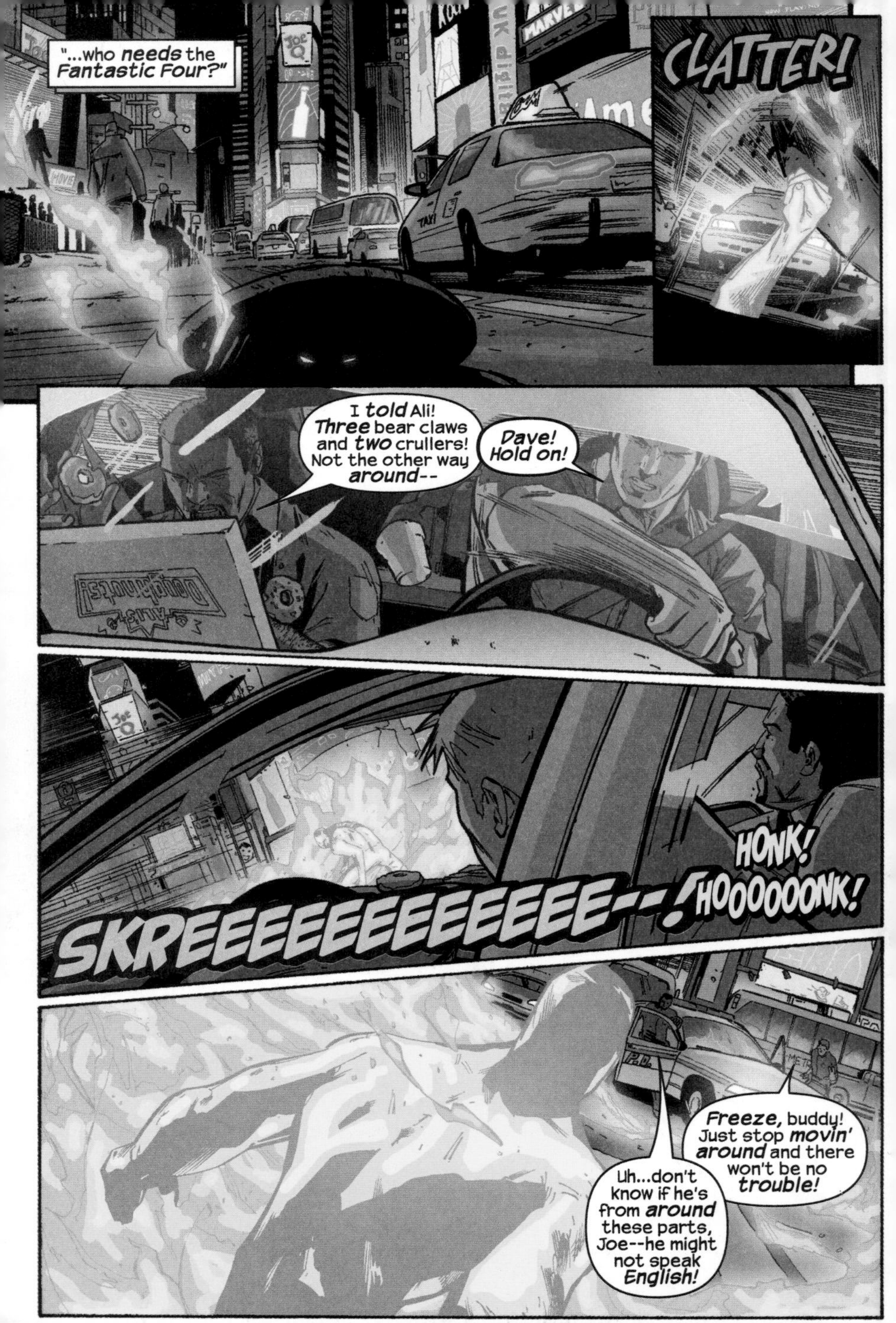
"...who needs the Fantastic Four?"
CLATTER!
I told Ali! Three bear claws and two crullers! Not the other way around--
Dave! Hold on!
HONK!
SKREEEEEEEEEEEEEE--!
HOOOOOONK!
Freeze, buddy! Just stop movin' around and there won't be no trouble!
Uh...don't know if he's from around these parts, Joe--he might not speak English!

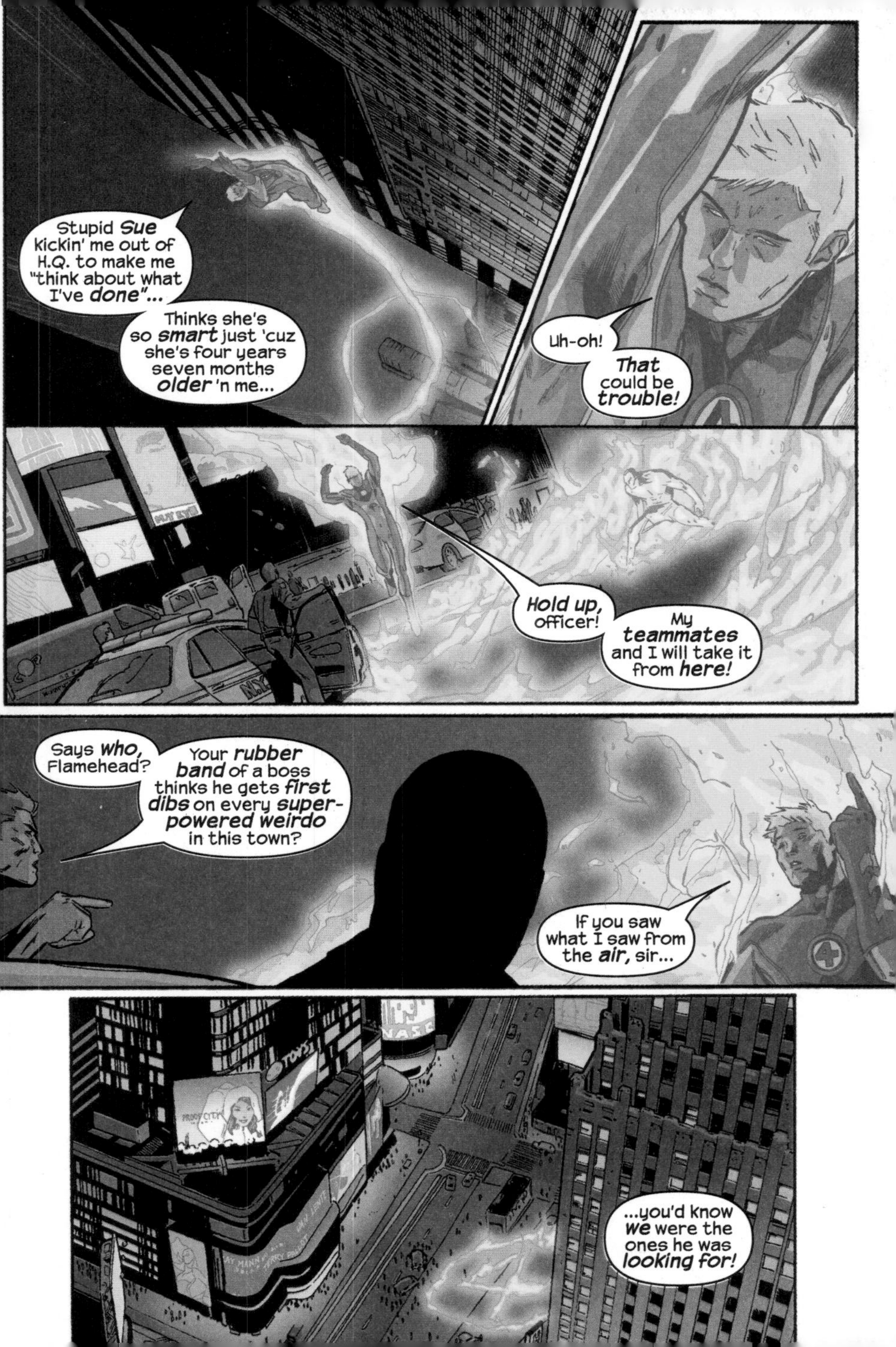
Stupid Sue kickin' me out of H.Q. to make me "think about what I've done"...
Thinks she's so smart just 'cuz she's four years seven months older 'n me...
Uh-oh! That could be trouble!
Hold up, officer!
My teammates and I will take it from here!
Says who, Flamehead?
Your rubber band of a boss thinks he gets first dibs on every super-powered weirdo in this town?
If you saw what I saw from the air, sir...
...you'd know we were the ones he was looking for!

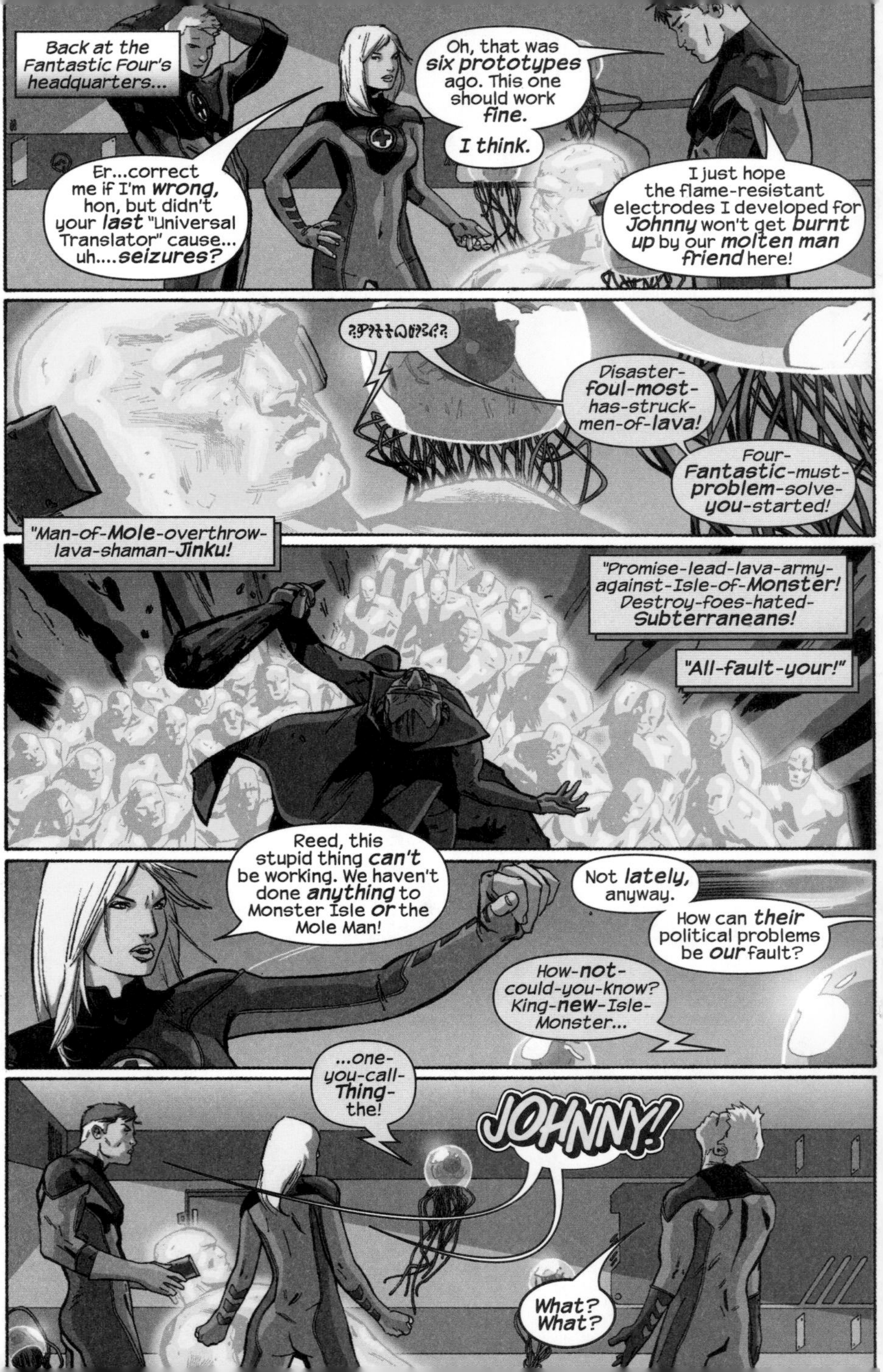
Back at the Fantastic Four's headquarters...
Oh, that was six prototypes ago. This one should work fine.
I think.
Er...correct me if I'm wrong, hon, but didn't your last "Universal Translator" cause... uh....seizures?
I just hope the flame-resistant electrodes I developed for Johnny won't get burnt up by our molten man friend here!
Disaster-foul-most-has-struck-men-of-lava!
Four-Fantastic-must-problem-solve-you-started!
"Man-of-Mole-overthrow-lava-shaman-Jinku!
"Promise-lead-lava-army-against-Isle-of-Monster! Destroy-foes-hated-Subterraneans!
"All-fault-your!"
Reed, this stupid thing can't be working. We haven't done anything to Monster Isle or the Mole Man!
Not lately, anyway.
How can their political problems be our fault?
How-not-could-you-know? King-new-Isle-Monster...
...one-you-call-Thing-the!
JOHNNY!
What? What?

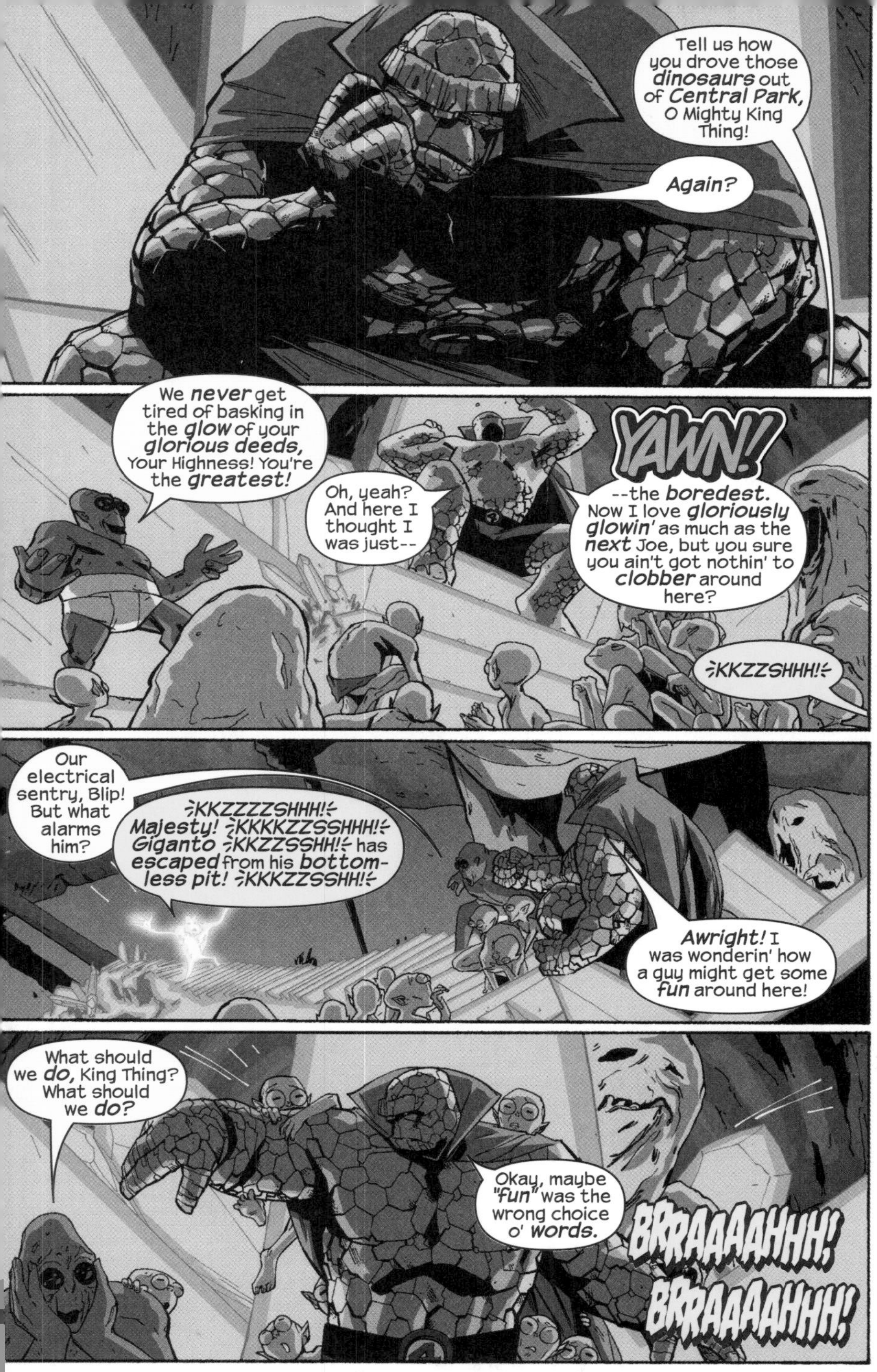
Tell us how you drove those dinosaurs out of Central Park, O Mighty King Thing!
Again?
We never get tired of basking in the glow of your glorious deeds, Your Highness! You're the greatest!
Oh, yeah? And here I thought I was just--
YAWN!
--the boredest. Now I love gloriously glowin' as much as the next Joe, but you sure you ain't got nothin' to clobber around here?
KKZZSHHH!
Our electrical sentry, Blip! But what alarms him?
KKZZZZSHHH! Majesty! KKKKZZSSHHH! Giganto KKZZSSHH! has escaped from his bottomless pit! KKKZZSSHH!
Awright! I was wonderin' how a guy might get some fun around here!
What should we do, King Thing? What should we do?
Okay, maybe "fun" was the wrong choice o' words.
BRRAAAAHHH!
BRRAAAAHHH!

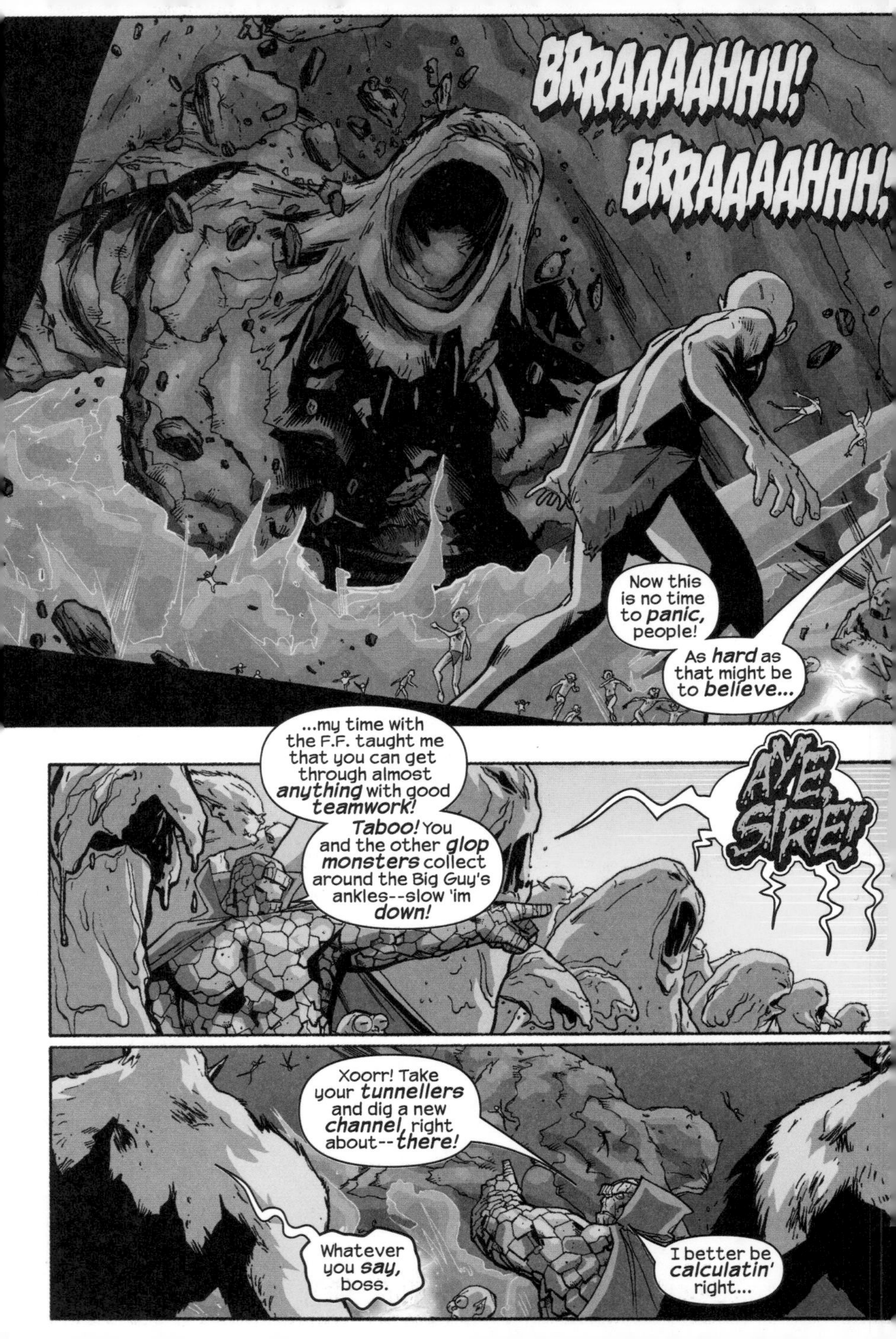
BRRAAAAHHH!
BRRAAAAHHH!
Now this is no time to panic, people!
As hard as that might be to believe...
...my time with the F.F. taught me that you can get through almost anything with good teamwork!
Taboo! You and the other glop monsters collect around the Big Guy's ankles--slow 'im down!
AYE, SIRE!
Xoorr! Take your tunnellers and dig a new channel, right about--there!
Whatever you say, boss.
I better be calculatin' right...

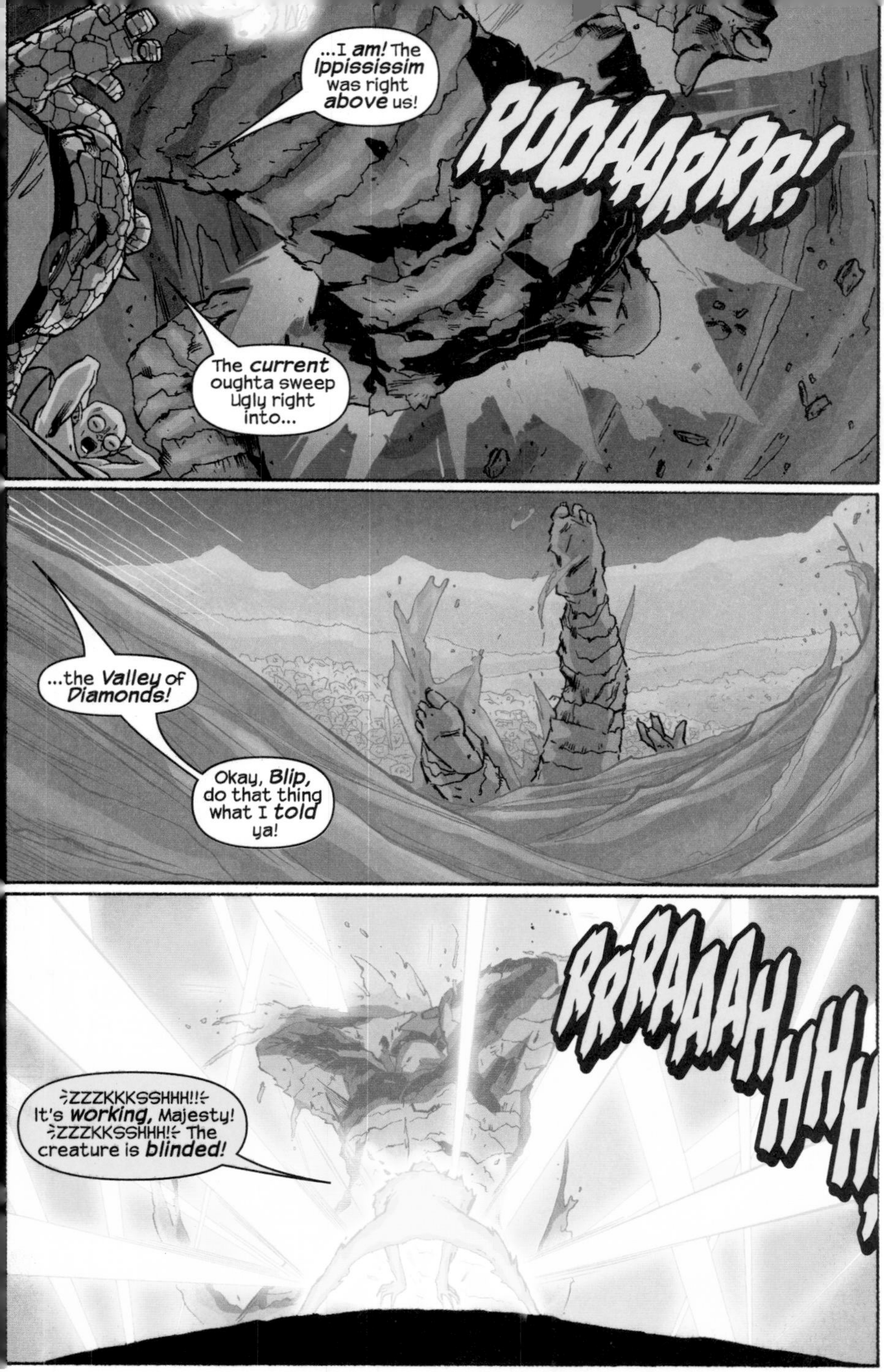
...I am! The Ippississim was right above us!
ROOAARRR!
The current oughta sweep ugly right into...
...the Valley of Diamonds!
Okay, Blip, do that thing what I told ya!
RRRAAAHHHH!
ZZZKKKSSHHH!!! It's working, Majesty! ZZZKKSSHHH! The creature is blinded!

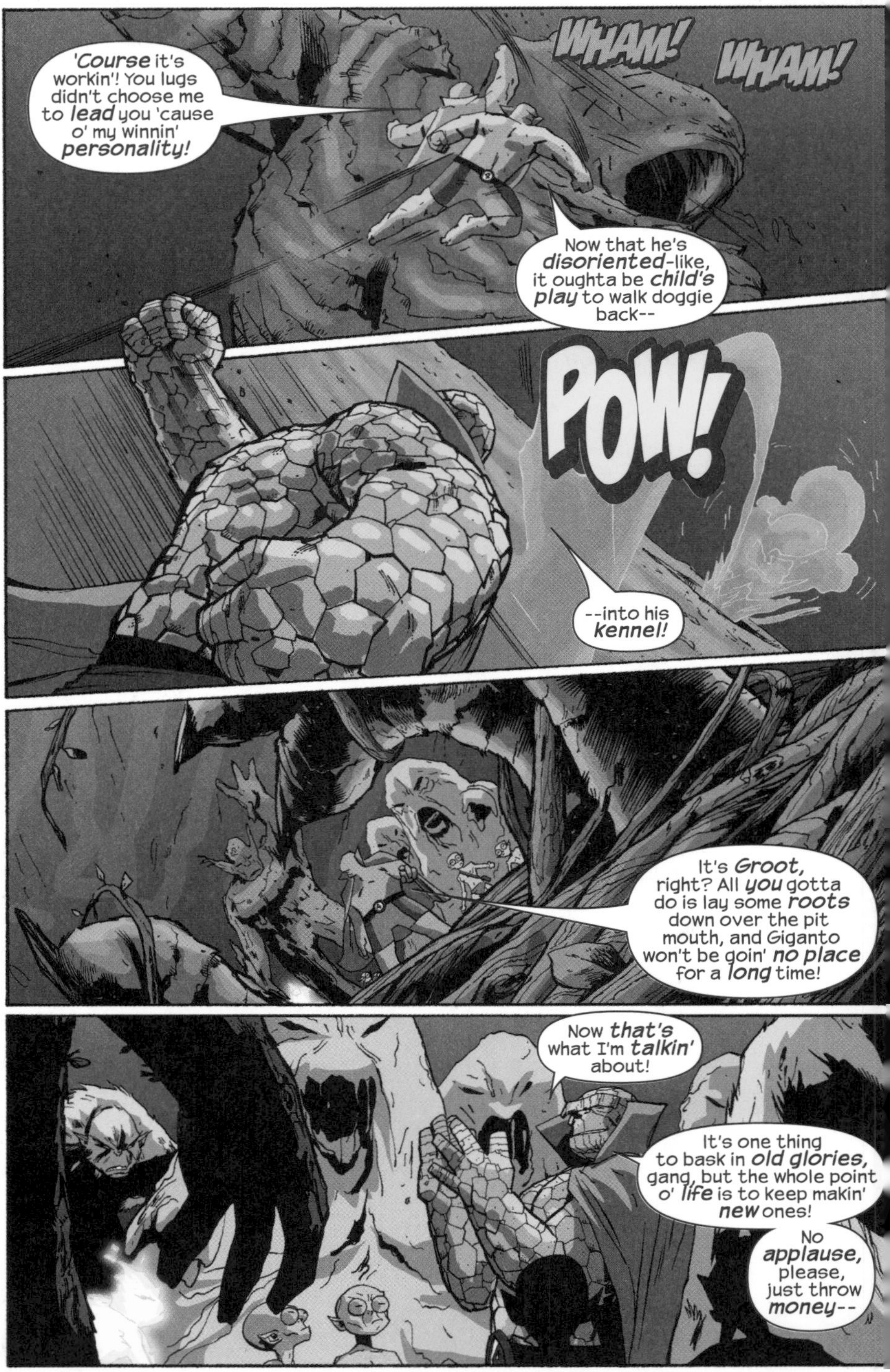

WHAM!
WHAM!
'Course it's workin'! You lugs didn't choose me to lead you 'cause o' my winnin' personality!
Now that he's disoriented-like, it oughta be child's play to walk doggie back--
POW!
--into his kennel!
It's Groot, right? All you gotta do is lay some roots down over the pit mouth, and Giganto won't be goin' no place for a long time!
Now that's what I'm talkin' about!
It's one thing to bask in old glories, gang, but the whole point o' life is to keep makin' new ones!
No applause, please, just throw money--

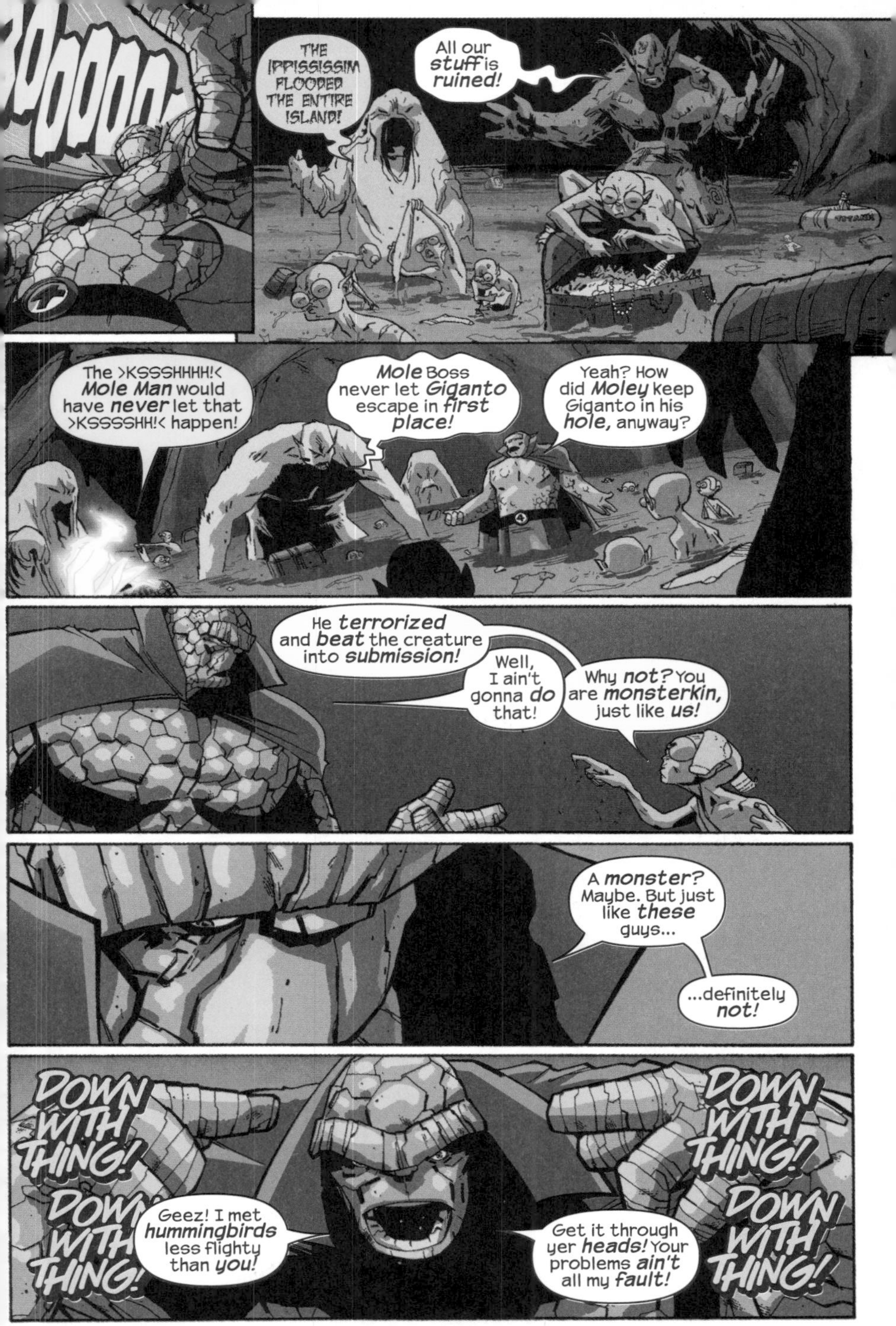
THE IPPISSISSIM FLOODED THE ENTIRE ISLAND!
All our stuff is ruined!
The >KSSSHHH!< Mole Man would have never let that >KSSSSHH!< happen!
Mole Boss never let Giganto escape in first place!
Yeah? How did Moley keep Giganto in his hole, anyway?
He terrorized and beat the creature into submission!
Well, I ain't gonna do that!
Why not? You are monsterkin, just like us!
A monster? Maybe. But just like these guys...
...definitely not!
DOWN WITH THING!
DOWN WITH THING!
DOWN WITH THING!
DOWN WITH THING!
Geez! I met hummingbirds less flighty than you!
Get it through yer heads! Your problems ain't all my fault!

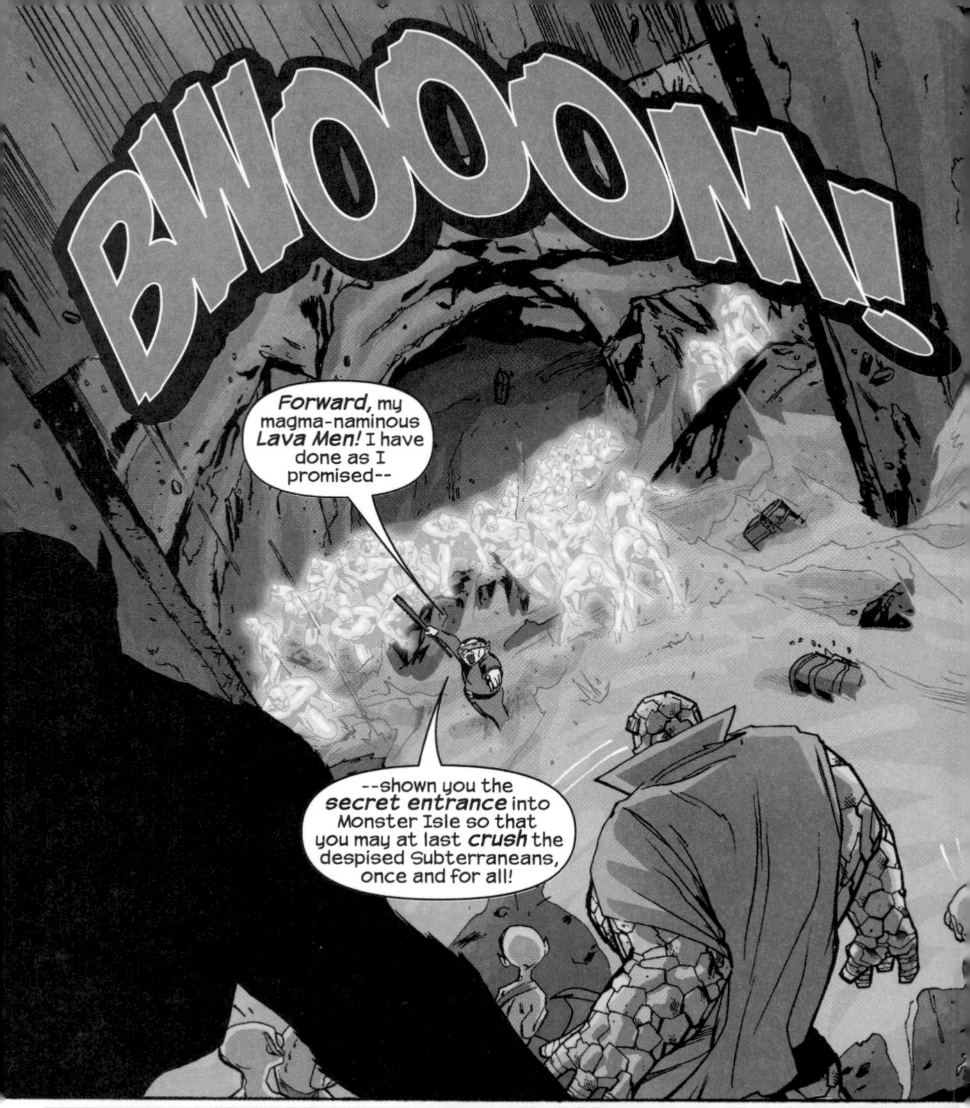
BWOOOM!!
Forward, my magma-naminous Lava Men! I have done as I promised--
--shown you the secret entrance into Monster Isle so that you may at last crush the despised Subterraneans, once and for all!

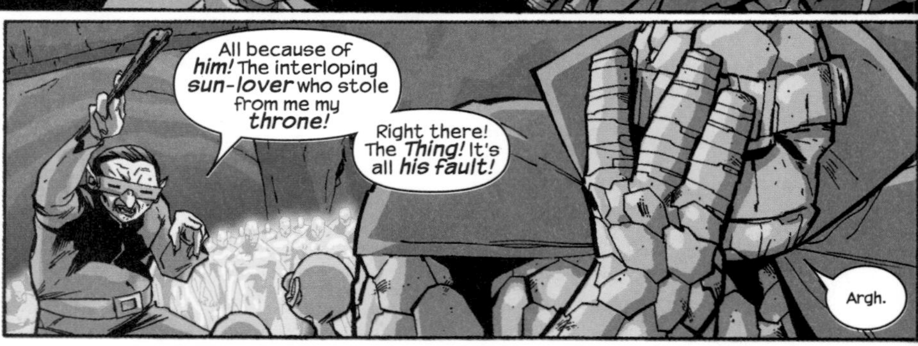
All because of him! The interloping sun-lover who stole from me my throne!
Right there! The Thing! It's all his fault!
Argh.

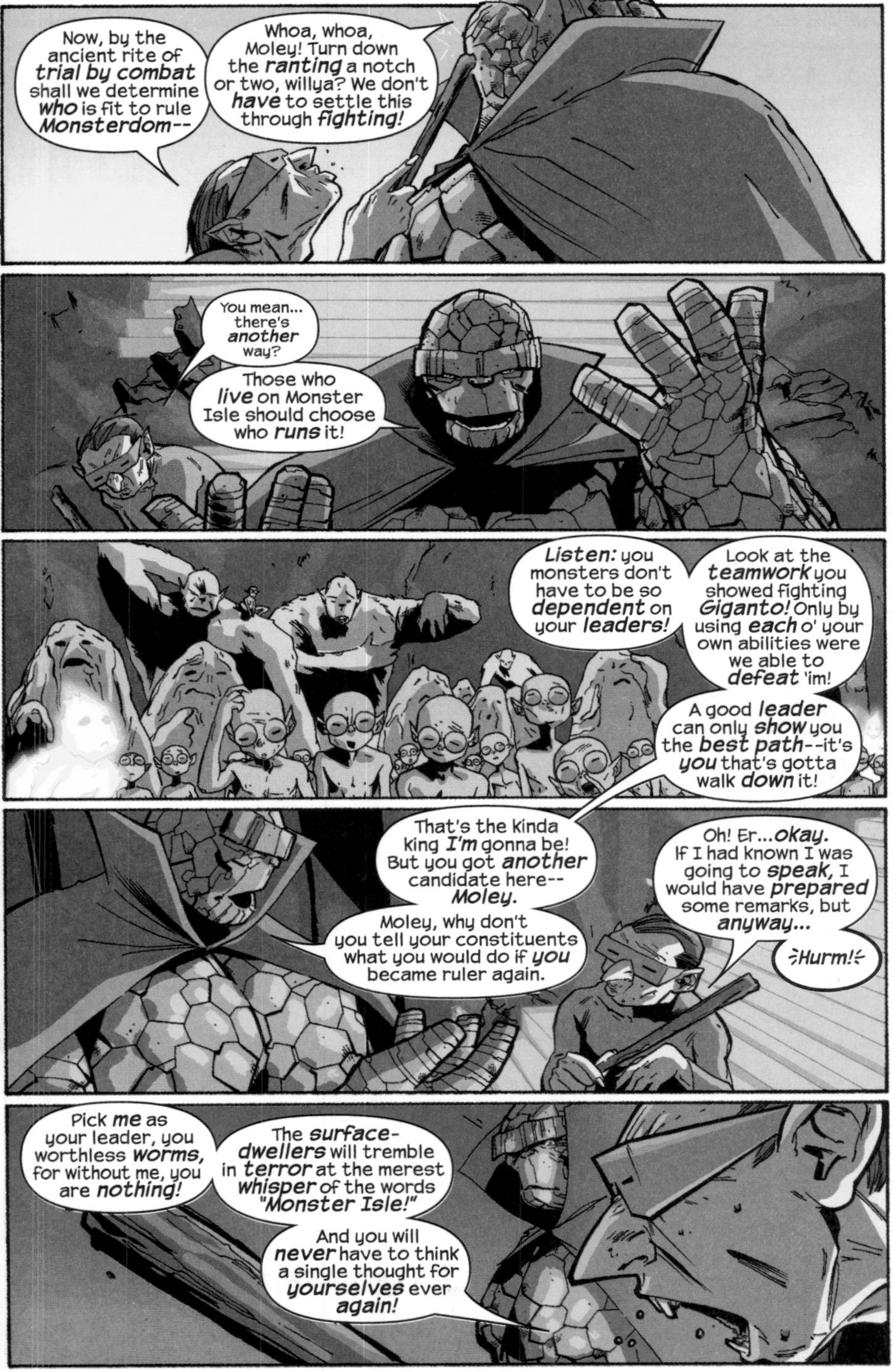

Now, by the ancient rite of trial by combat shall we determine who is fit to rule Monsterdom--
Whoa, whoa, Moley! Turn down the ranting a notch or two, willya? We don't have to settle this through fighting!
You mean... there's another way?
Those who live on Monster Isle should choose who runs it!
Listen: you monsters don't have to be so dependent on your leaders!
Look at the teamwork you showed fighting Giganto! Only by using each o' your own abilities were we able to defeat 'im!
A good leader can only show you the best path--it's you that's gotta walk down it!
That's the kinda king I'm gonna be! But you got another candidate here-- Moley.
Moley, why don't you tell your constituents what you would do if you became ruler again.
Oh! Er...okay. If I had known I was going to speak, I would have prepared some remarks, but anyway...
Hurm!
Pick me as your leader, you worthless worms, for without me, you are nothing!
The surface-dwellers will tremble in terror at the merest whisper of the words "Monster Isle!"
And you will never have to think a single thought for yourselves ever again!

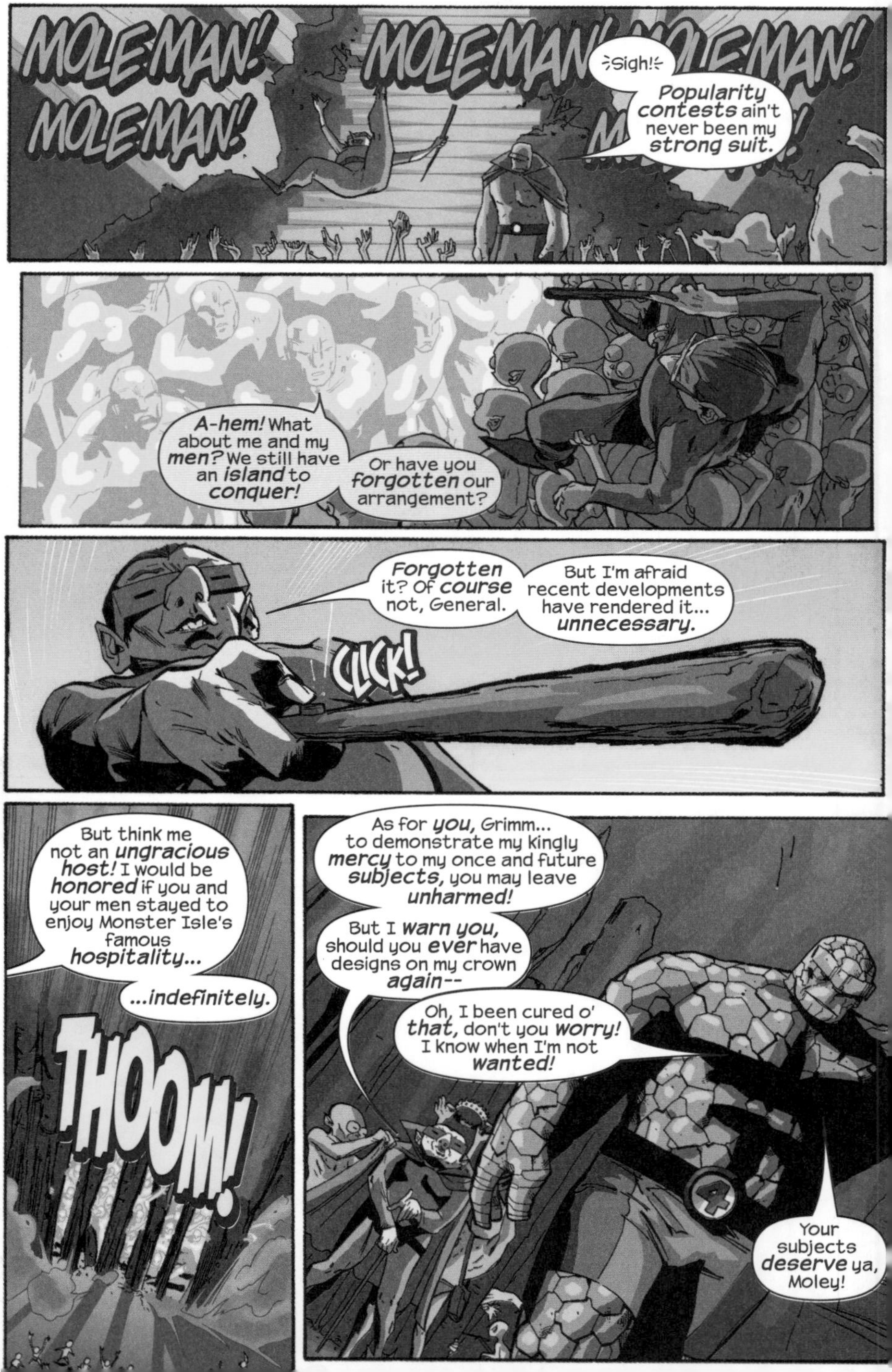
MOLE MAN! MOLE MAN!
MOLE MAN! MOLE MAN! MOLE MAN!
Sigh!
Popularity contests ain't never been my strong suit.
A-hem! What about me and my men? We still have an island to conquer!
Or have you forgotten our arrangement?
Forgotten it? Of course not, General.
But I'm afraid recent developments have rendered it... unnecessary.
CLICK!
But think me not an ungracious host! I would be honored if you and your men stayed to enjoy Monster Isle's famous hospitality...
...indefinitely.
THOOM!
As for you, Grimm... to demonstrate my kingly mercy to my once and future subjects, you may leave unharmed!
But I warn you, should you ever have designs on my crown again--
Oh, I been cured o' that, don't you worry! I know when I'm not wanted!
Your subjects deserve ya, Moley!

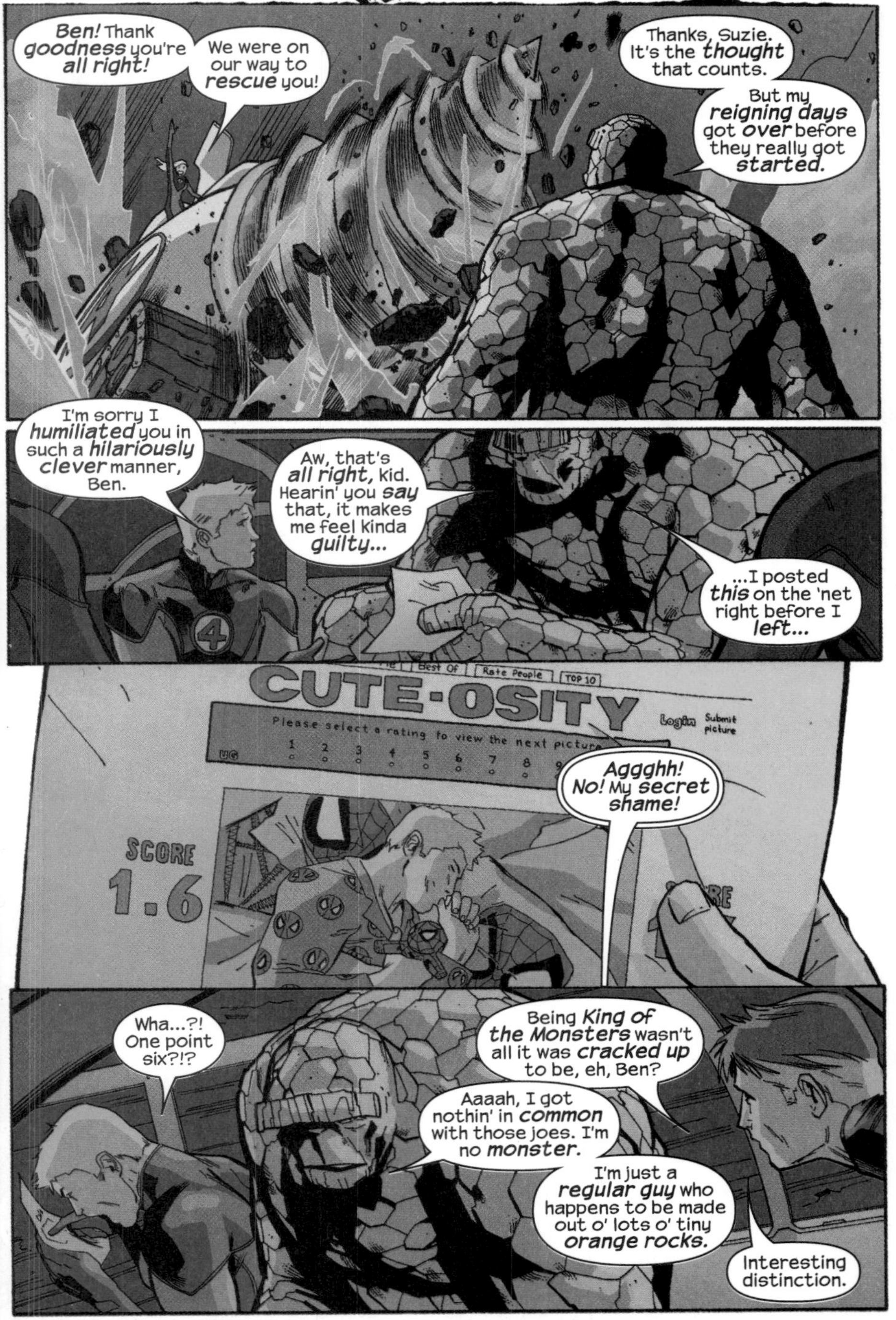

Ben! Thank goodness you're all right!
We were on our way to rescue you!
Thanks, Suzie. It's the thought that counts.
But my reigning days got over before they really got started.
I'm sorry I humiliated you in such a hilariously clever manner, Ben.
Aw, that's all right, kid. Hearin' you say that, it makes me feel kinda guilty...
...I posted this on the 'net right before I left...
Best Of
Rate People
TOP 10
CUTE-OSITY
Login
Submit picture
Please select a rating to view the next picture
UG
1
2
3
4
5
6
7
8
SCORE
1.6
Aggghh! No! My secret shame!
Wha...?! One point six?!?
Being King of the Monsters wasn't all it was cracked up to be, eh, Ben?
Aaaah, I got nothin' in common with those joes. I'm no monster.
I'm just a regular guy who happens to be made out o' lots o' tiny orange rocks.
Interesting distinction.

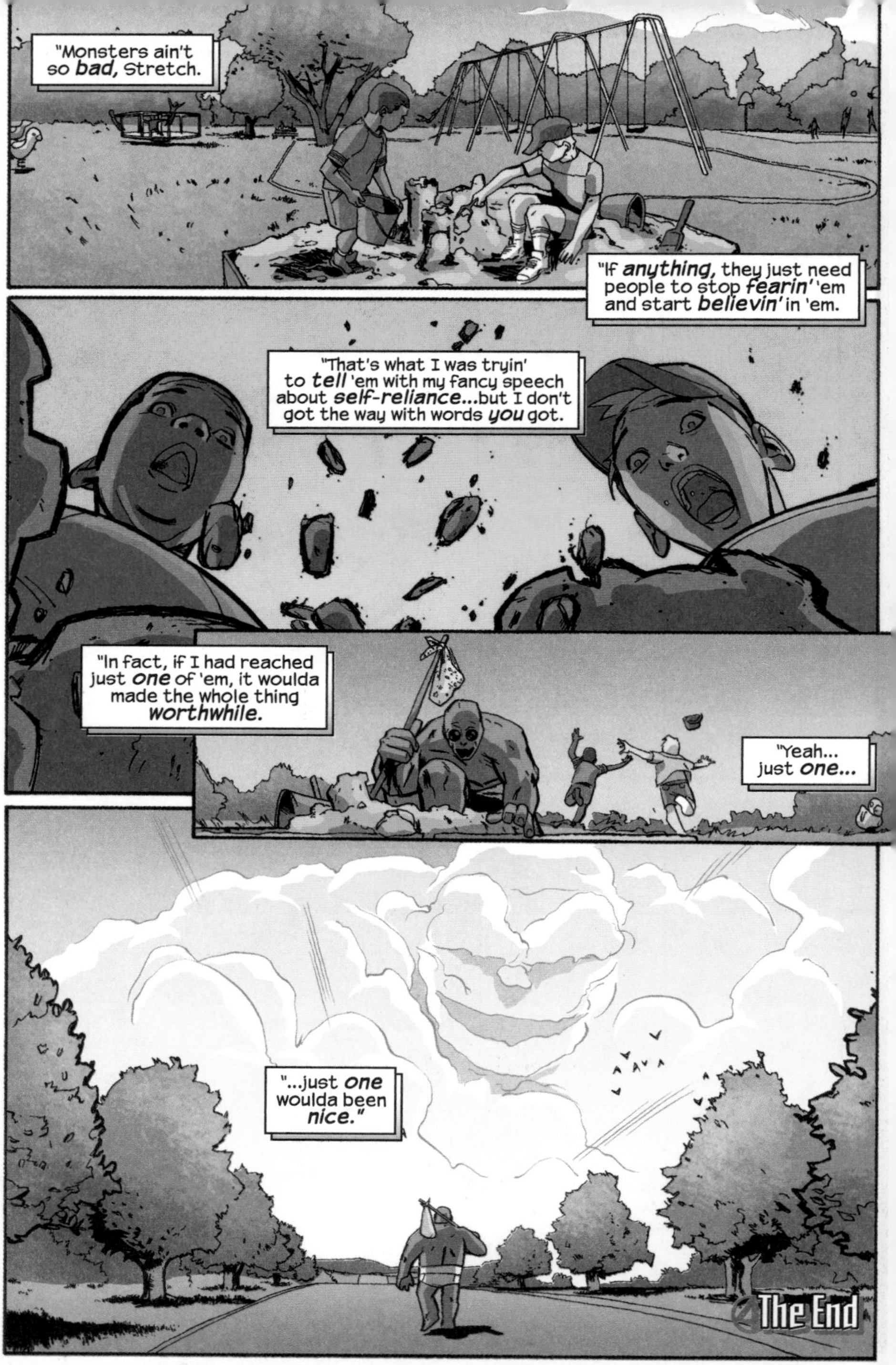
"Monsters ain't so bad, Stretch.
"If anything, they just need people to stop fearin' 'em and start believin' in 'em.
"That's what I was tryin' to tell 'em with my fancy speech about self-reliance...but I don't got the way with words you got.
"In fact, if I had reached just one of 'em, it woulda made the whole thing worthwhile.
"Yeah... just one...
"...just one woulda been nice."
The End

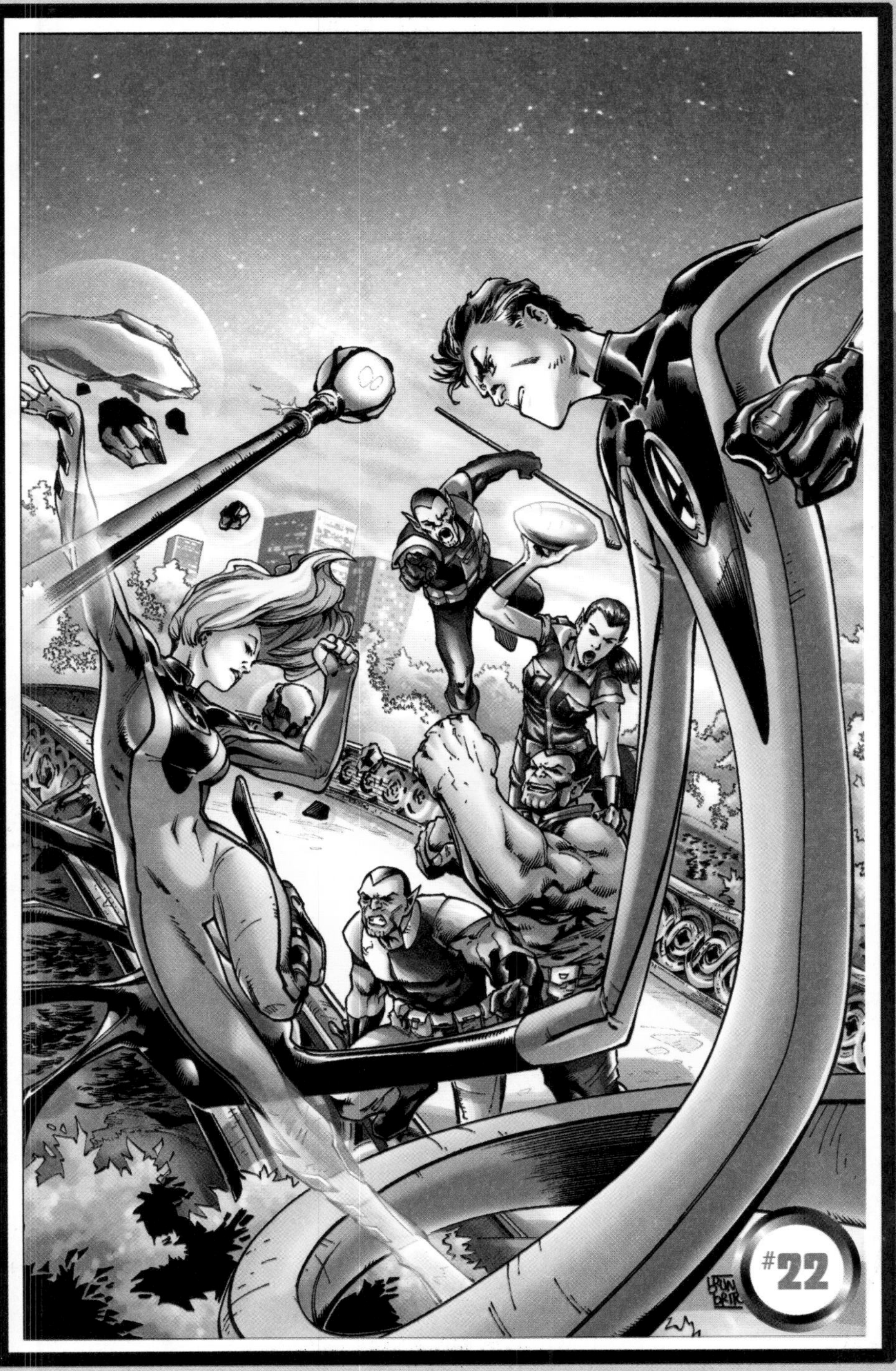
#22

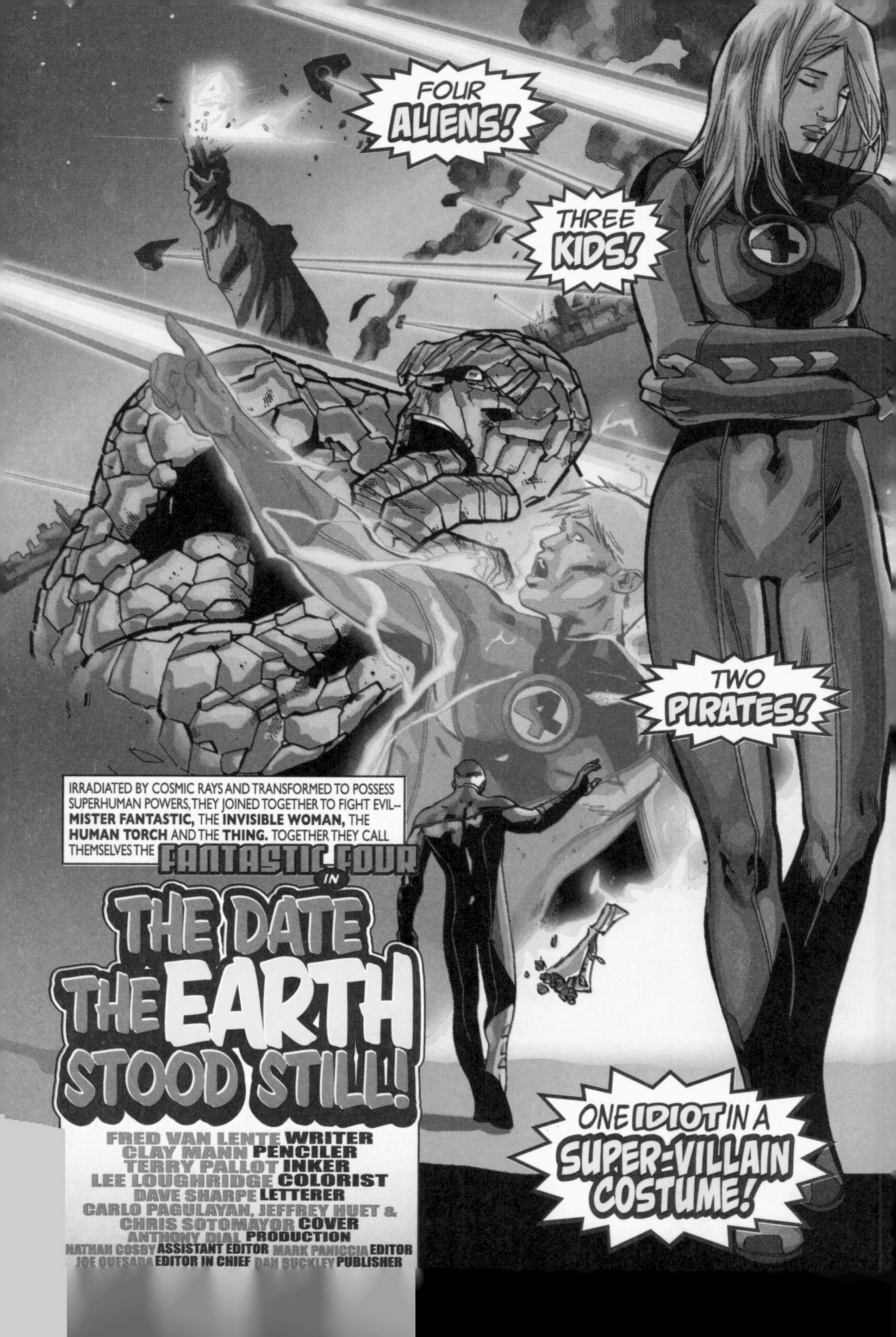
FOUR ALIENS!
THREE KIDS!
TWO PIRATES!
ONE IDIOT IN A SUPER-VILLAIN COSTUME!
IRRADIATED BY COSMIC RAYS AND TRANSFORMED TO POSSESS SUPERHUMAN POWERS, THEY JOINED TOGETHER TO FIGHT EVIL-- MISTER FANTASTIC, THE INVISIBLE WOMAN, THE HUMAN TORCH AND THE THING. TOGETHER THEY CALL THEMSELVES THE
FANTASTIC FOUR
IN
THE DATE THE EARTH STOOD STILL!
FRED VAN LENTE WRITER
CLAY MANN PENCILER
TERRY PALLOT INKER
LEE LOUGHRIDGE COLORIST
DAVE SHARPE LETTERER
CARLO PAGULAYAN, JEFFREY HUET & CHRIS SOTOMAYOR COVER
ANTHONY DIAL PRODUCTION
NATHAN COSBY ASSISTANT EDITOR MARK PANICCIA EDITOR
JOE QUESADA EDITOR IN CHIEF DAN BUCKLEY PUBLISHER

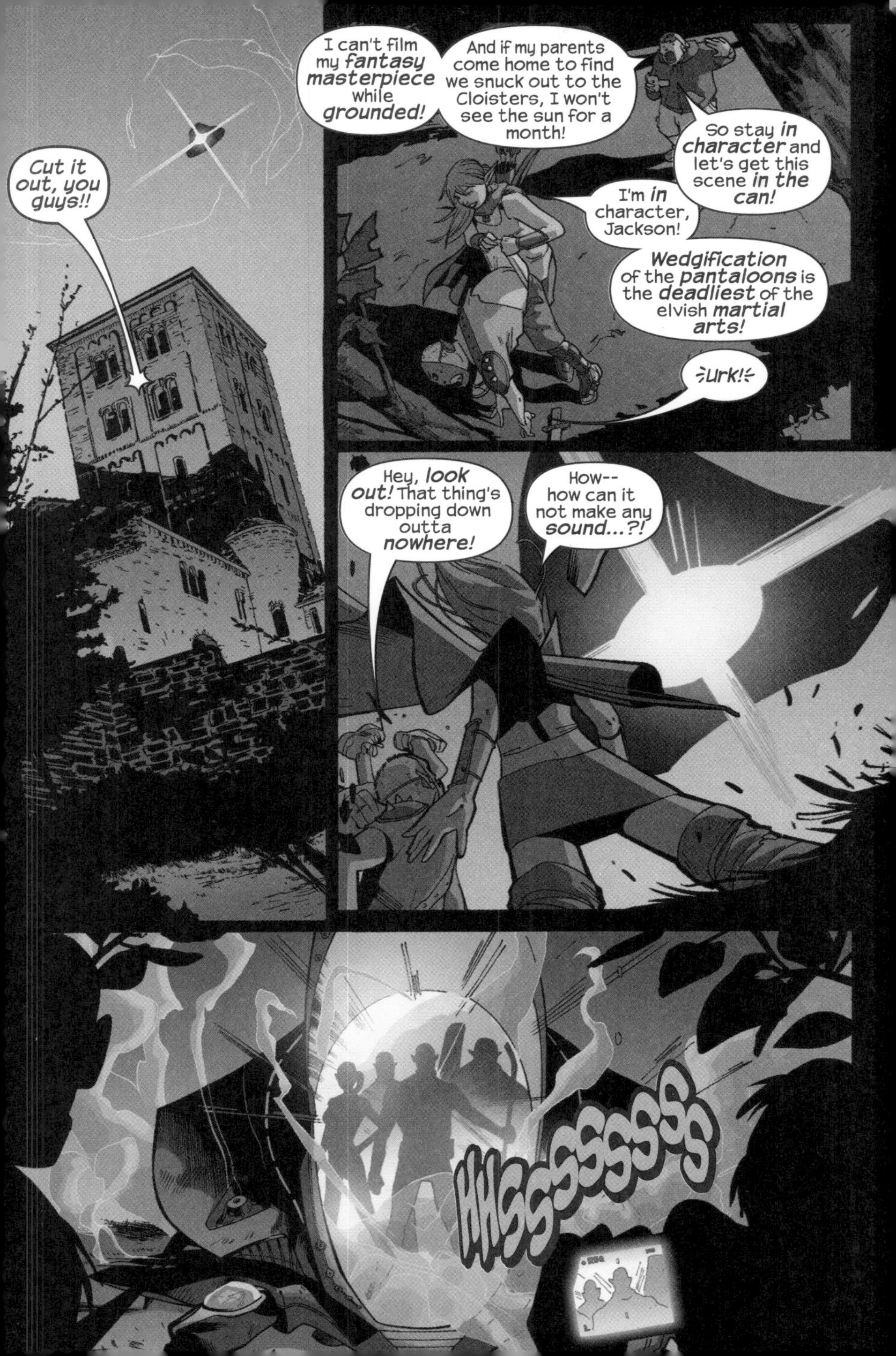

Cut it out, you guys!!
I can't film my fantasy masterpiece while grounded!
And if my parents come home to find we snuck out to the Cloisters, I won't see the sun for a month!
So stay in character and let's get this scene in the can!
I'm in character, Jackson!
Wedgification of the pantaloons is the deadliest of the elvish martial arts!
Urk!
Hey, look out! That thing's dropping down outta nowhere!
How-- how can it not make any sound...?!
HHSSSSSSSS

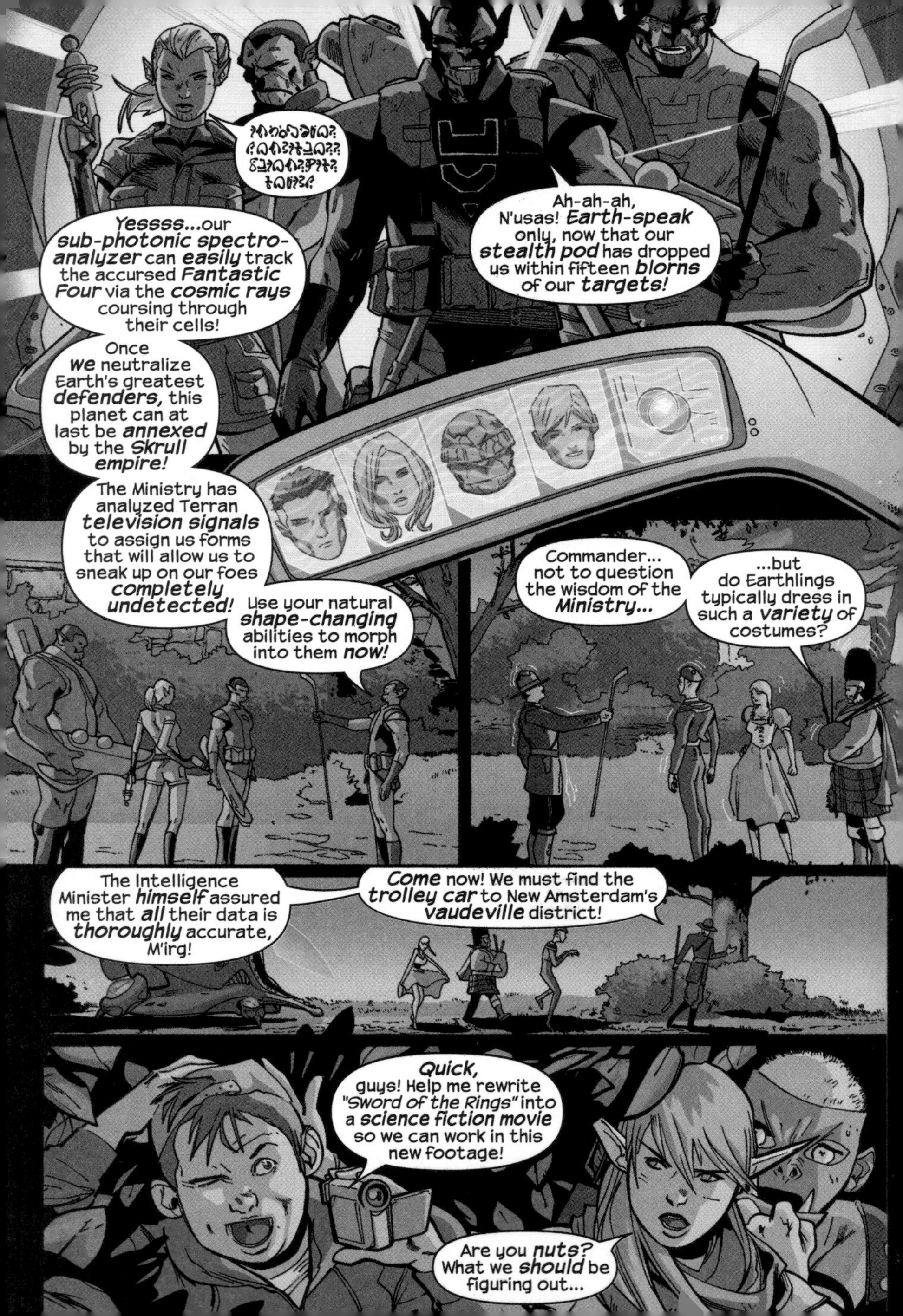

Yessss...our sub-photonic spectro-analyzer can easily track the accursed Fantastic Four via the cosmic rays coursing through their cells!
Ah-ah-ah, N'usas! Earth-speak only, now that our stealth pod has dropped us within fifteen blorns of our targets!
Once we neutralize Earth's greatest defenders, this planet can at last be annexed by the Skrull empire!
The Ministry has analyzed Terran television signals to assign us forms that will allow us to sneak up on our foes completely undetected!
Use your natural shape-changing abilities to morph into them now!
Commander... not to question the wisdom of the Ministry...
...but do Earthlings typically dress in such a variety of costumes?
The Intelligence Minister himself assured me that all their data is thoroughly accurate, M'irg!
Come now! We must find the trolley car to New Amsterdam's vaudeville district!
Quick, guys! Help me rewrite "Sword of the Rings" into a science fiction movie so we can work in this new footage!
Are you nuts? What we should be figuring out...

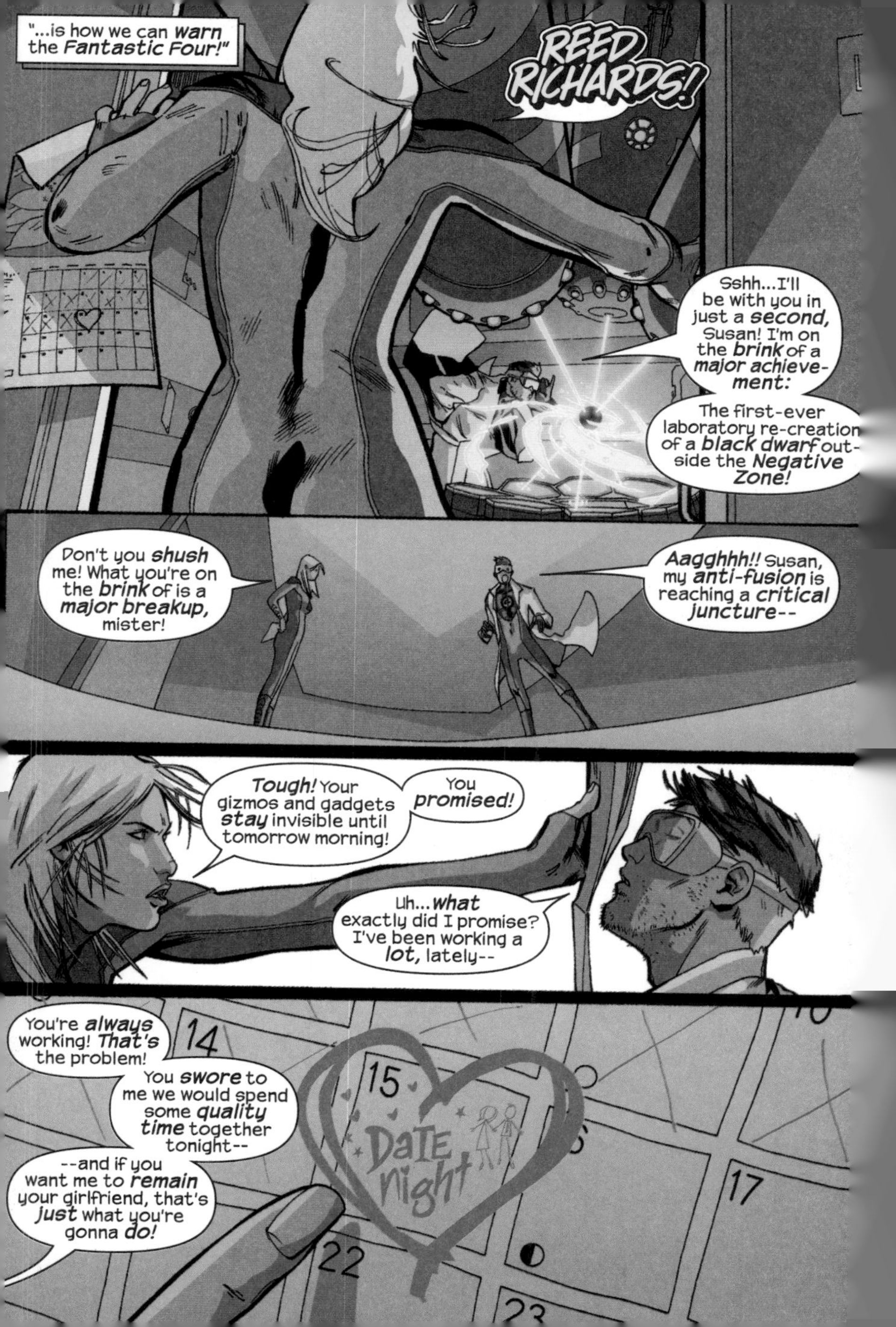
"...is how we can warn the Fantastic Four!"
REED RICHARDS!
Sshh...I'll be with you in just a second, Susan! I'm on the brink of a major achievement:
The first-ever laboratory re-creation of a black dwarf outside the Negative Zone!
Don't you shush me! What you're on the brink of is a major breakup, mister!
Aagghhh!! Susan, my anti-fusion is reaching a critical juncture--
Tough! Your gizmos and gadgets stay invisible until tomorrow morning!
You promised!
Uh...what exactly did I promise? I've been working a lot, lately--
You're always working! That's the problem!
You swore to me we would spend some quality time together tonight--
--and if you want me to remain your girlfriend, that's just what you're gonna do!
14
15
DaTE night
17
22
23

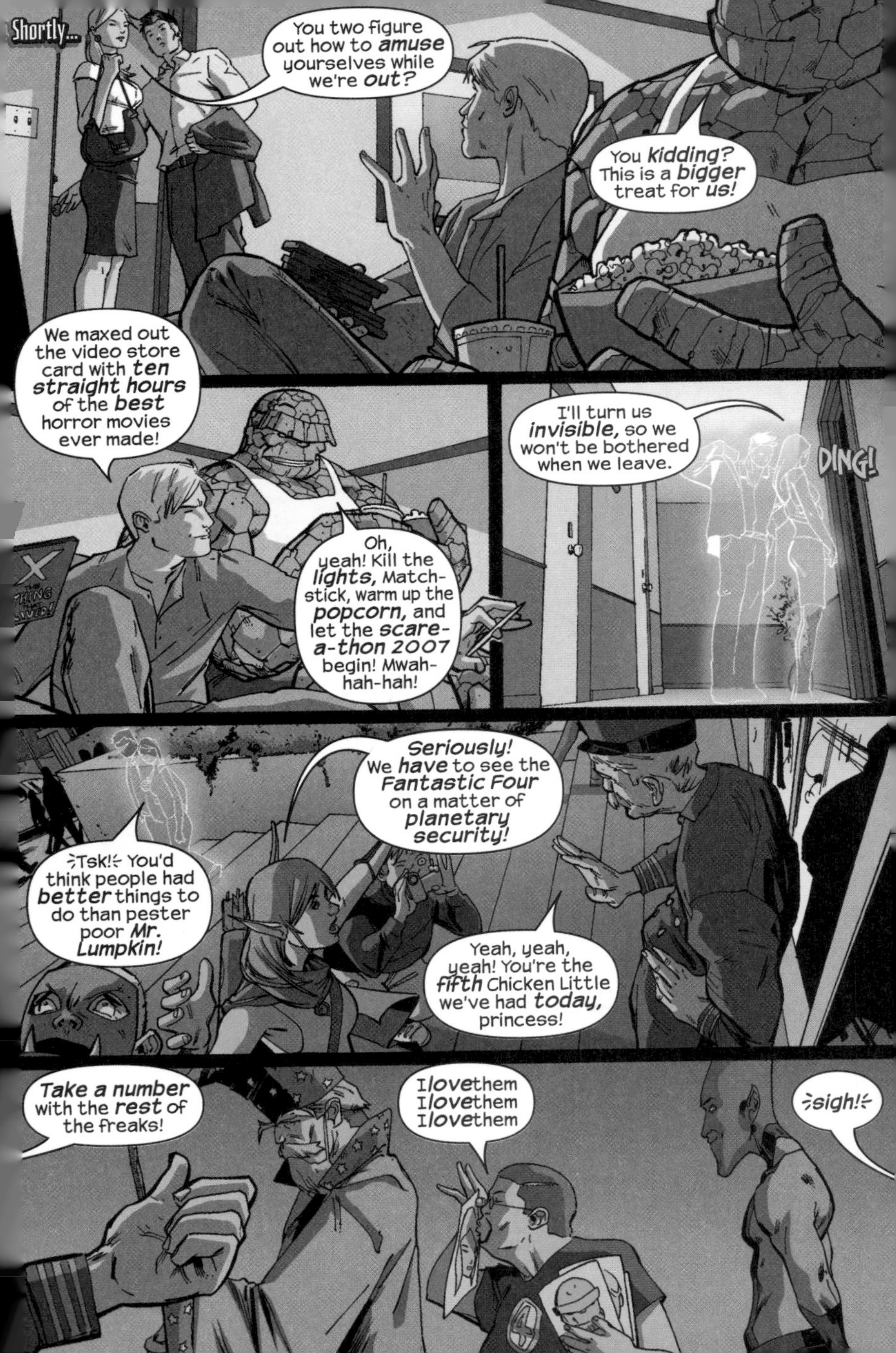
Shortly...
You two figure out how to amuse yourselves while we're out?
You kidding? This is a bigger treat for us!
We maxed out the video store card with ten straight hours of the best horror movies ever made!
Oh, yeah! Kill the lights, Match-stick, warm up the popcorn, and let the scare-a-thon 2007 begin! Mwah-hah-hah!
I'll turn us invisible, so we won't be bothered when we leave.
DING!
Seriously! We have to see the Fantastic Four on a matter of planetary security!
Tsk! You'd think people had better things to do than pester poor Mr. Lumpkin!
Yeah, yeah, yeah! You're the fifth Chicken Little we've had today, princess!
Take a number with the rest of the freaks!
Ilovethem Ilovethem Ilovethem
sigh!

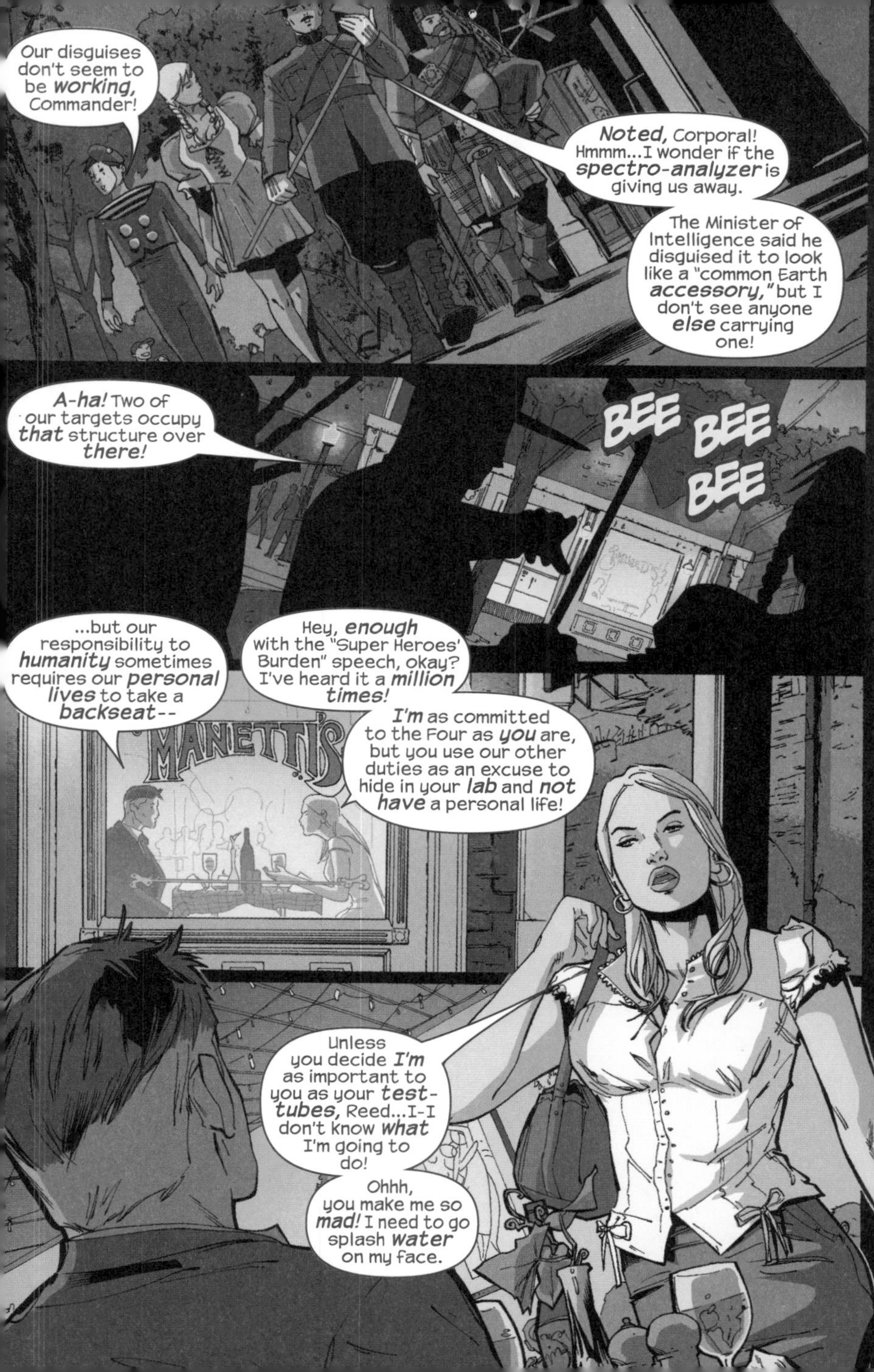

Our disguises don't seem to be working, Commander!
Noted, Corporal! Hmmm...I wonder if the spectro-analyzer is giving us away.
The Minister of Intelligence said he disguised it to look like a "common Earth accessory," but I don't see anyone else carrying one!
A-ha! Two of our targets occupy that structure over there!
BEE BEE BEE
...but our responsibility to humanity sometimes requires our personal lives to take a backseat--
Hey, enough with the "Super Heroes' Burden" speech, okay? I've heard it a million times!
I'm as committed to the Four as you are, but you use our other duties as an excuse to hide in your lab and not have a personal life!
MANETTI'S
Unless you decide I'm as important to you as your test-tubes, Reed...I-I don't know what I'm going to do!
Ohhh, you make me so mad! I need to go splash water on my face.

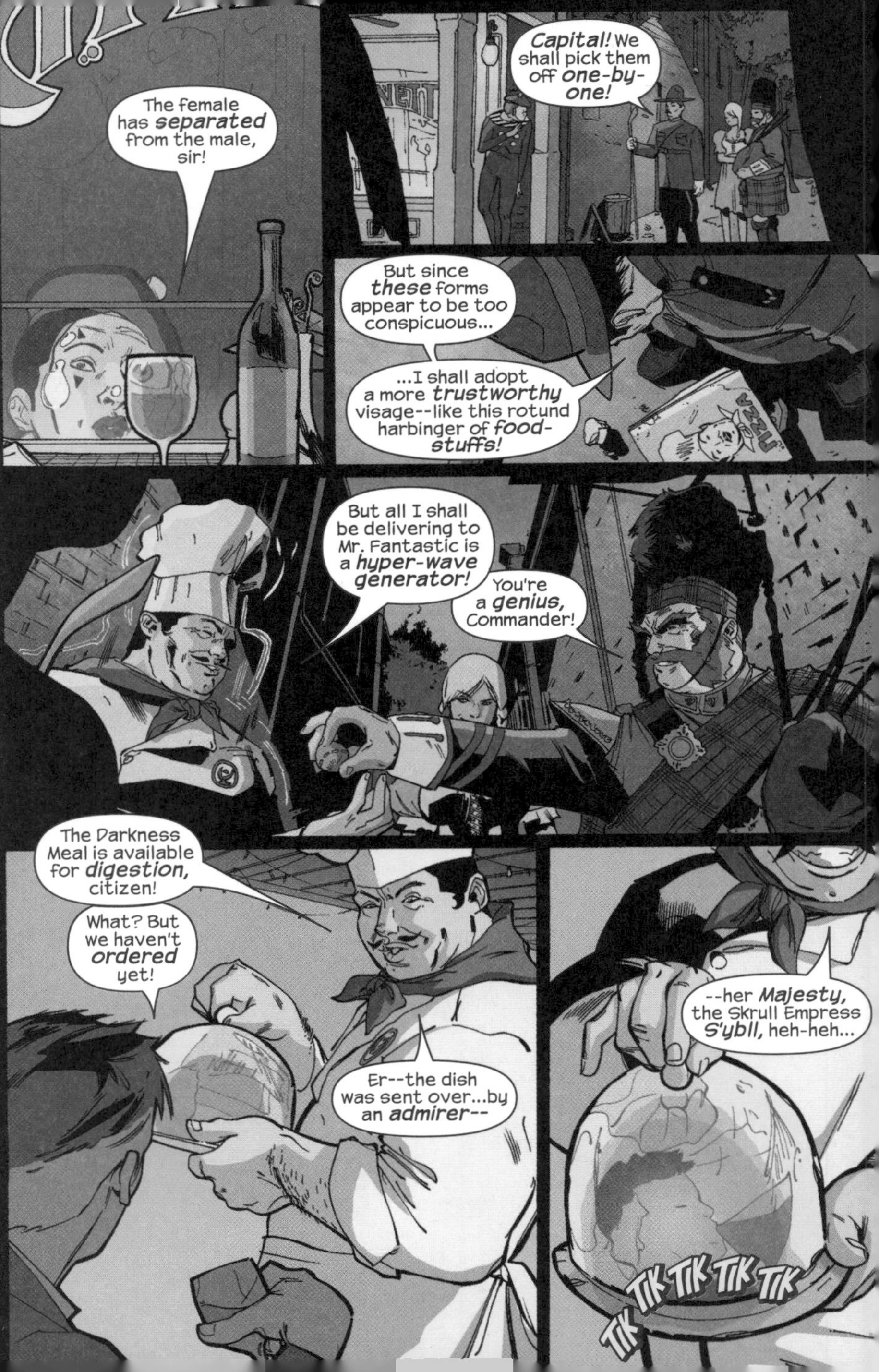
The female has separated from the male, sir!
Capital! We shall pick them off one-by-one!
But since these forms appear to be too conspicuous...
...I shall adopt a more trustworthy visage--like this rotund harbinger of food-stuffs!
PIZZA
But all I shall be delivering to Mr. Fantastic is a hyper-wave generator!
You're a genius, Commander!
The Darkness Meal is available for digestion, citizen!
What? But we haven't ordered yet!
Er--the dish was sent over...by an admirer--
--her Majesty, the Skrull Empress S'ybll, heh-heh...
TIK TIK TIK TIK TIK

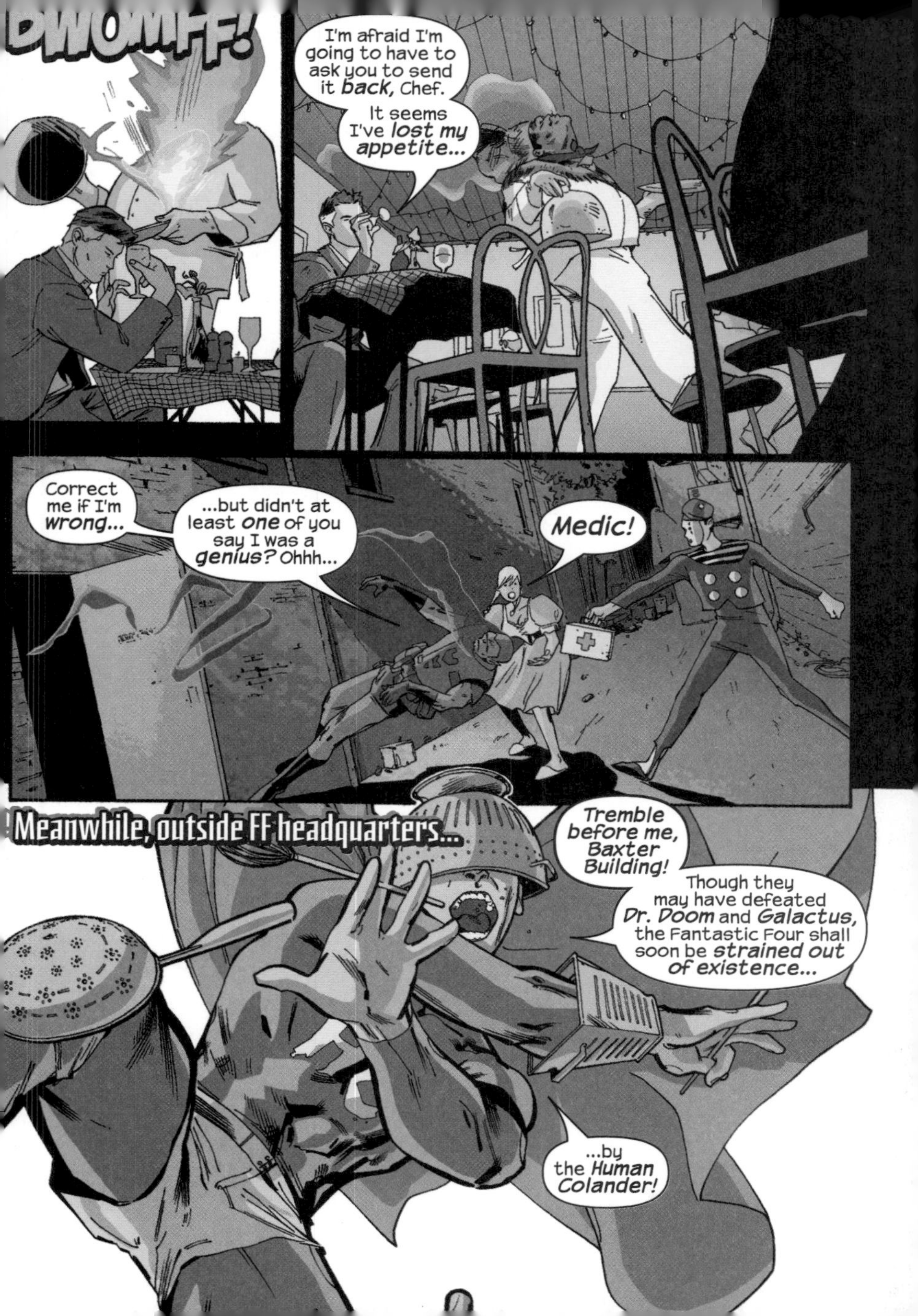
DWOMFF!
I'm afraid I'm going to have to ask you to send it back, Chef.
It seems I've lost my appetite...
Correct me if I'm wrong...
...but didn't at least one of you say I was a genius? Ohhh...
Medic!
Meanwhile, outside FF headquarters...
Tremble before me, Baxter Building!
Though they may have defeated Dr. Doom and Galactus, the Fantastic Four shall soon be strained out of existence...
...by the Human Colander!

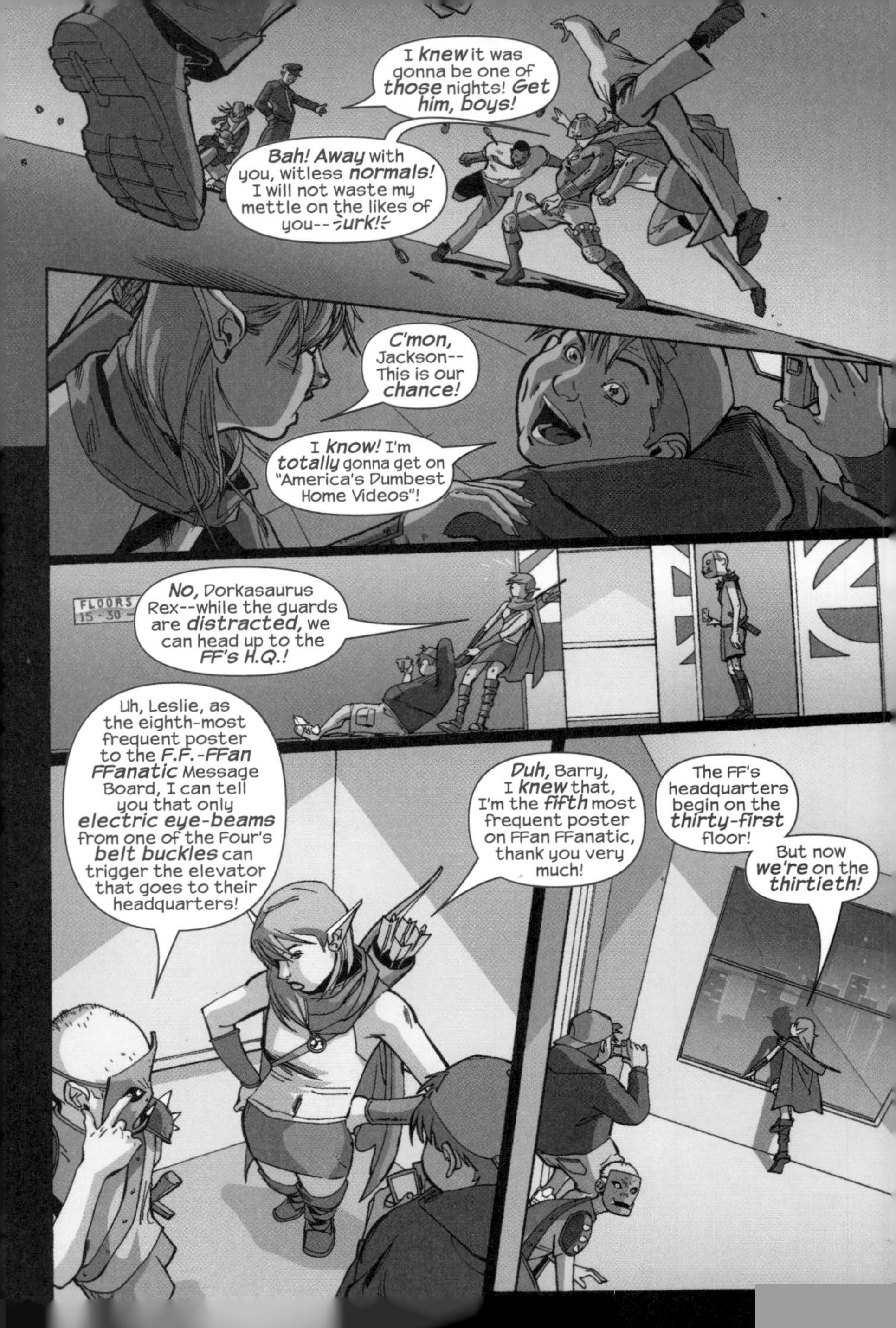
I knew it was gonna be one of those nights! Get him, boys!
Bah! Away with you, witless normals! I will not waste my mettle on the likes of you-- urk!
C'mon, Jackson-- This is our chance!
I know! I'm totally gonna get on "America's Dumbest Home Videos"!
FLOORS 15 - 30
No, Dorkasaurus Rex--while the guards are distracted, we can head up to the FF's H.Q.!
Uh, Leslie, as the eighth-most frequent poster to the F.F.-FFan FFanatic Message Board, I can tell you that only electric eye-beams from one of the Four's belt buckles can trigger the elevator that goes to their headquarters!
Duh, Barry, I knew that, I'm the fifth most frequent poster on FFan FFanatic, thank you very much!
The FF's headquarters begin on the thirty-first floor!
But now we're on the thirtieth!

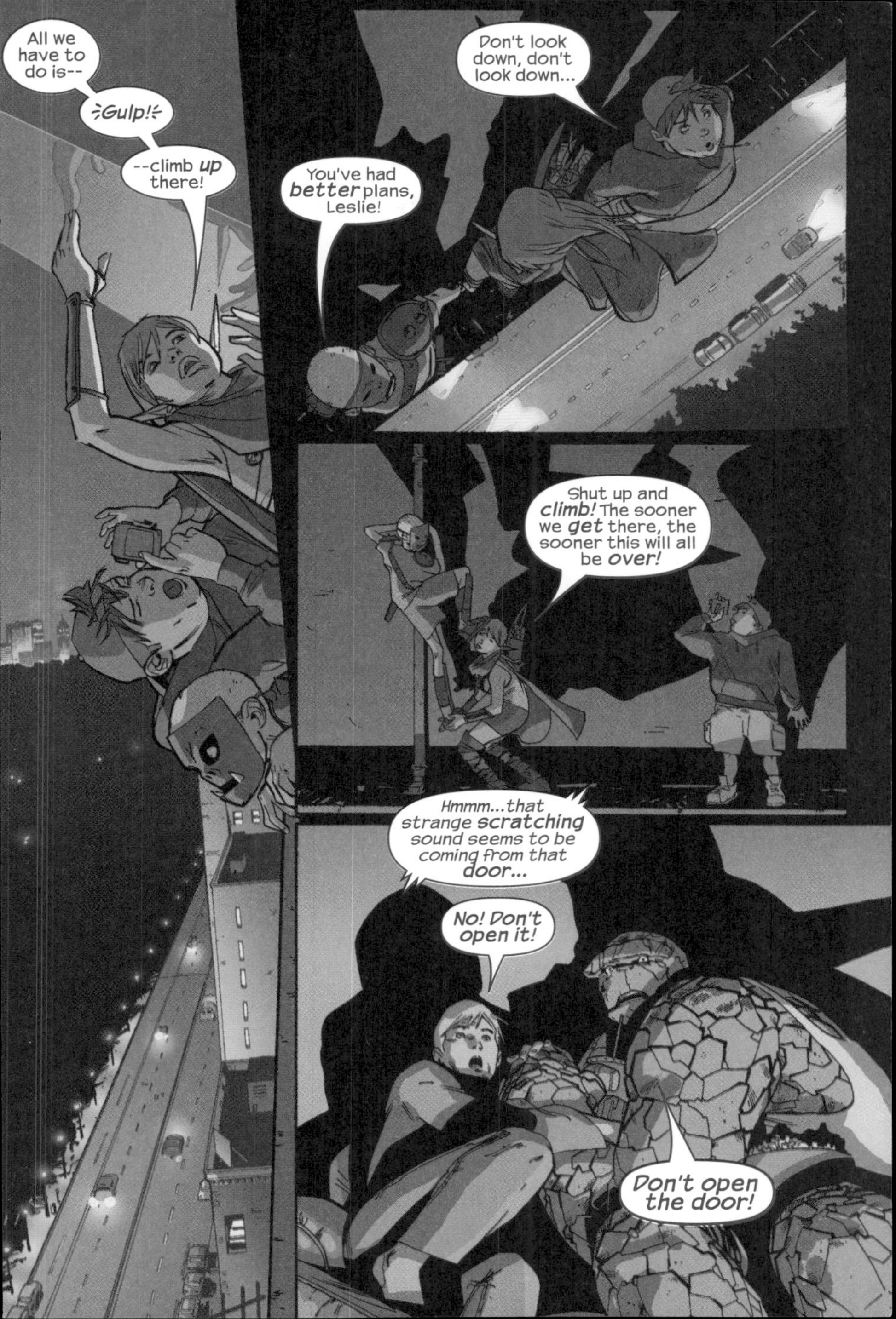
All we have to do is--
Gulp!
--climb up there!
Don't look down, don't look down...
You've had better plans, Leslie!
Shut up and climb! The sooner we get there, the sooner this will all be over!
Hmmm...that strange scratching sound seems to be coming from that door...
No! Don't open it!
Don't open the door!

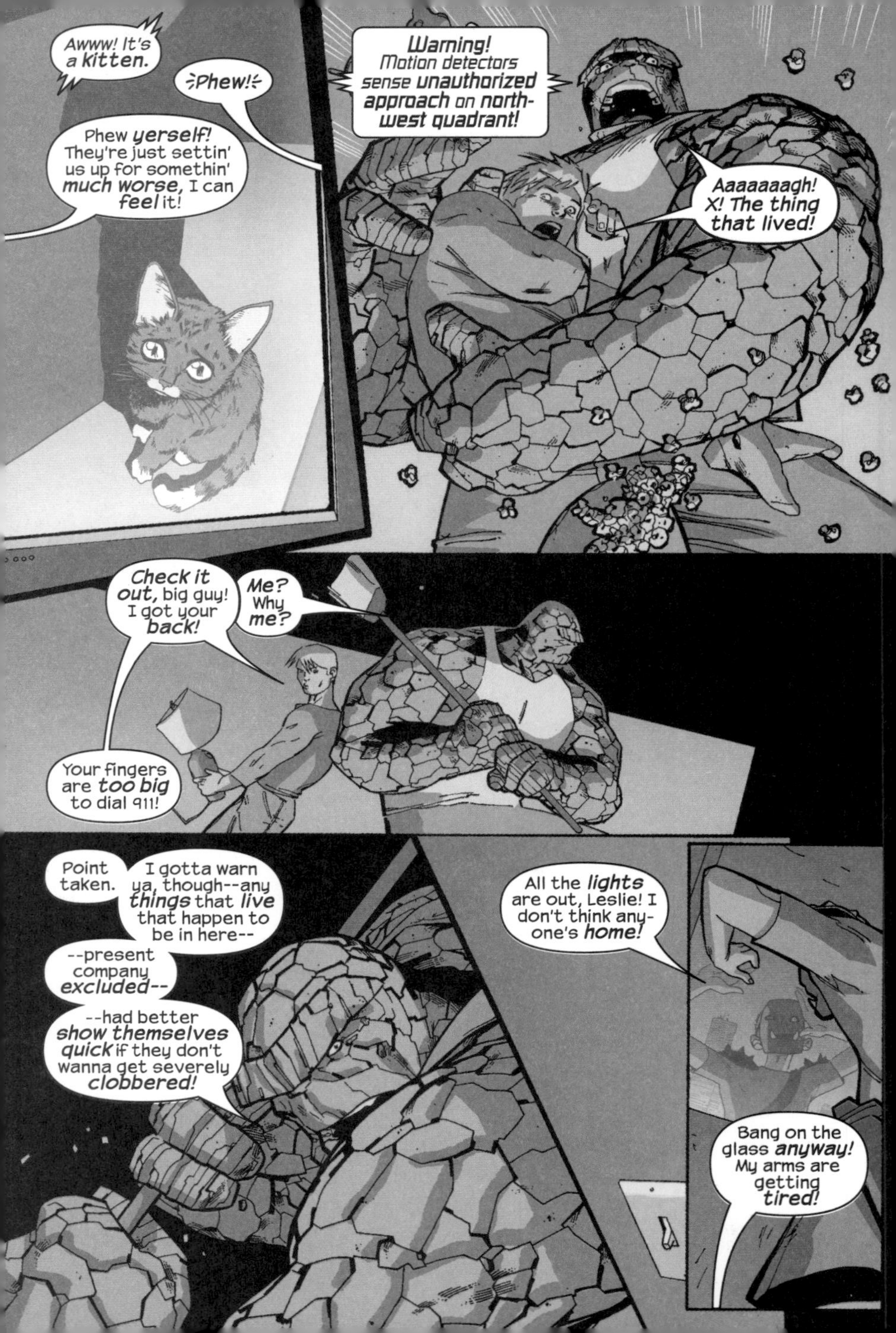

Awww! It's a kitten.
Phew!
Phew yerself! They're just settin' us up for somethin' much worse, I can feel it!
Warning! Motion detectors sense unauthorized approach on north-west quadrant!
Aaaaaaagh! X! The thing that lived!
Check it out, big guy! I got your back!
Me? Why me?
Your fingers are too big to dial 911!
Point taken.
I gotta warn ya, though--any things that live that happen to be in here--
--present company excluded--
--had better show themselves quick if they don't wanna get severely clobbered!
All the lights are out, Leslie! I don't think any-one's home!
Bang on the glass anyway! My arms are getting tired!

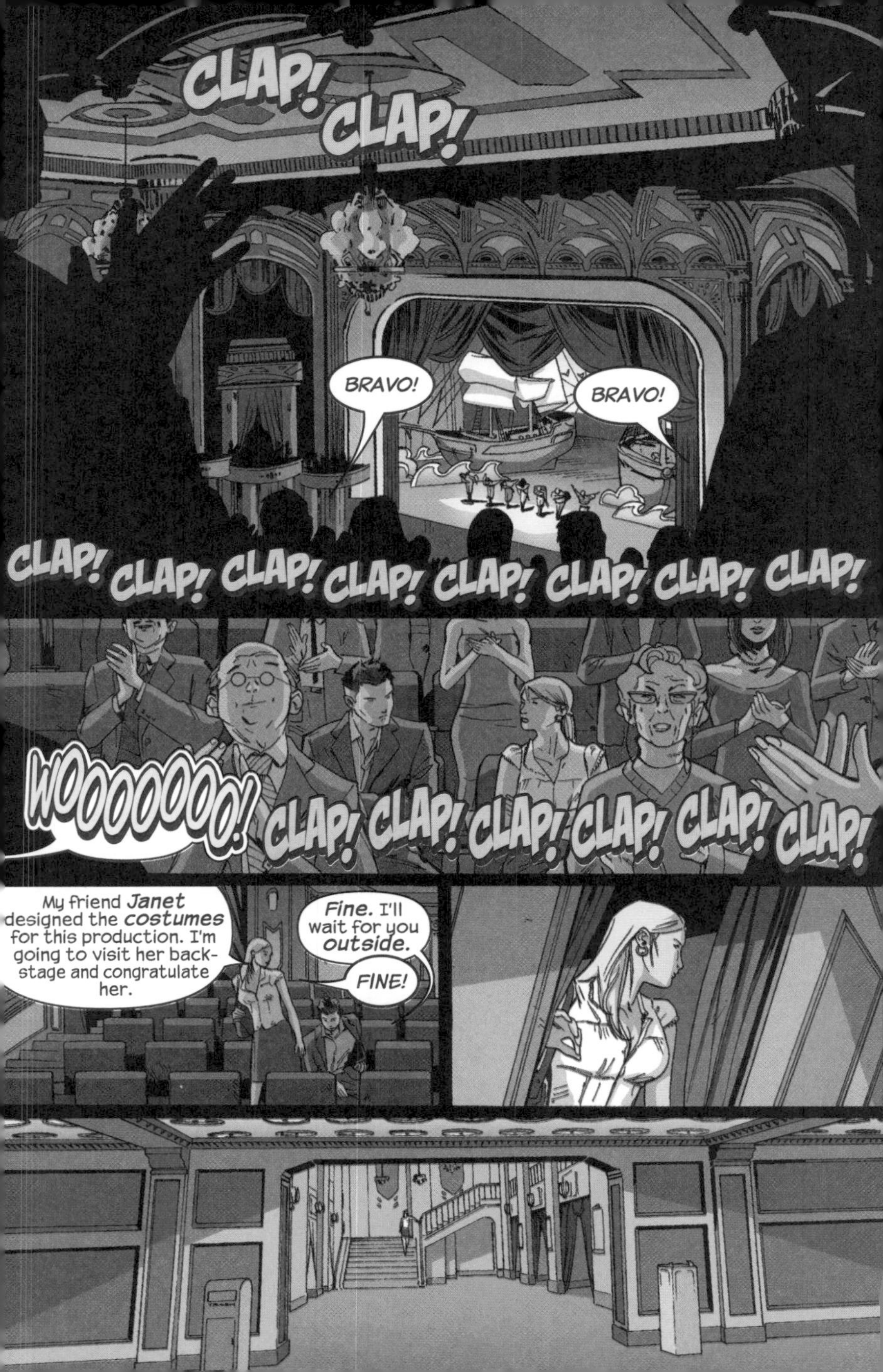
CLAP! CLAP!
BRAVO!
BRAVO!
CLAP! CLAP! CLAP! CLAP! CLAP! CLAP! CLAP! CLAP!
WOOOOOOO!
CLAP! CLAP! CLAP! CLAP! CLAP! CLAP!
My friend Janet designed the costumes for this production. I'm going to visit her backstage and congratulate her.
Fine. I'll wait for you outside.
FINE!

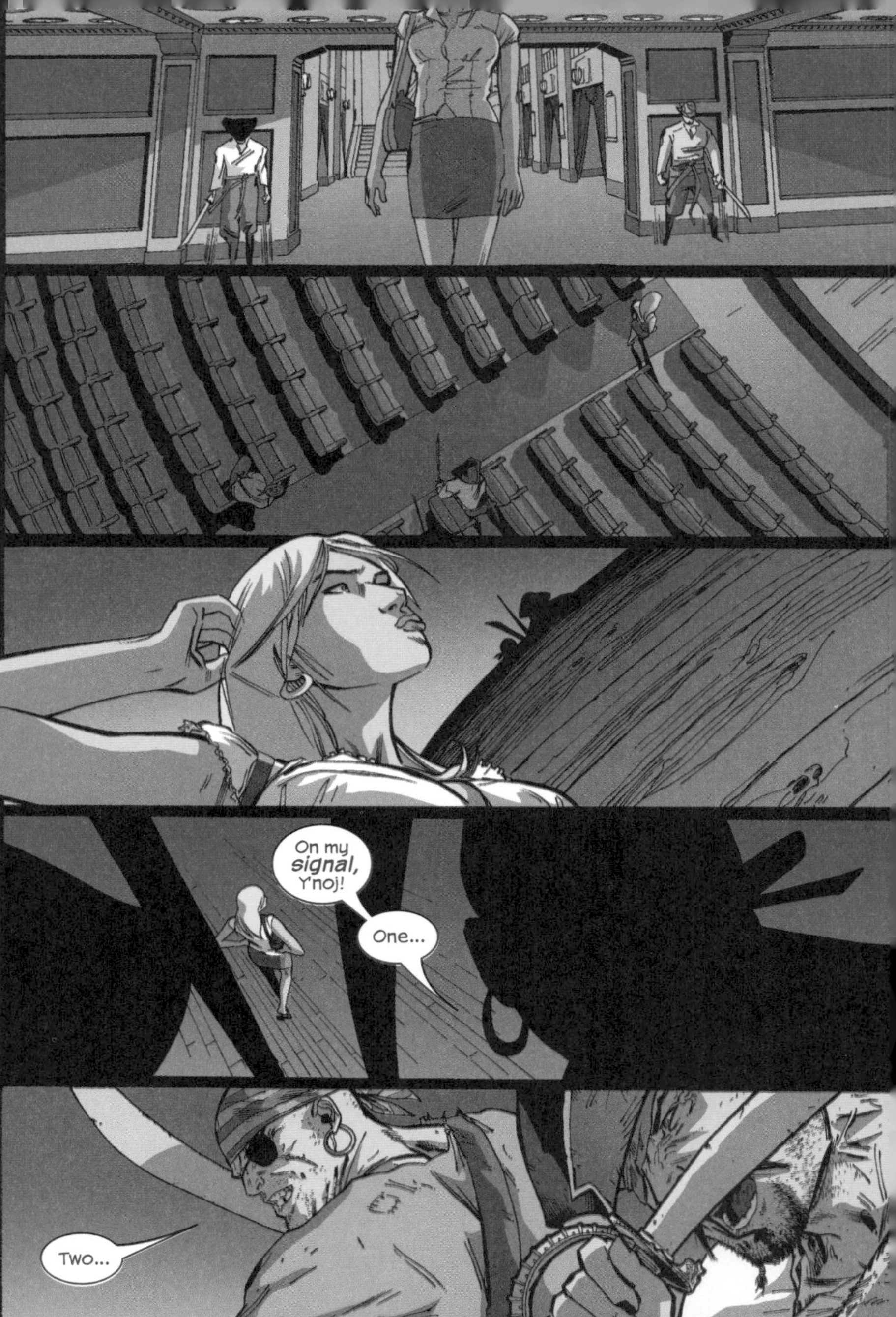

On my *signal,* Y'noj!
One...
Two...

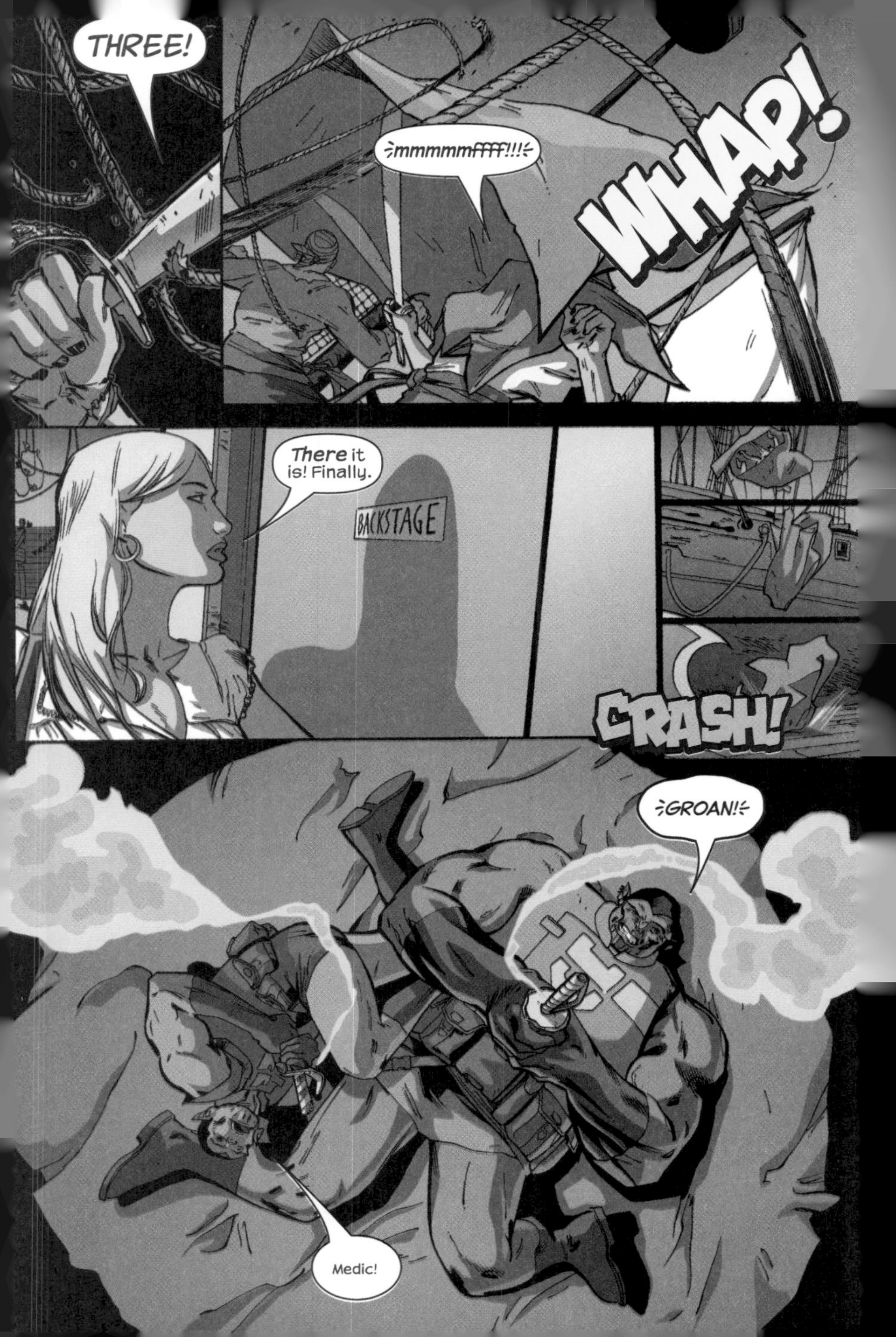
THREE!
mmmmmffff!!!
WHAP!
There it is! Finally.
BACKSTAGE
CRASH!
GROAN!
Medic!

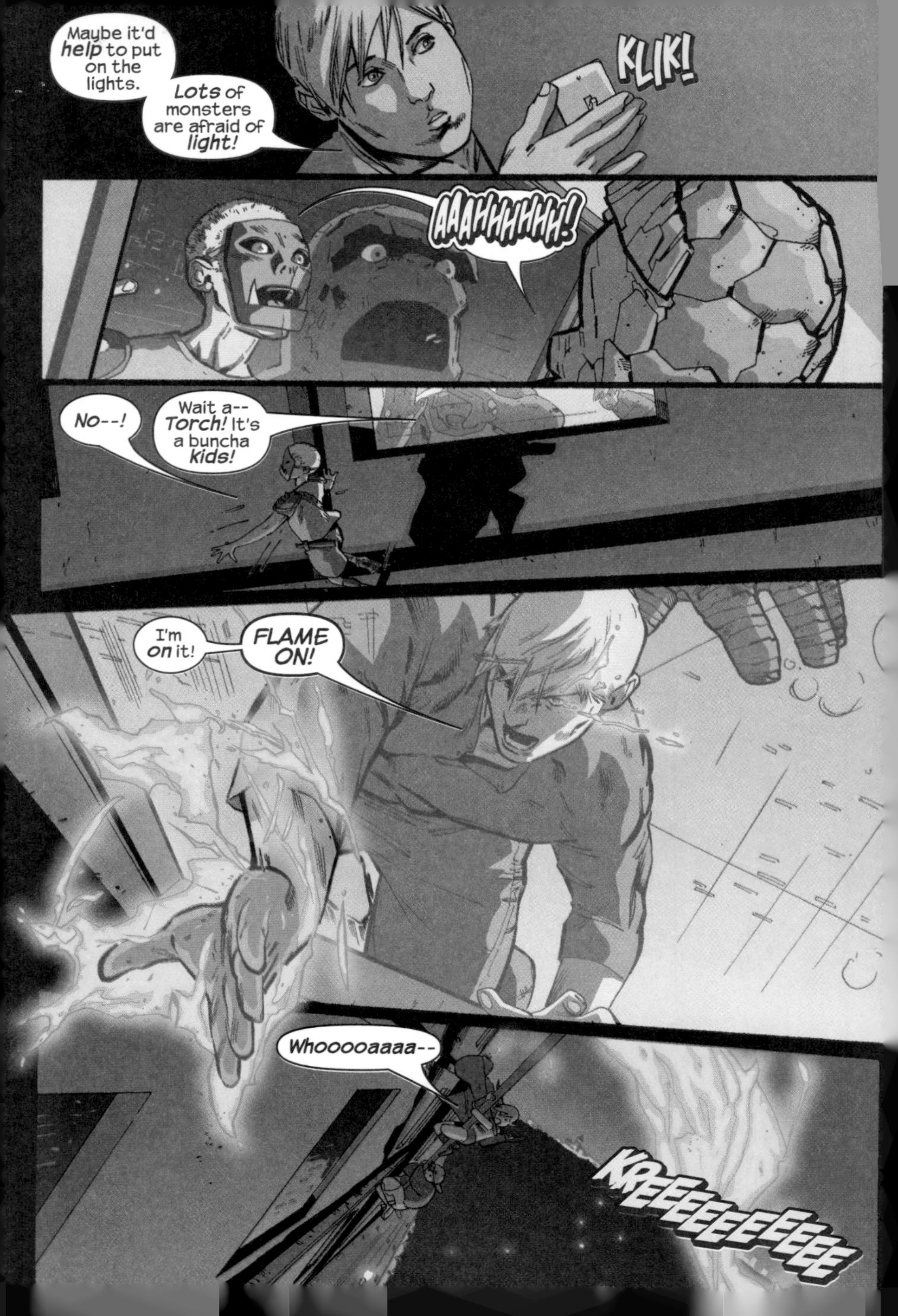
Maybe it'd help to put on the lights.
Lots of monsters are afraid of light!
KLIK!
AAAHHHHHH!
No--!
Wait a-- Torch! It's a buncha kids!
I'm on it!
FLAME ON!
Whoooaaaa--
KREEEEEEEEEE

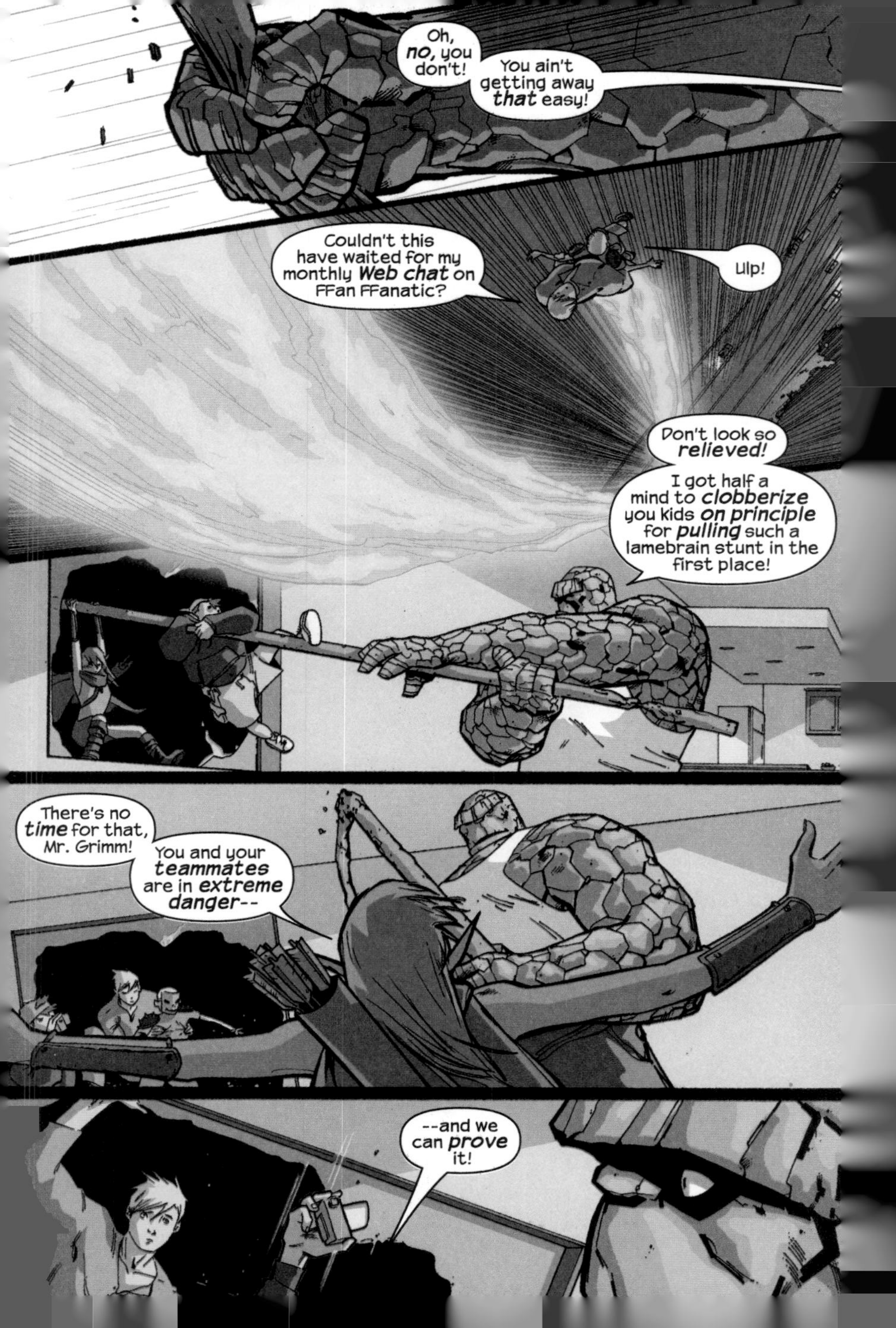
Oh, *no,* you don't!
You ain't getting away *that* easy!
Couldn't this have waited for my monthly *Web chat* on FFan FFanatic?
Ulp!
Don't look so *relieved!*
I got half a mind to *clobberize* you kids *on principle* for *pulling* such a lamebrain stunt in the first place!
There's no *time* for that, Mr. Grimm!
You and your *teammates* are in *extreme danger*--
--and we can *prove* it!

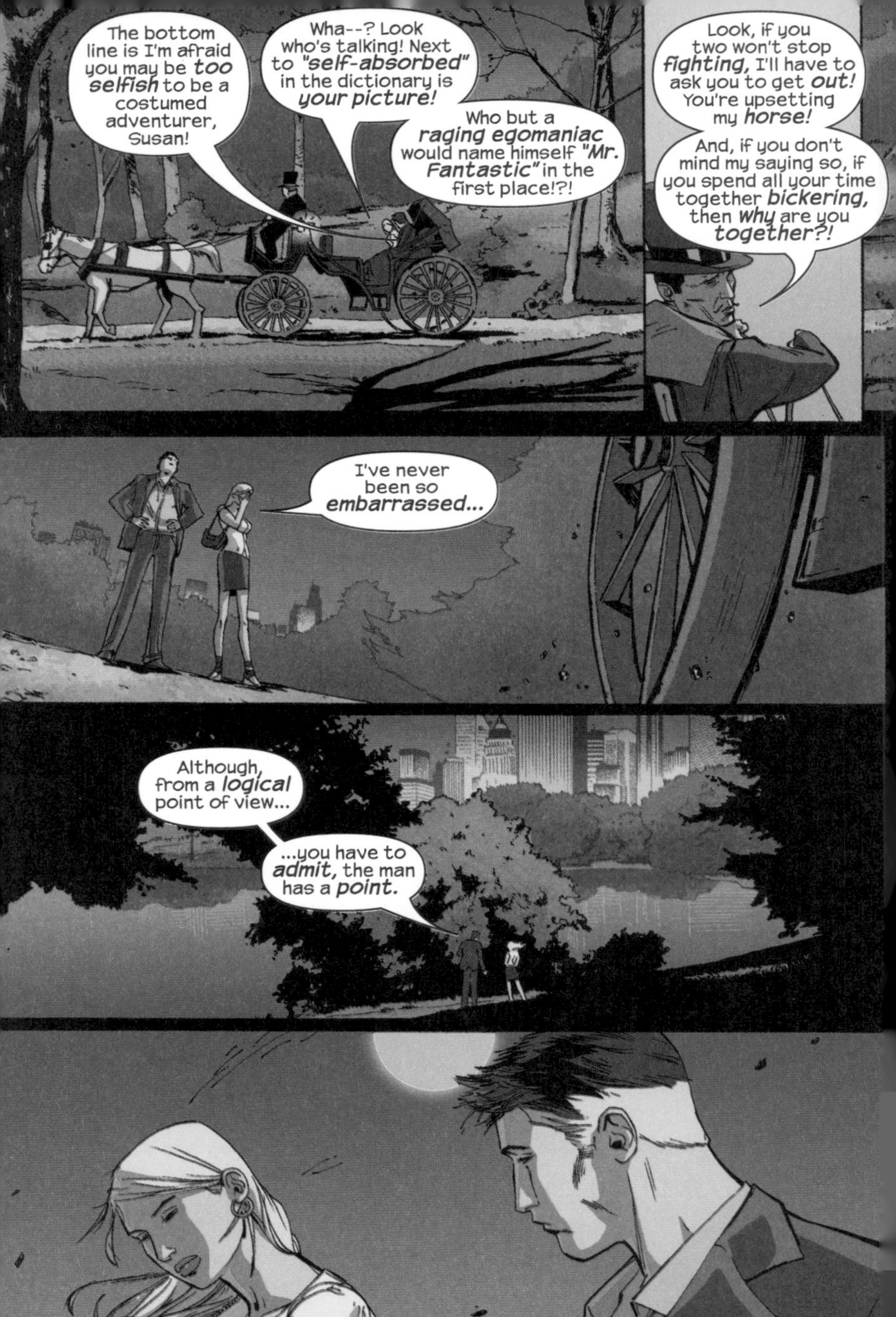
The bottom line is I'm afraid you may be too selfish to be a costumed adventurer, Susan!
Wha--? Look who's talking! Next to "self-absorbed" in the dictionary is your picture!
Who but a raging egomaniac would name himself "Mr. Fantastic" in the first place!?!
Look, if you two won't stop fighting, I'll have to ask you to get out! You're upsetting my horse!
And, if you don't mind my saying so, if you spend all your time together bickering, then why are you together?!
I've never been so embarrassed...
Although, from a logical point of view...
...you have to admit, the man has a point.

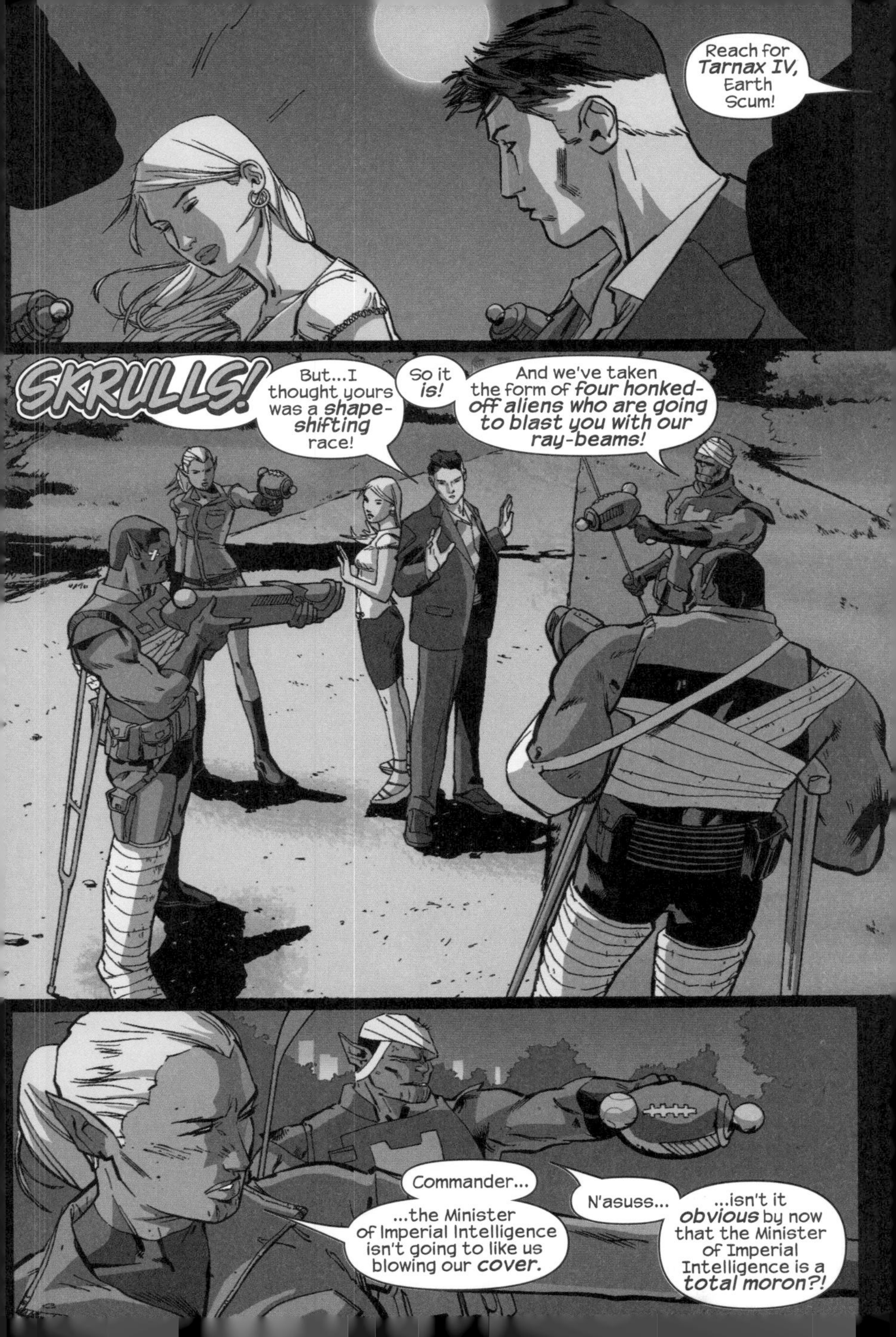
Reach for Tarnax IV, Earth Scum!
SKRULLS!
But...I thought yours was a shape-shifting race!
So it is!
And we've taken the form of four honked-off aliens who are going to blast you with our ray-beams!
Commander...
...the Minister of Imperial Intelligence isn't going to like us blowing our cover.
N'asuss...
...isn't it obvious by now that the Minister of Imperial Intelligence is a total moron?!

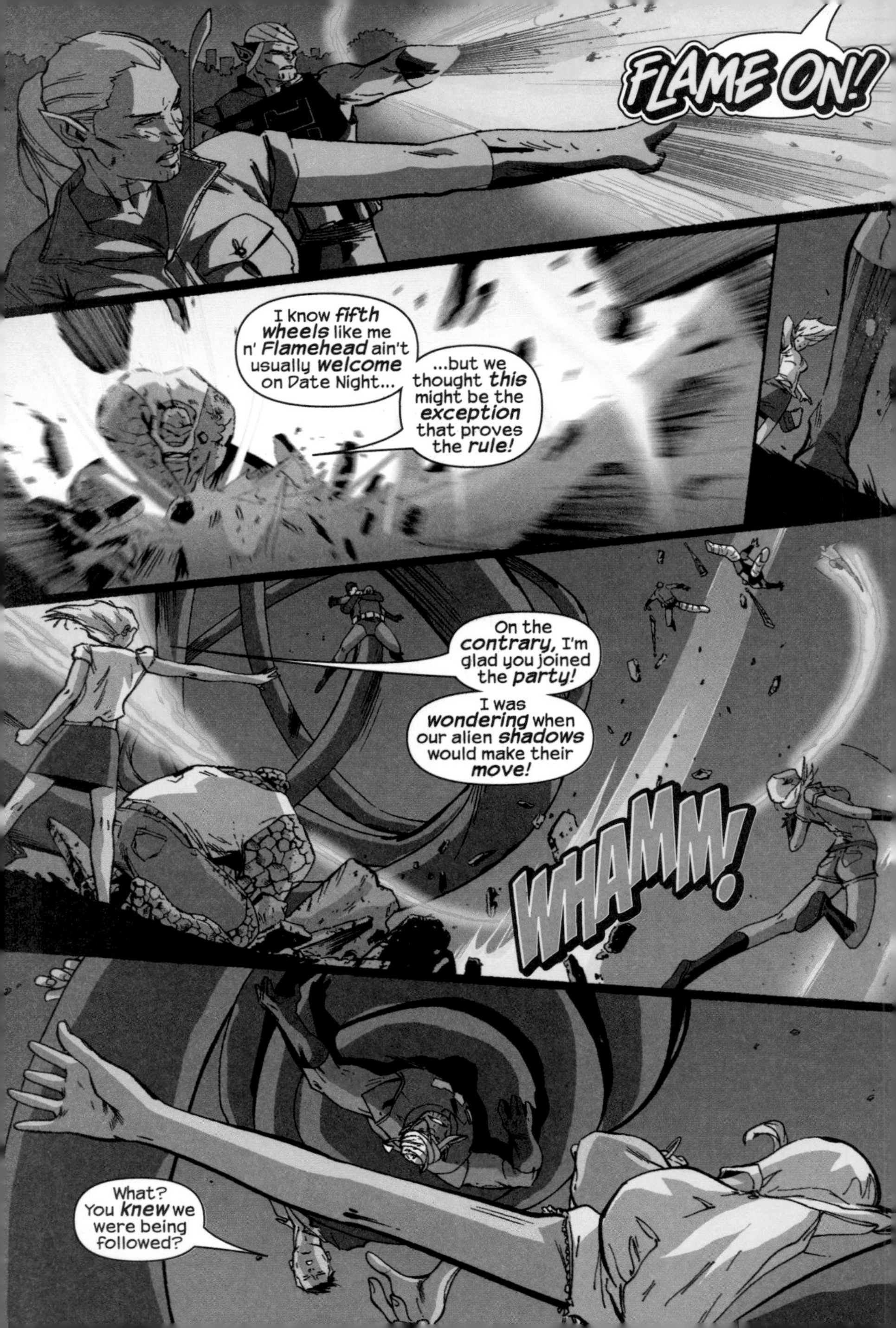
FLAME ON!
I know fifth wheels like me n' Flamehead ain't usually welcome on Date Night...
...but we thought this might be the exception that proves the rule!
On the contrary, I'm glad you joined the party!
I was wondering when our alien shadows would make their move!
WHAMM!
What? You knew we were being followed?

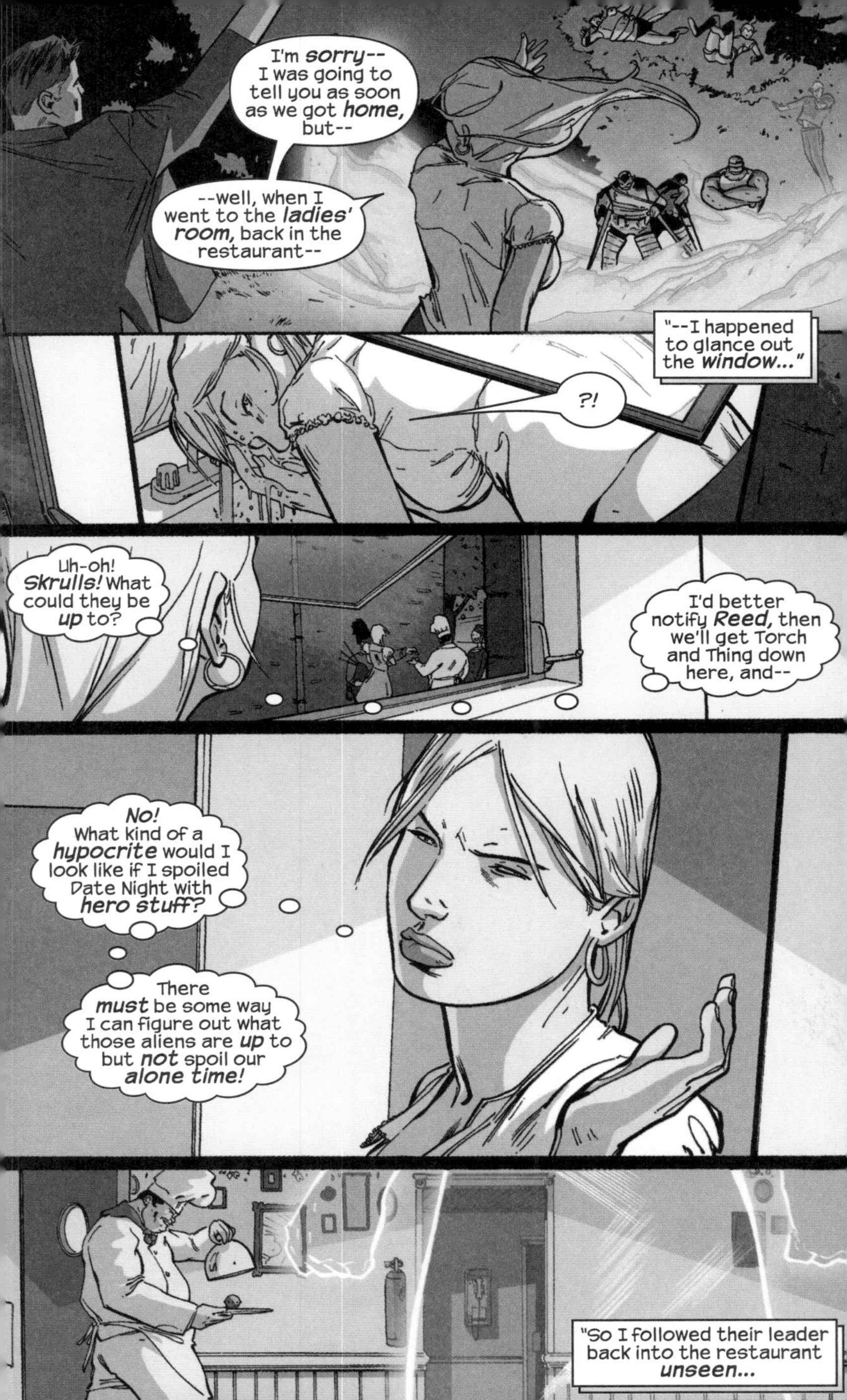
I'm sorry-- I was going to tell you as soon as we got home, but--
--well, when I went to the ladies' room, back in the restaurant--
"--I happened to glance out the window..."
?!
Uh-oh! Skrulls! What could they be up to?
I'd better notify Reed, then we'll get Torch and Thing down here, and--
No! What kind of a hypocrite would I look like if I spoiled Date Night with hero stuff?
There must be some way I can figure out what those aliens are up to but not spoil our alone time!
"So I followed their leader back into the restaurant unseen...

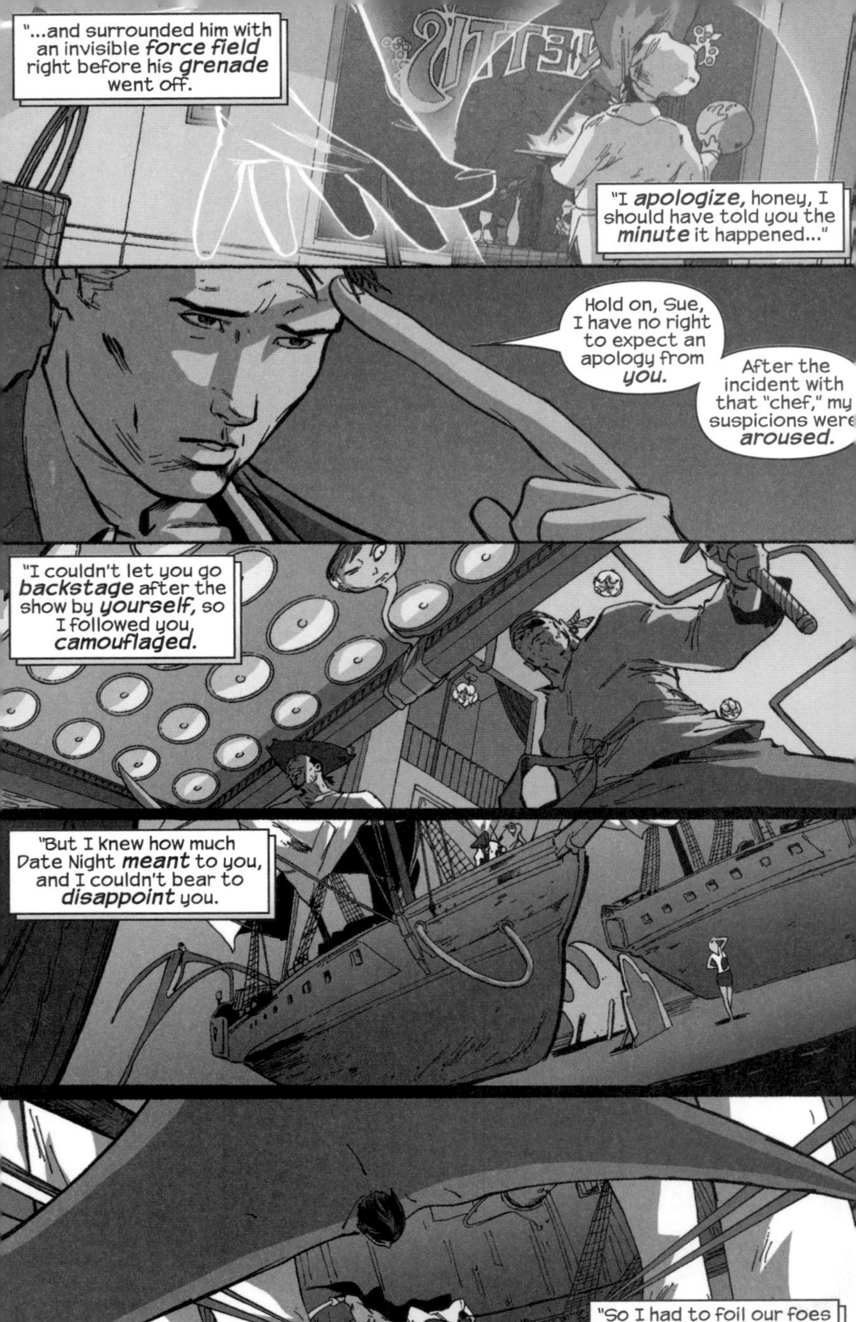
"...and surrounded him with an invisible force field right before his grenade went off.
"I apologize, honey, I should have told you the minute it happened..."
Hold on, Sue, I have no right to expect an apology from you.
After the incident with that "chef," my suspicions were aroused.
"I couldn't let you go backstage after the show by yourself, so I followed you, camouflaged.
"But I knew how much Date Night meant to you, and I couldn't bear to disappoint you.
"So I had to foil our foes in a way that couldn't be traced back to me."

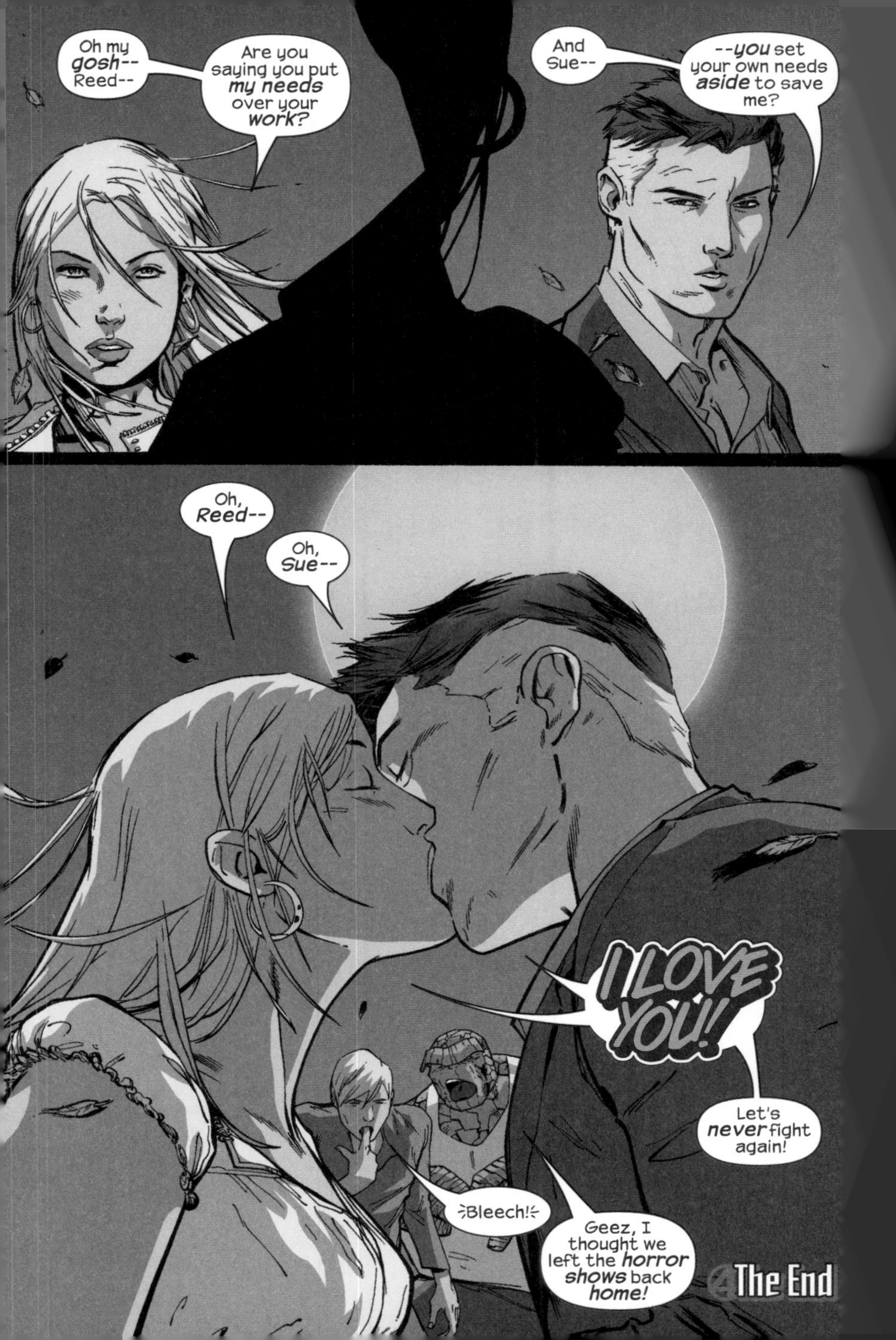
Oh my gosh-- Reed--
Are you saying you put my needs over your work?
And Sue--
--you set your own needs aside to save me?
Oh, Reed--
Oh, Sue--
I LOVE YOU!
Let's never fight again!
Bleech!
Geez, I thought we left the horror shows back home!
The End

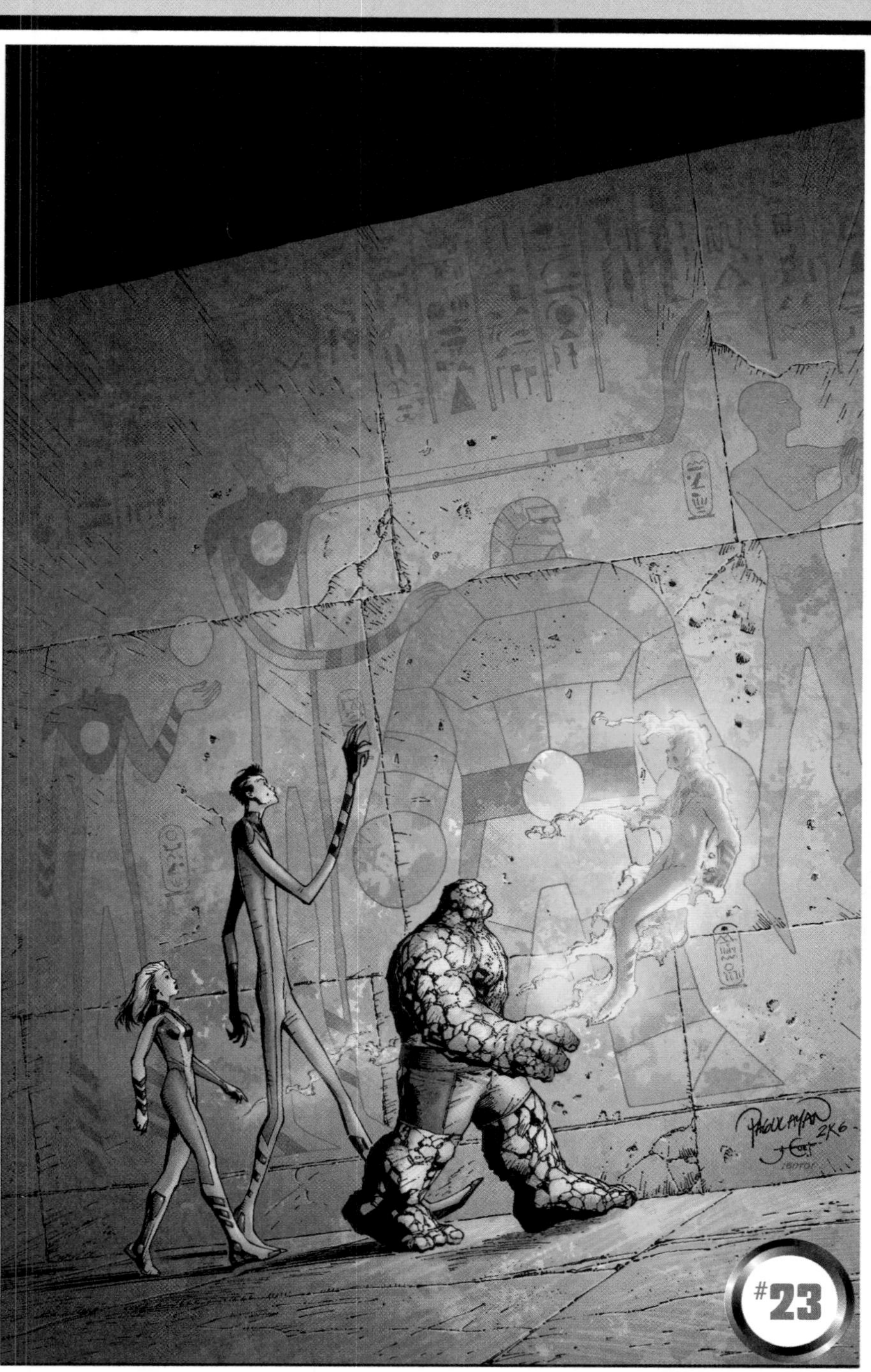
#23

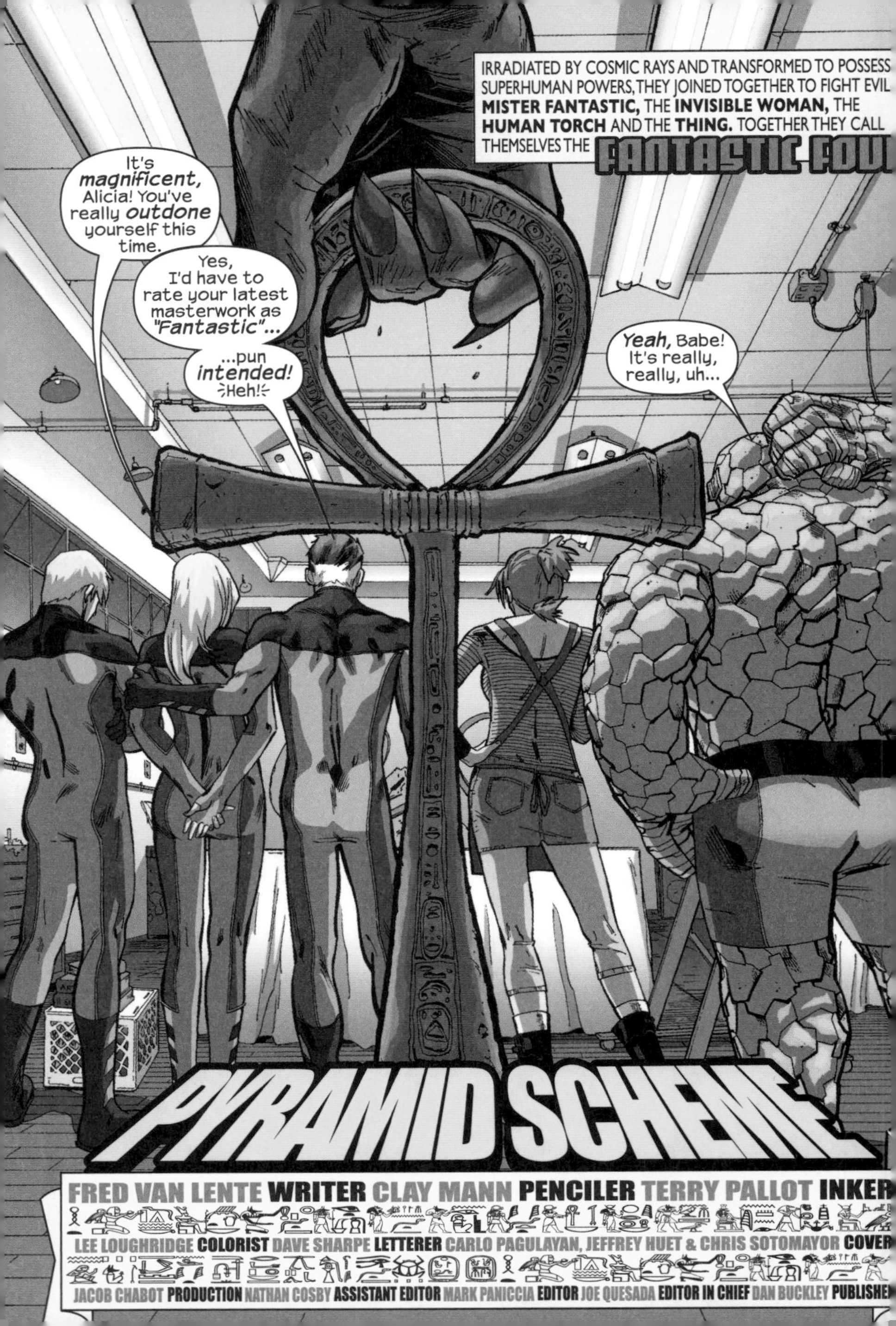
IRRADIATED BY COSMIC RAYS AND TRANSFORMED TO POSSESS SUPERHUMAN POWERS, THEY JOINED TOGETHER TO FIGHT EVIL: MISTER FANTASTIC, THE INVISIBLE WOMAN, THE HUMAN TORCH AND THE THING. TOGETHER THEY CALL THEMSELVES THE FANTASTIC FOUR
It's magnificent, Alicia! You've really outdone yourself this time.
Yes, I'd have to rate your latest masterwork as "Fantastic"...
...pun intended! Heh!
Yeah, Babe! It's really, really, uh...
PYRAMID SCHEME
FRED VAN LENTE WRITER CLAY MANN PENCILER TERRY PALLOT INKER
LEE LOUGHRIDGE COLORIST DAVE SHARPE LETTERER CARLO PAGULAYAN, JEFFREY HUET & CHRIS SOTOMAYOR COVER
JACOB CHABOT PRODUCTION NATHAN COSBY ASSISTANT EDITOR MARK PANICCIA EDITOR JOE QUESADA EDITOR IN CHIEF DAN BUCKLEY PUBLISHER

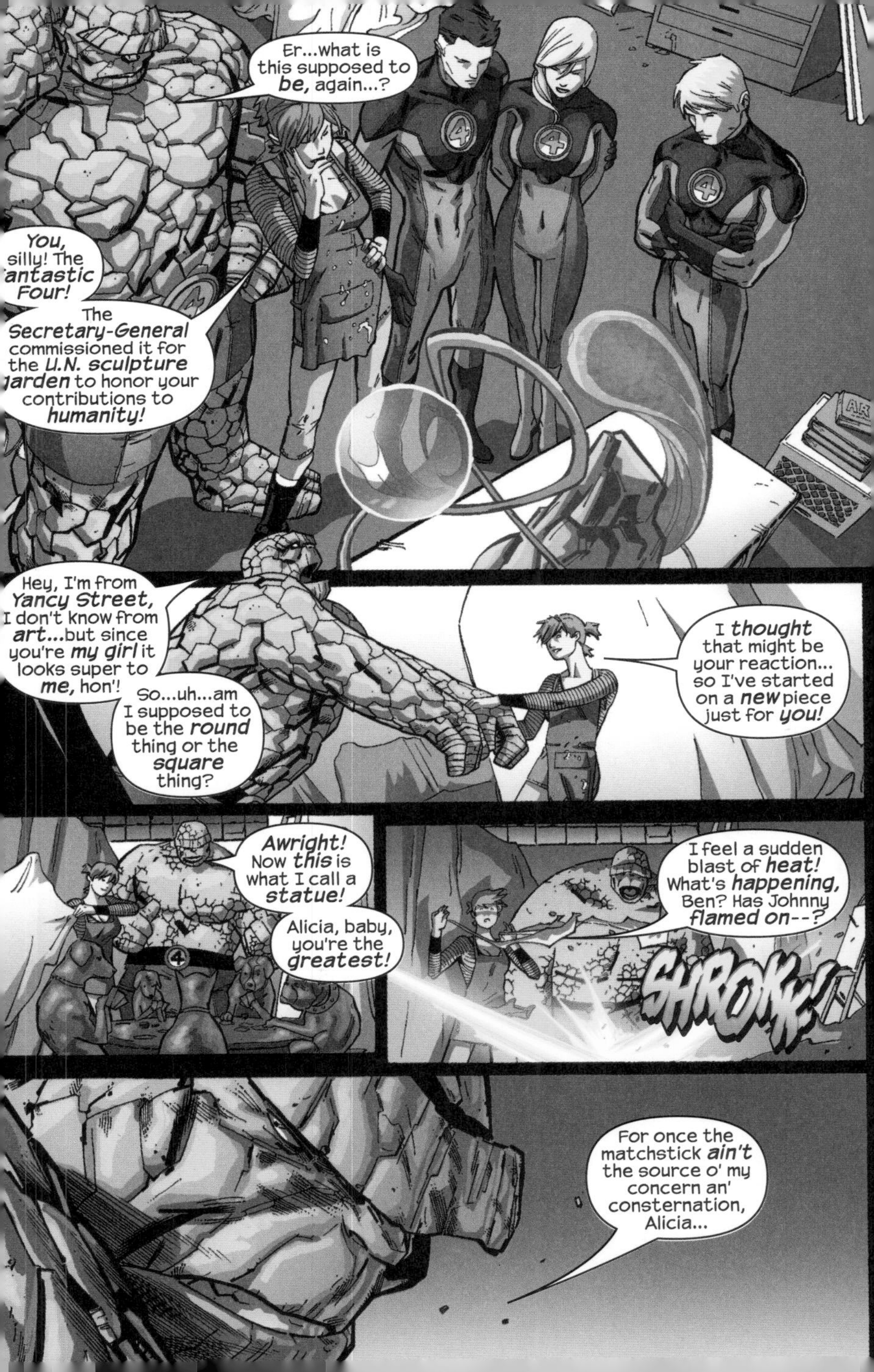
Er...what is this supposed to be, again...?
You, silly! The antastic Four!
The Secretary-General commissioned it for the U.N. sculpture arden to honor your contributions to humanity!
Hey, I'm from Yancy Street, I don't know from art...but since you're my girl it looks super to me, hon'!
So...uh...am I supposed to be the round thing or the square thing?
I thought that might be your reaction... so I've started on a new piece just for you!
Awright! Now this is what I call a statue!
Alicia, baby, you're the greatest!
I feel a sudden blast of heat! What's happening, Ben? Has Johnny flamed on--?
SHROKK!
For once the matchstick ain't the source o' my concern an' consternation, Alicia...

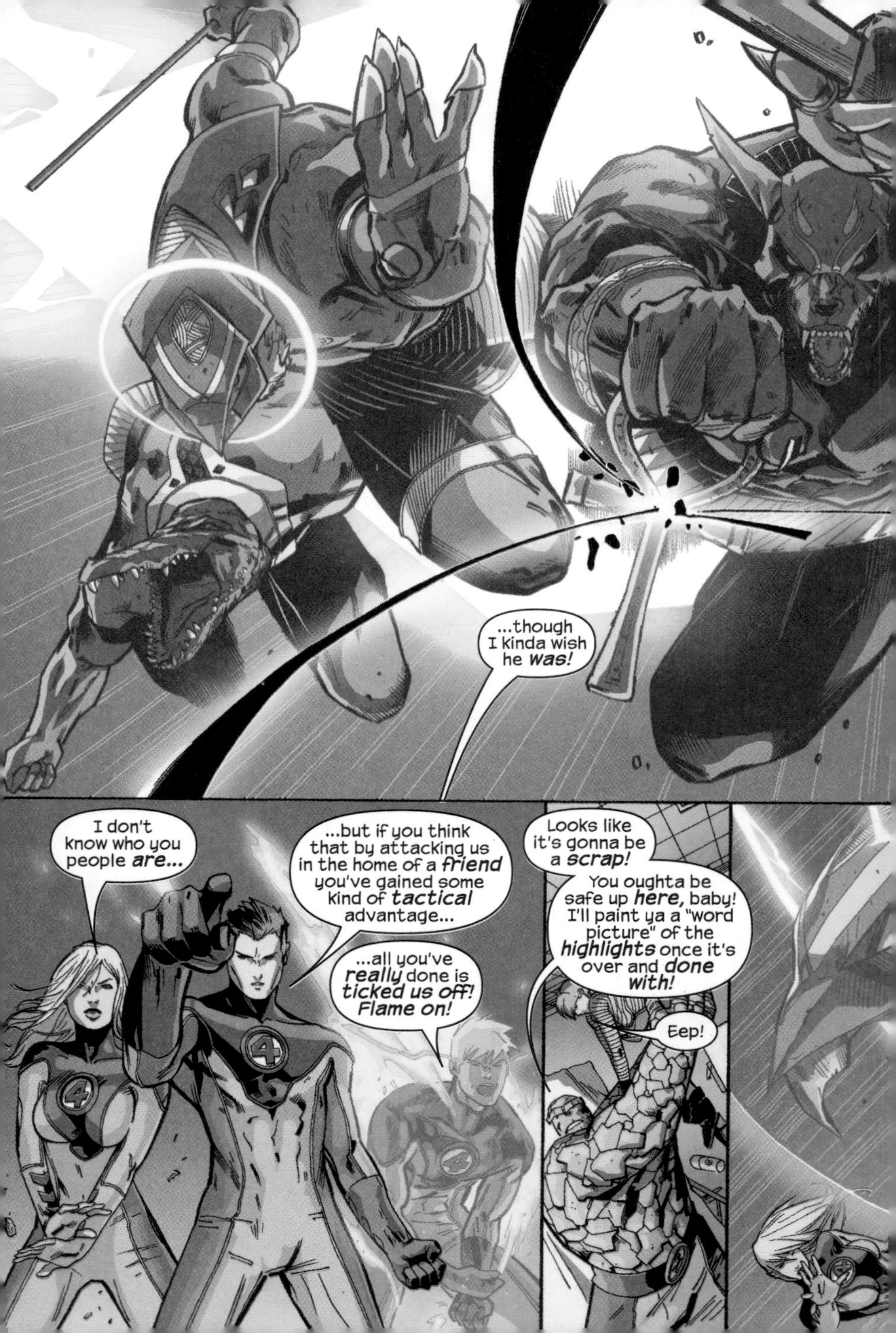
...though I kinda wish he *was!*
I don't know who you people *are...*
...but if you think that by attacking us in the home of a *friend* you've gained some kind of *tactical* advantage...
...all you've *really* done is *ticked us off! Flame on!*
Looks like it's gonna be a *scrap!*
You oughta be safe up *here,* baby! I'll paint ya a "word picture" of the *highlights* once it's over and *done with!*
Eep!

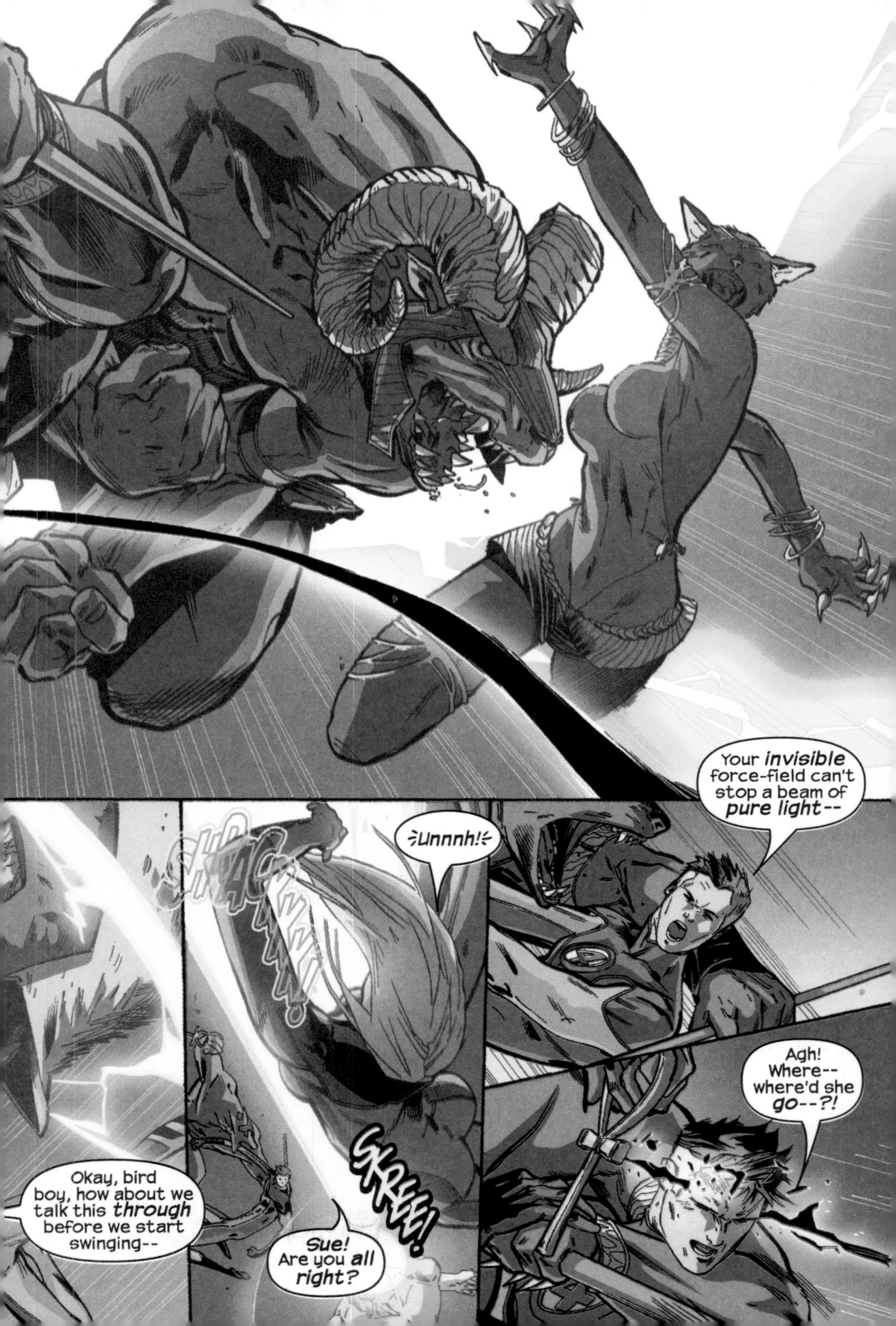
Your invisible force-field can't stop a beam of pure light--
Okay, bird boy, how about we talk this through before we start swinging--
SHHAAK!
Unnnh!
SKREE!
Sue! Are you all right?
Agh! Where-- where'd she go--?!

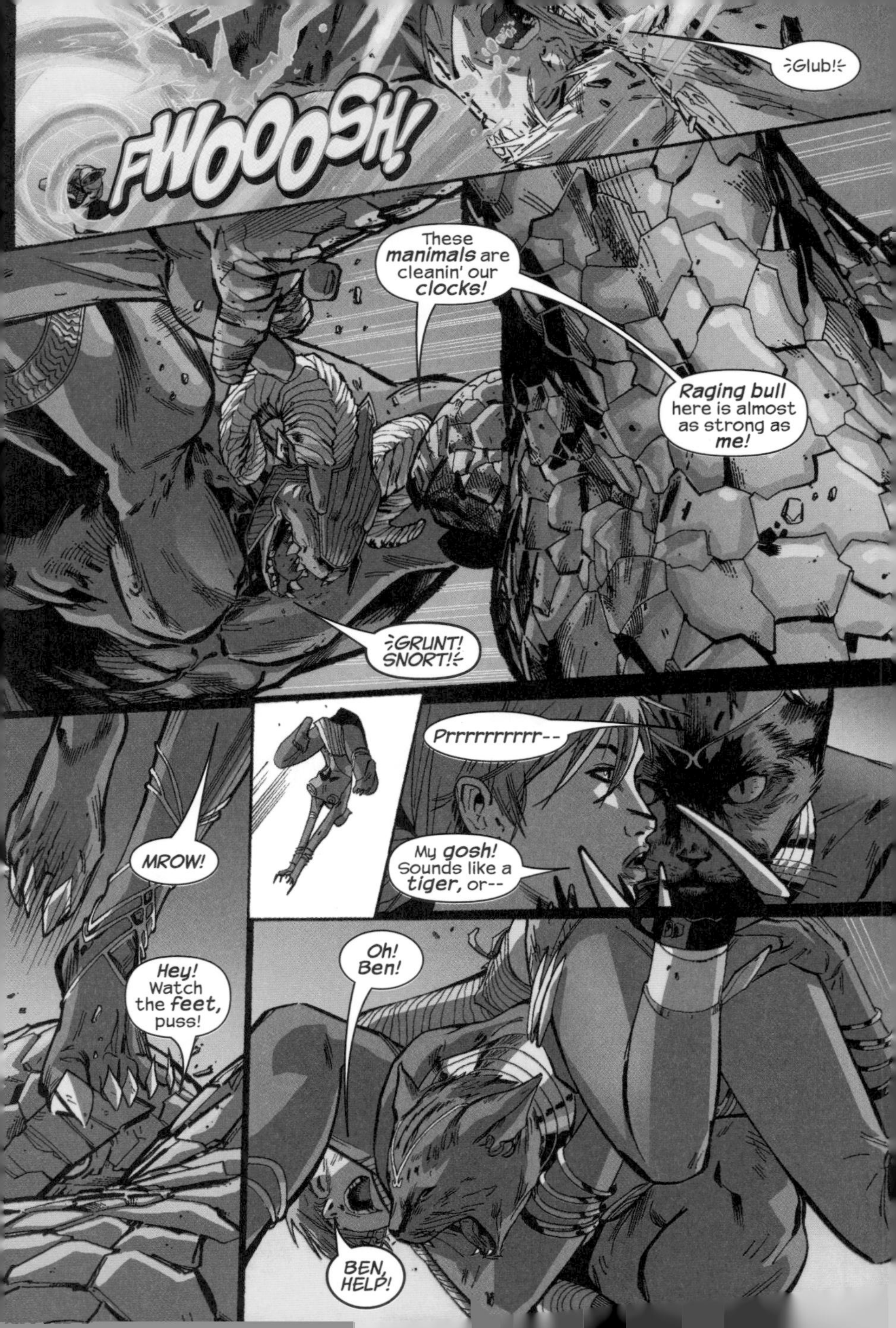

FWOOOSH!
Glub!
These manimals are cleanin' our clocks!
Raging bull here is almost as strong as me!
GRUNT! SNORT!
MROW!
Prrrrrrrrr--
My gosh! Sounds like a tiger, or--
Hey! Watch the feet, puss!
Oh! Ben!
BEN, HELP!

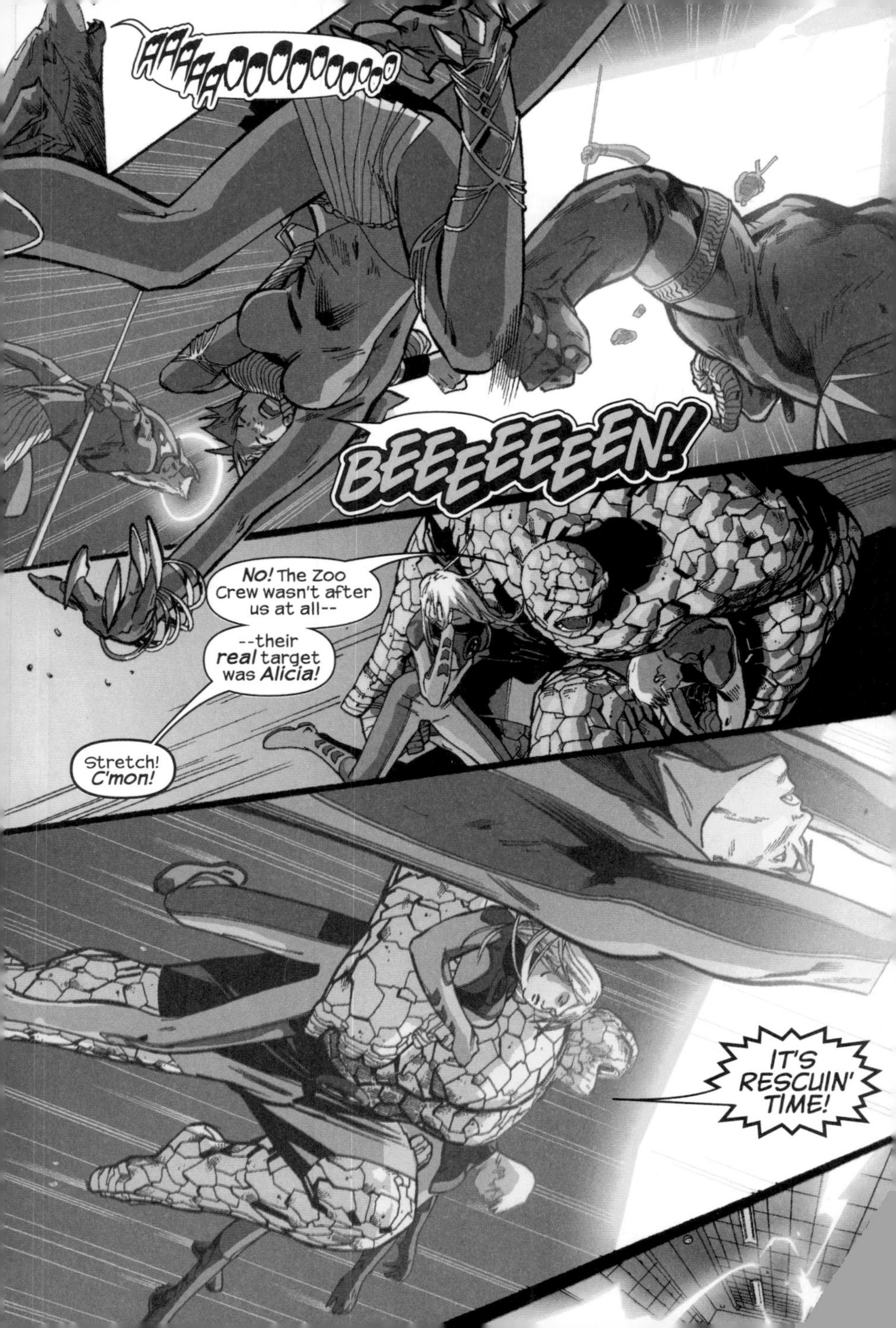
AAAAAOOOOOOOOOOO
BEEEEEEEEN!
No! The Zoo Crew wasn't after us at all--
--their real target was Alicia!
Stretch! C'mon!
IT'S RESCUIN' TIME!

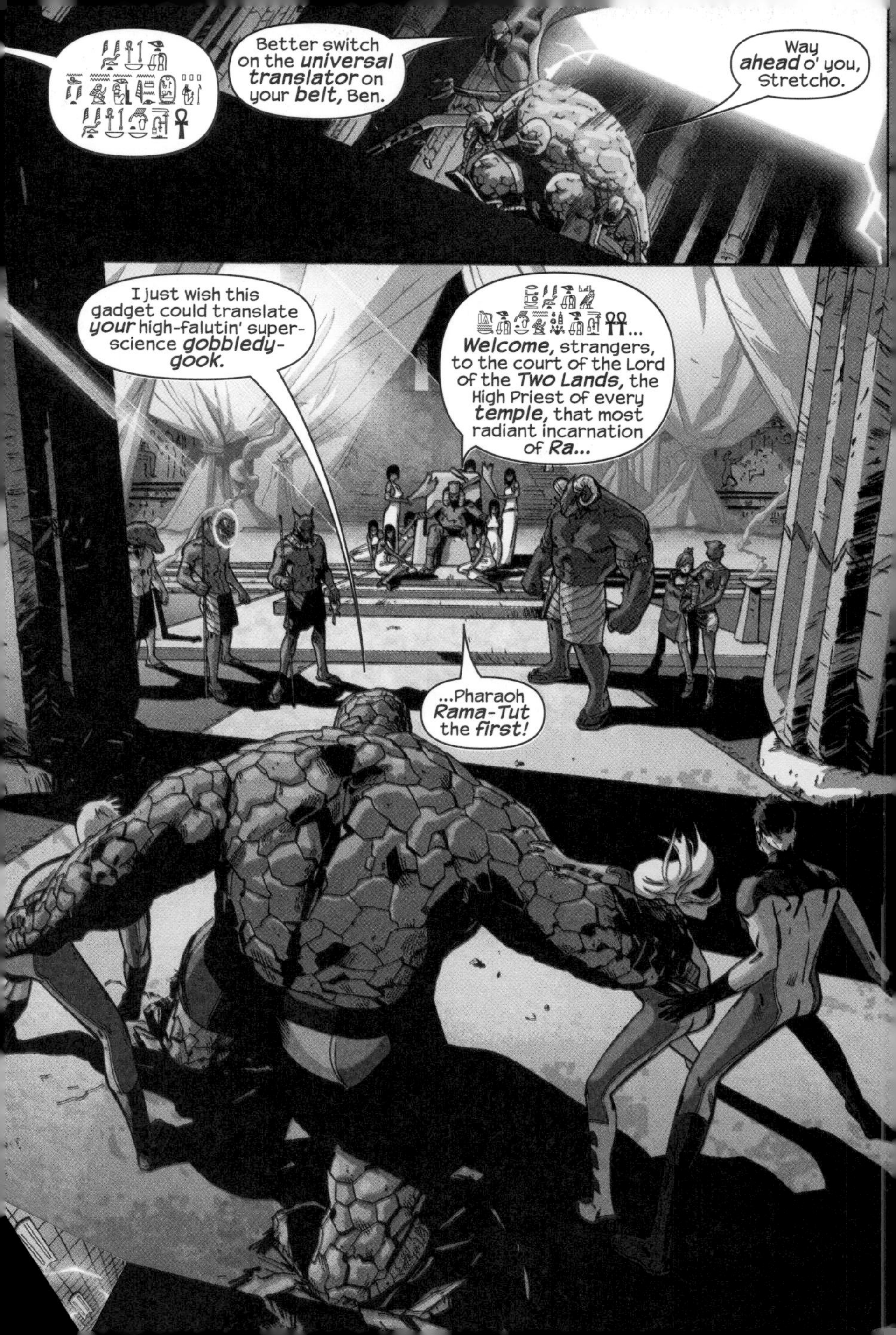

Better switch on the universal translator on your belt, Ben.
Way ahead o' you, Stretcho.
I just wish this gadget could translate your high-falutin' super-science gobbledy-gook.
...Welcome, strangers, to the court of the Lord of the Two Lands, the High Priest of every temple, that most radiant incarnation of Ra...
...Pharaoh Rama-Tut the first!

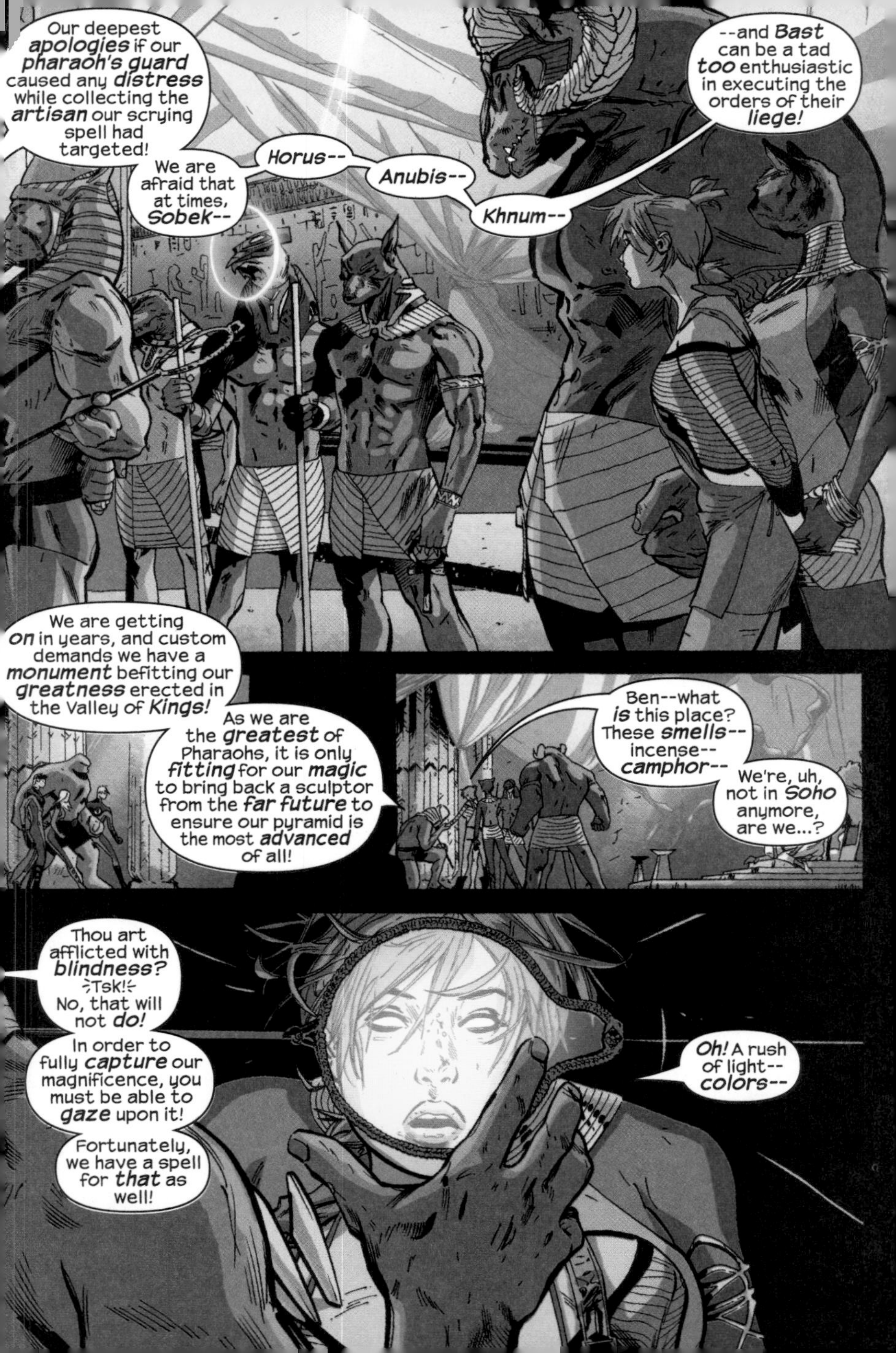
Our deepest apologies if our pharaoh's guard caused any distress while collecting the artisan our scrying spell had targeted!
We are afraid that at times, Sobek--
Horus--
Anubis--
Khnum--
--and Bast can be a tad too enthusiastic in executing the orders of their liege!
We are getting on in years, and custom demands we have a monument befitting our greatness erected in the Valley of Kings!
As we are the greatest of Pharaohs, it is only fitting for our magic to bring back a sculptor from the far future to ensure our pyramid is the most advanced of all!
Ben--what is this place? These smells--incense--camphor--
We're, uh, not in Soho anymore, are we...?
Thou art afflicted with blindness? Tsk! No, that will not do!
In order to fully capture our magnificence, you must be able to gaze upon it!
Fortunately, we have a spell for that as well!
Oh! A rush of light--colors--

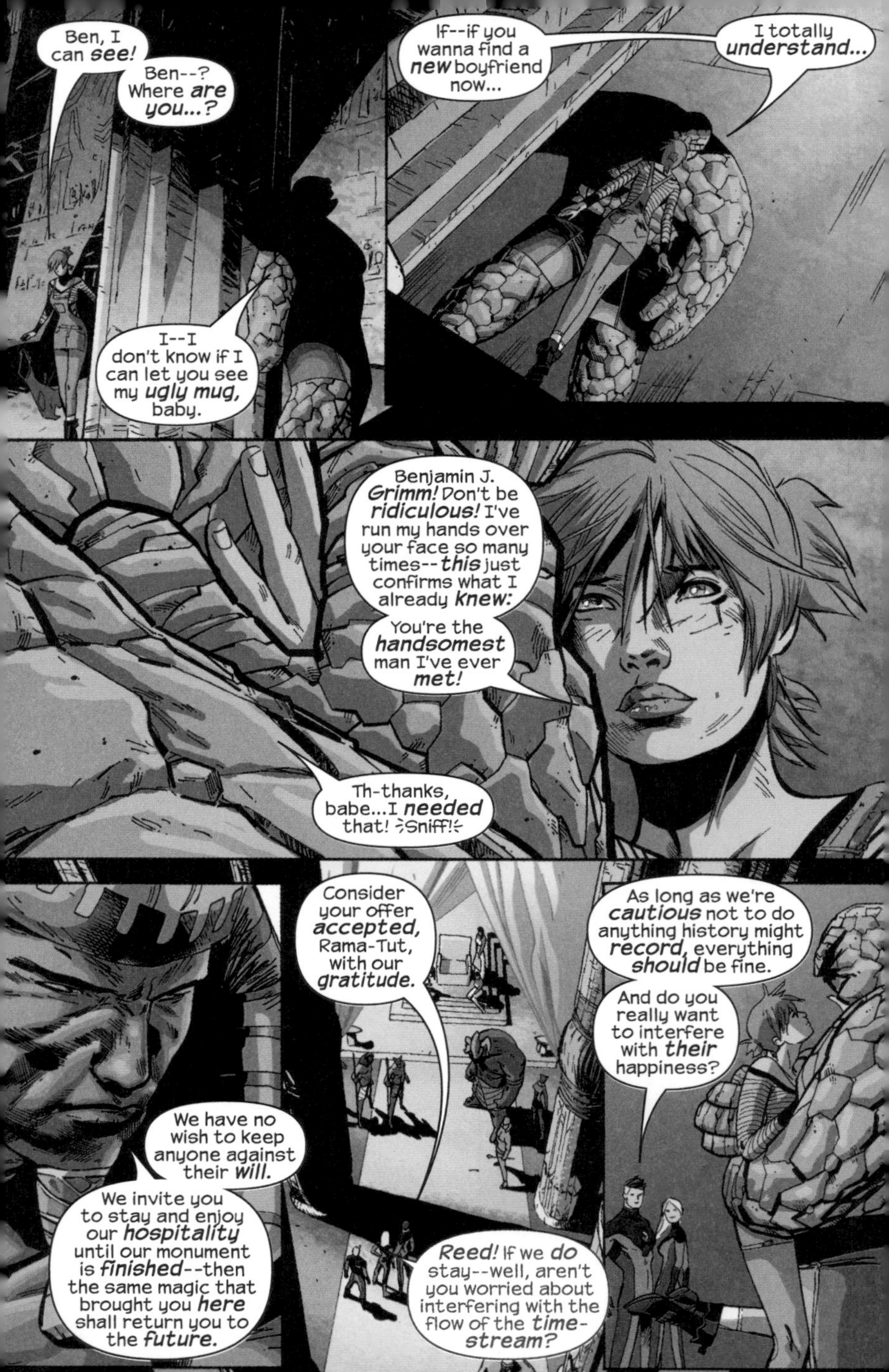

Ben, I can see!
Ben--? Where are you...?
I--I don't know if I can let you see my ugly mug, baby.
If--if you wanna find a new boyfriend now...
I totally understand...
Benjamin J. Grimm! Don't be ridiculous! I've run my hands over your face so many times--this just confirms what I already knew:
You're the handsomest man I've ever met!
Th-thanks, babe...I needed that! Sniff!
We have no wish to keep anyone against their will.
We invite you to stay and enjoy our hospitality until our monument is finished--then the same magic that brought you here shall return you to the future.
Consider your offer accepted, Rama-Tut, with our gratitude.
Reed! If we do stay--well, aren't you worried about interfering with the flow of the time-stream?
As long as we're cautious not to do anything history might record, everything should be fine.
And do you really want to interfere with their happiness?

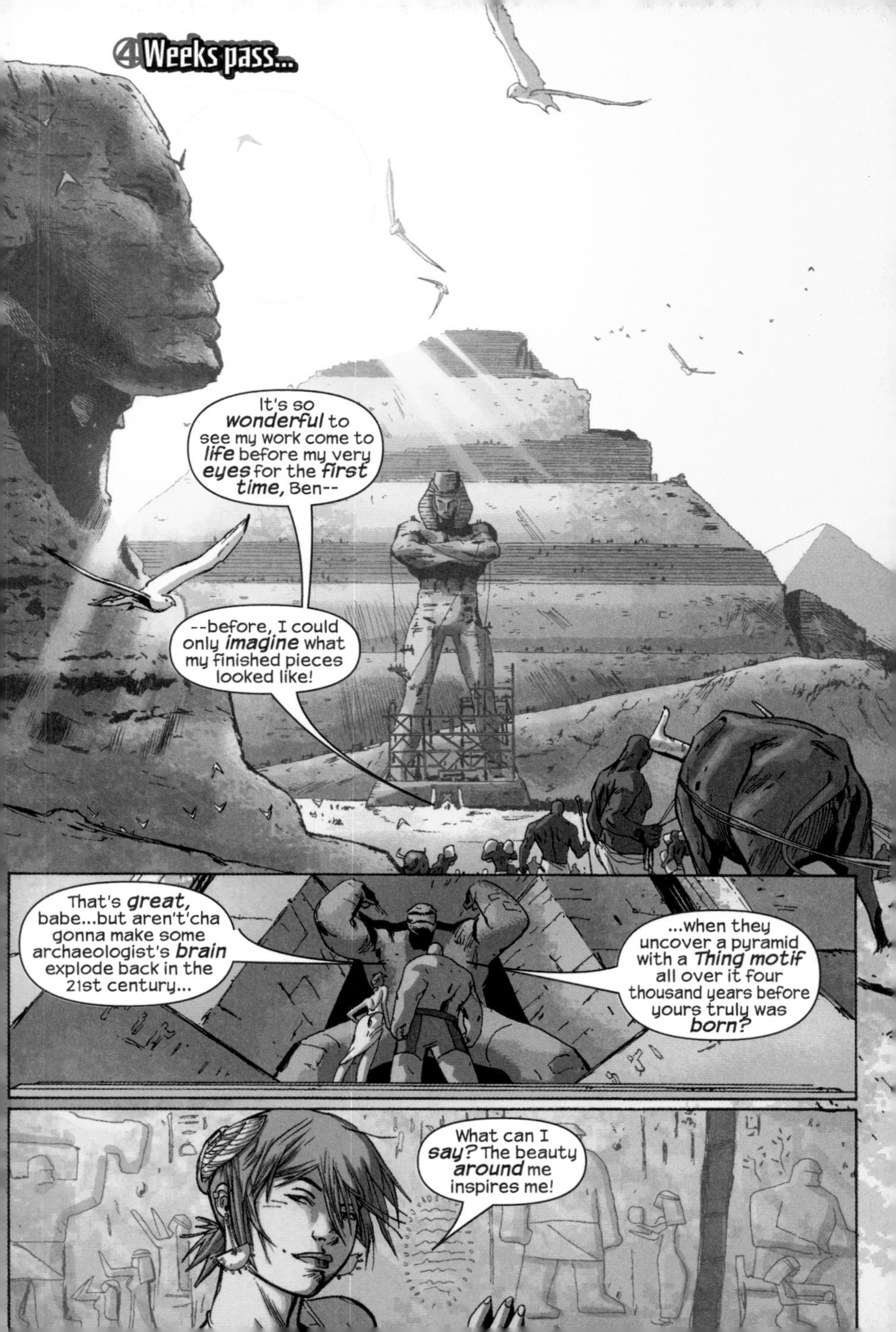
Weeks pass...
It's so wonderful to see my work come to life before my very eyes for the first time, Ben--
--before, I could only imagine what my finished pieces looked like!
That's great, babe...but aren't'cha gonna make some archaeologist's brain explode back in the 21st century...
...when they uncover a pyramid with a Thing motif all over it four thousand years before yours truly was born?
What can I say? The beauty around me inspires me!

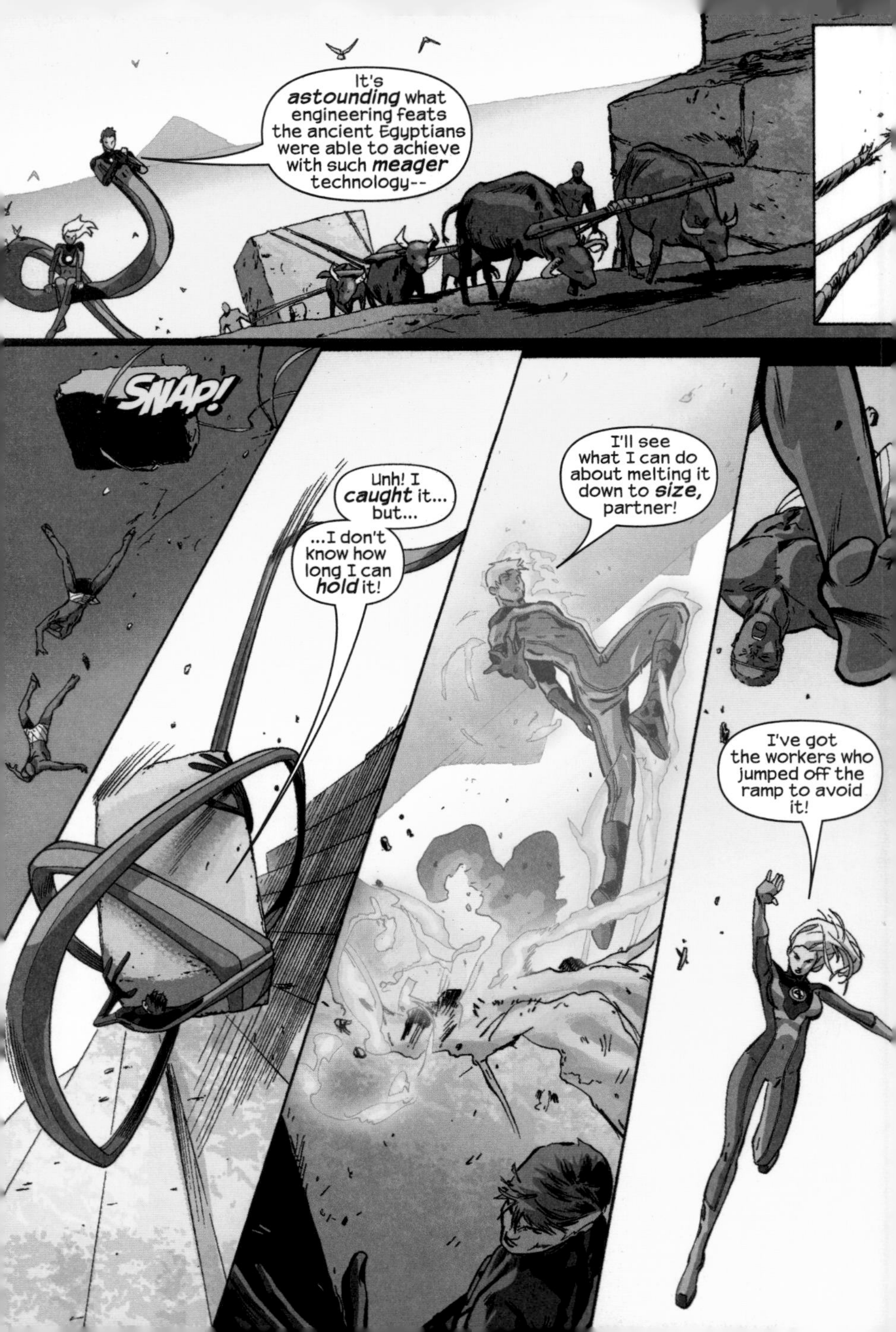
It's astounding what engineering feats the ancient Egyptians were able to achieve with such meager technology--
SNAP!
Unh! I caught it... but...
...I don't know how long I can hold it!
I'll see what I can do about melting it down to size, partner!
I've got the workers who jumped off the ramp to avoid it!

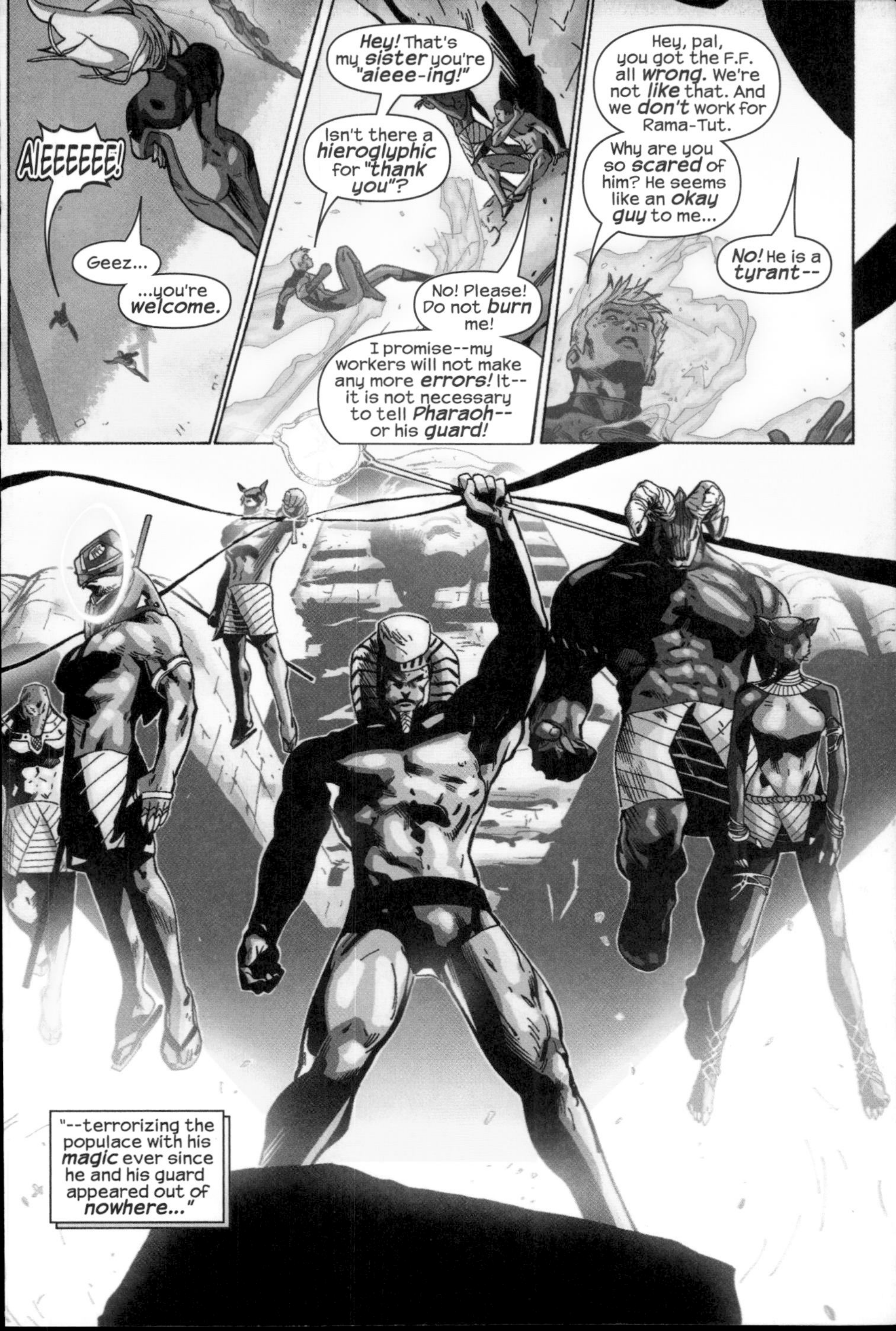
AIEEEEEE!
Geez...
...you're welcome.
Hey! That's my sister you're "aieee-ing!"
Isn't there a hieroglyphic for "thank you"?
No! Please! Do not burn me!
I promise--my workers will not make any more errors! It--it is not necessary to tell Pharaoh--or his guard!
Hey, pal, you got the F.F. all wrong. We're not like that. And we don't work for Rama-Tut.
Why are you so scared of him? He seems like an okay guy to me...
No! He is a tyrant--
"--terrorizing the populace with his magic ever since he and his guard appeared out of nowhere..."

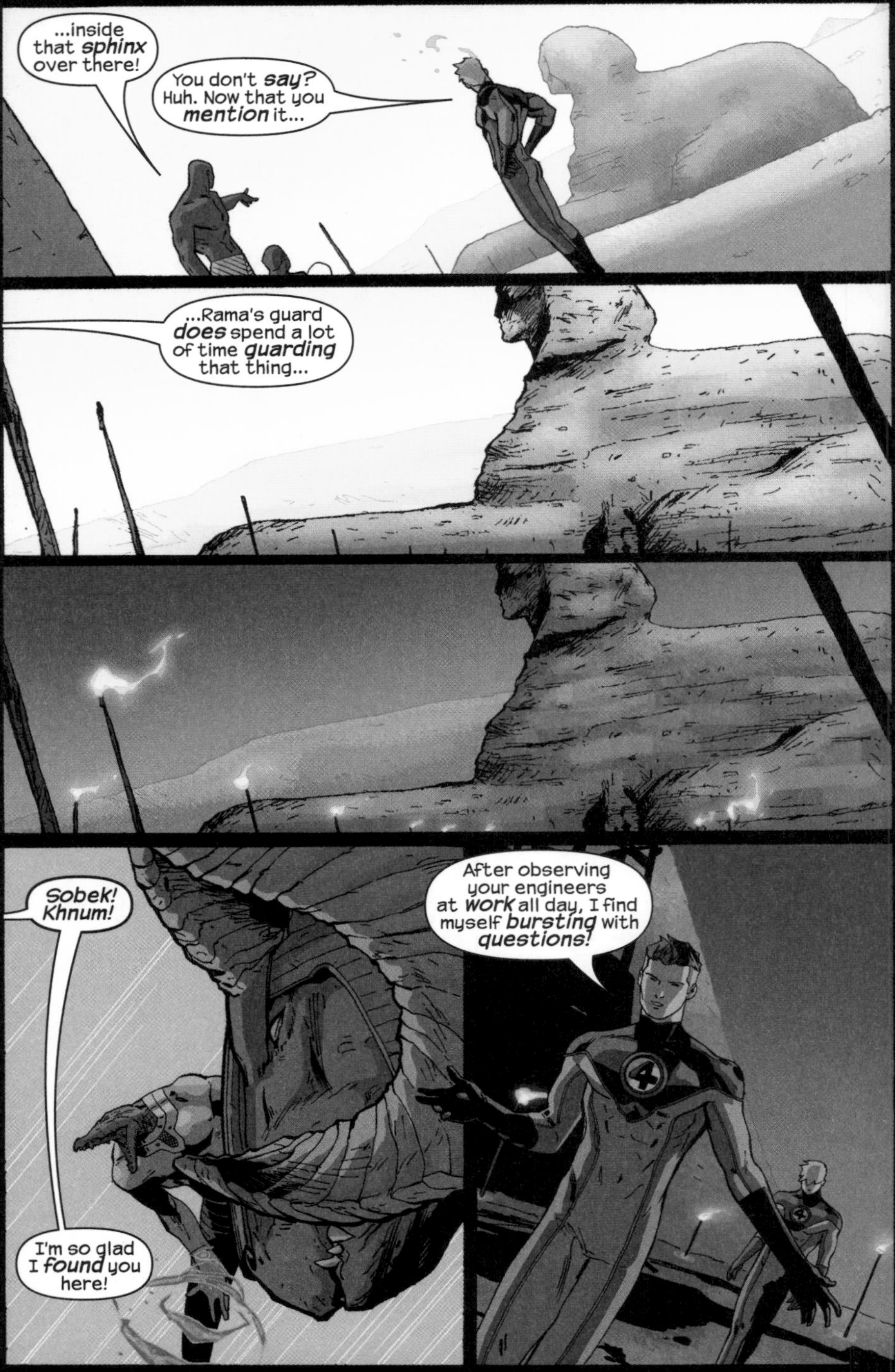
...inside that sphinx over there!
You don't say? Huh. Now that you mention it...
...Rama's guard does spend a lot of time guarding that thing...
Sobek! Khnum!
I'm so glad I found you here!
After observing your engineers at work all day, I find myself bursting with questions!

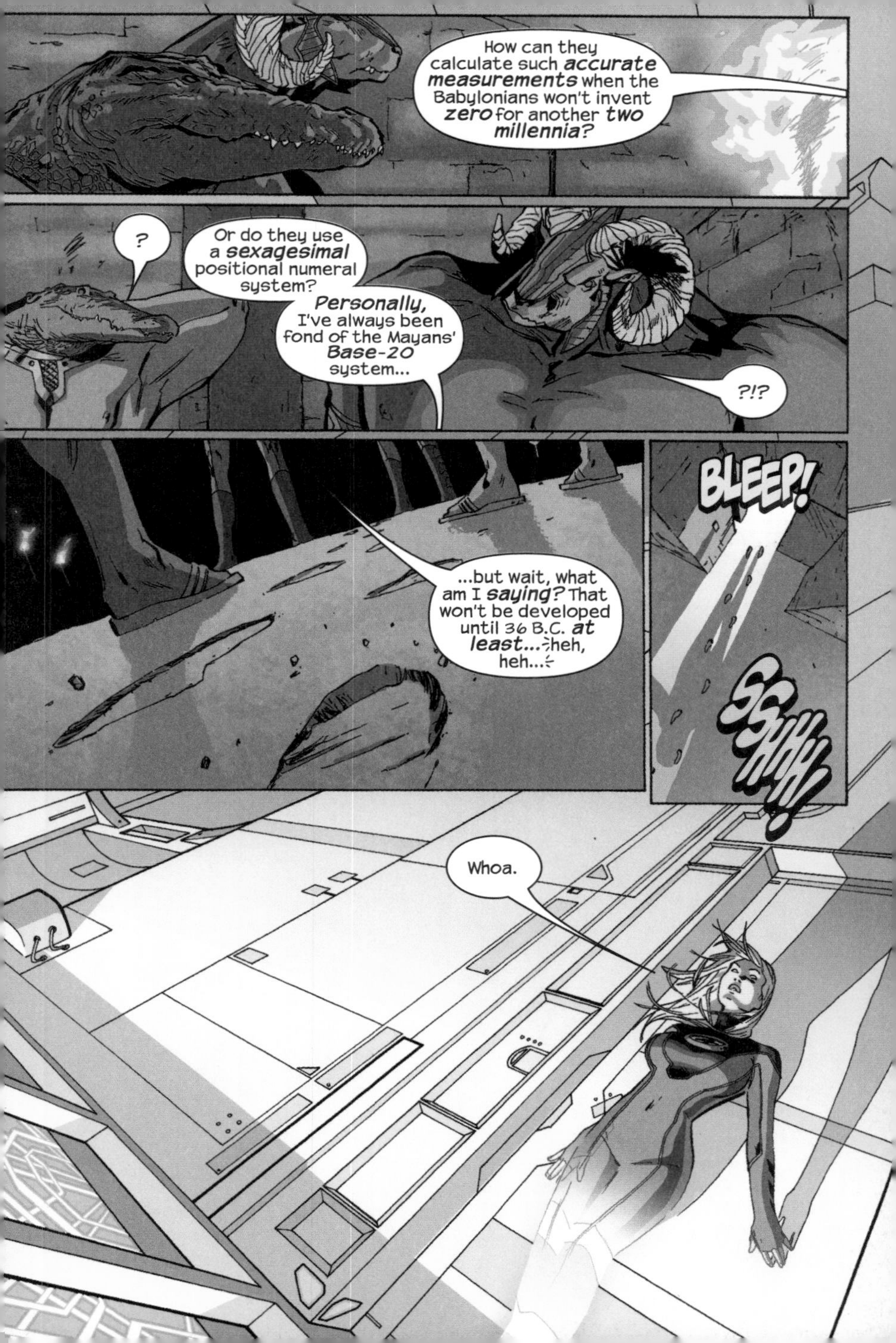
How can they calculate such accurate measurements when the Babylonians won't invent zero for another two millennia?
?
Or do they use a sexagesimal positional numeral system?
Personally, I've always been fond of the Mayans' Base-20 system...
?!?
...but wait, what am I saying? That won't be developed until 36 B.C. at least... heh, heh...
BLEEP!
SSHHH!
Whoa.

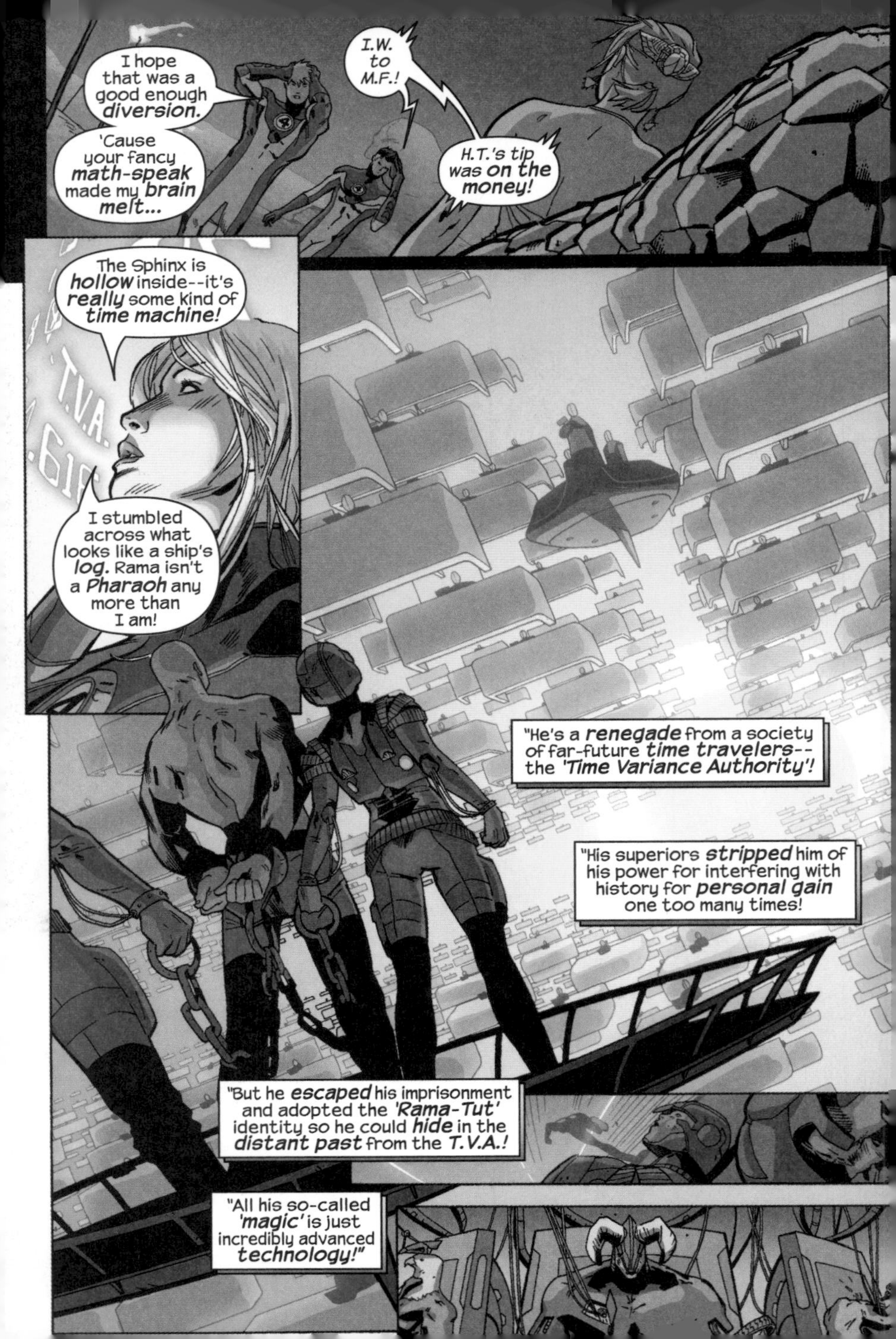
I hope that was a good enough diversion.
'Cause your fancy math-speak made my brain melt...
I.W. to M.F.!
H.T.'s tip was on the money!
The Sphinx is hollow inside--it's really some kind of time machine!
T.V.A.
I stumbled across what looks like a ship's log. Rama isn't a Pharaoh any more than I am!
"He's a renegade from a society of far-future time travelers-- the 'Time Variance Authority'!
"His superiors stripped him of his power for interfering with history for personal gain one too many times!
"But he escaped his imprisonment and adopted the 'Rama-Tut' identity so he could hide in the distant past from the T.V.A.!
"All his so-called 'magic' is just incredibly advanced technology!"

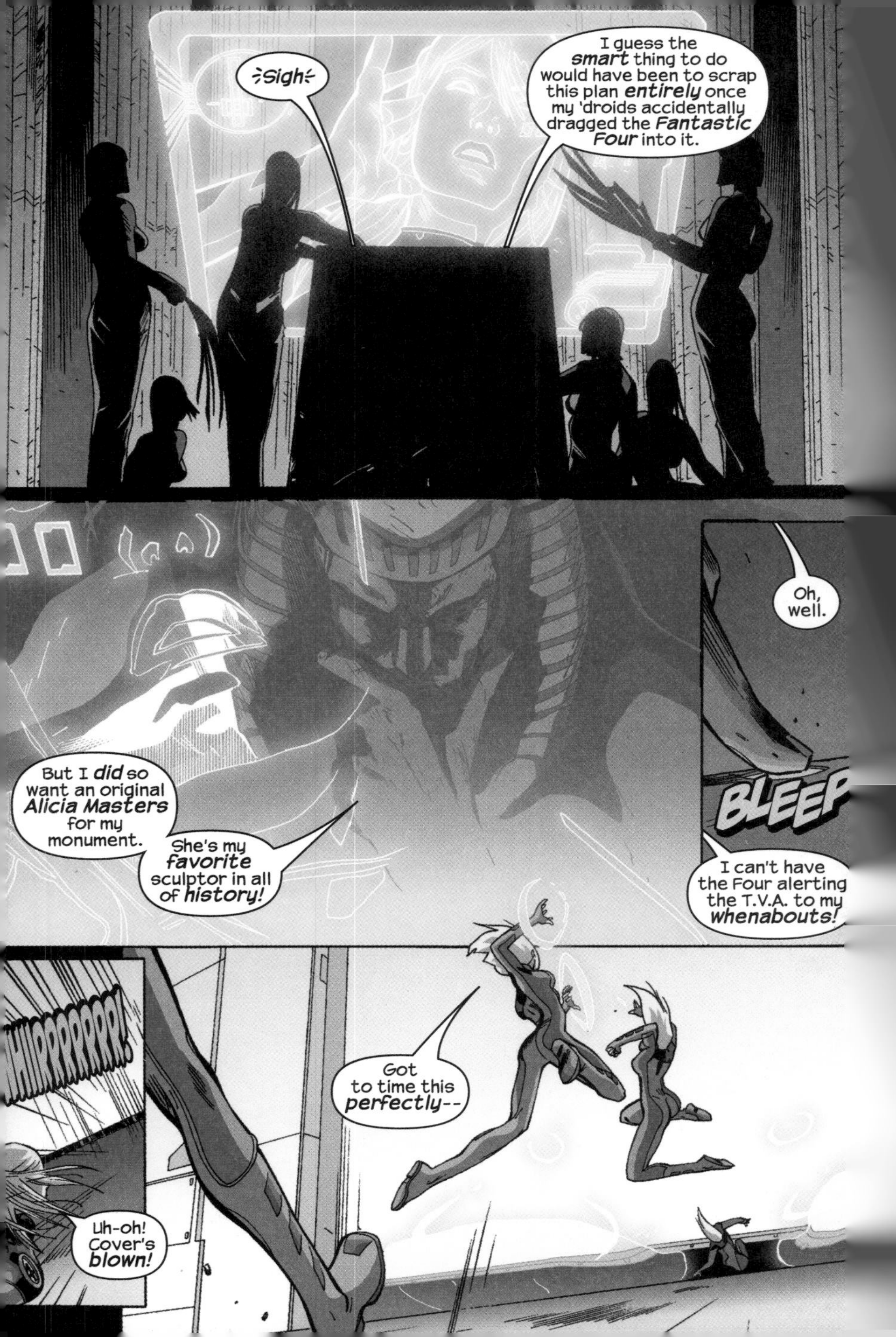

~Sigh~
I guess the smart thing to do would have been to scrap this plan entirely once my 'droids accidentally dragged the Fantastic Four into it.
Oh, well.
But I did so want an original Alicia Masters for my monument.
She's my favorite sculptor in all of history!
BLEEP
I can't have the Four alerting the T.V.A. to my whenabouts!
HIIRRRRRRR!
Got to time this perfectly--
Uh-oh! Cover's blown!

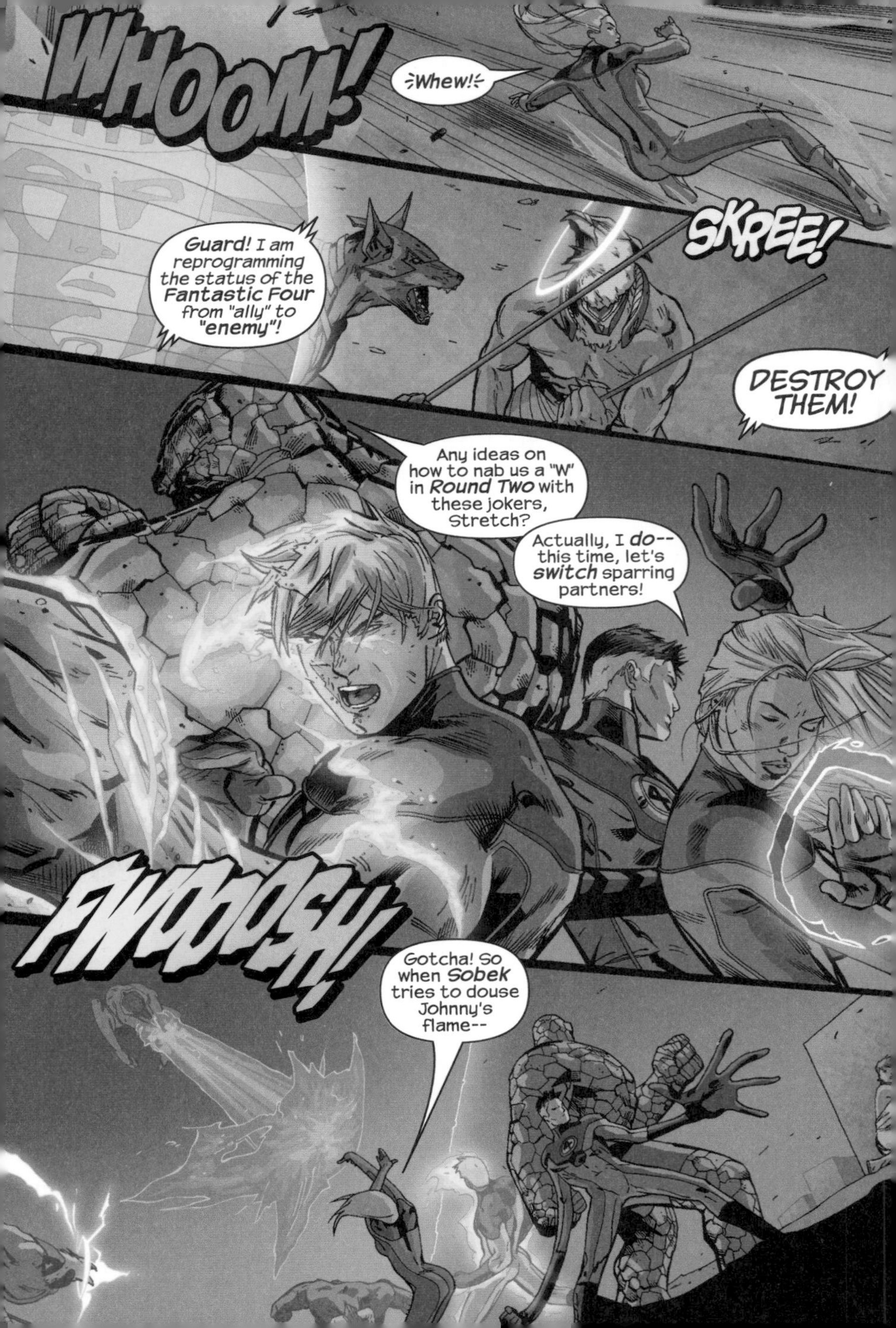
WHOOM!
Whew!
Guard! I am reprogramming the status of the Fantastic Four from "ally" to "enemy"!
SKREE!
DESTROY THEM!
Any ideas on how to nab us a "W" in Round Two with these jokers, Stretch?
Actually, I do-- this time, let's switch sparring partners!
FWOOOSH!
Gotcha! So when Sobek tries to douse Johnny's flame--

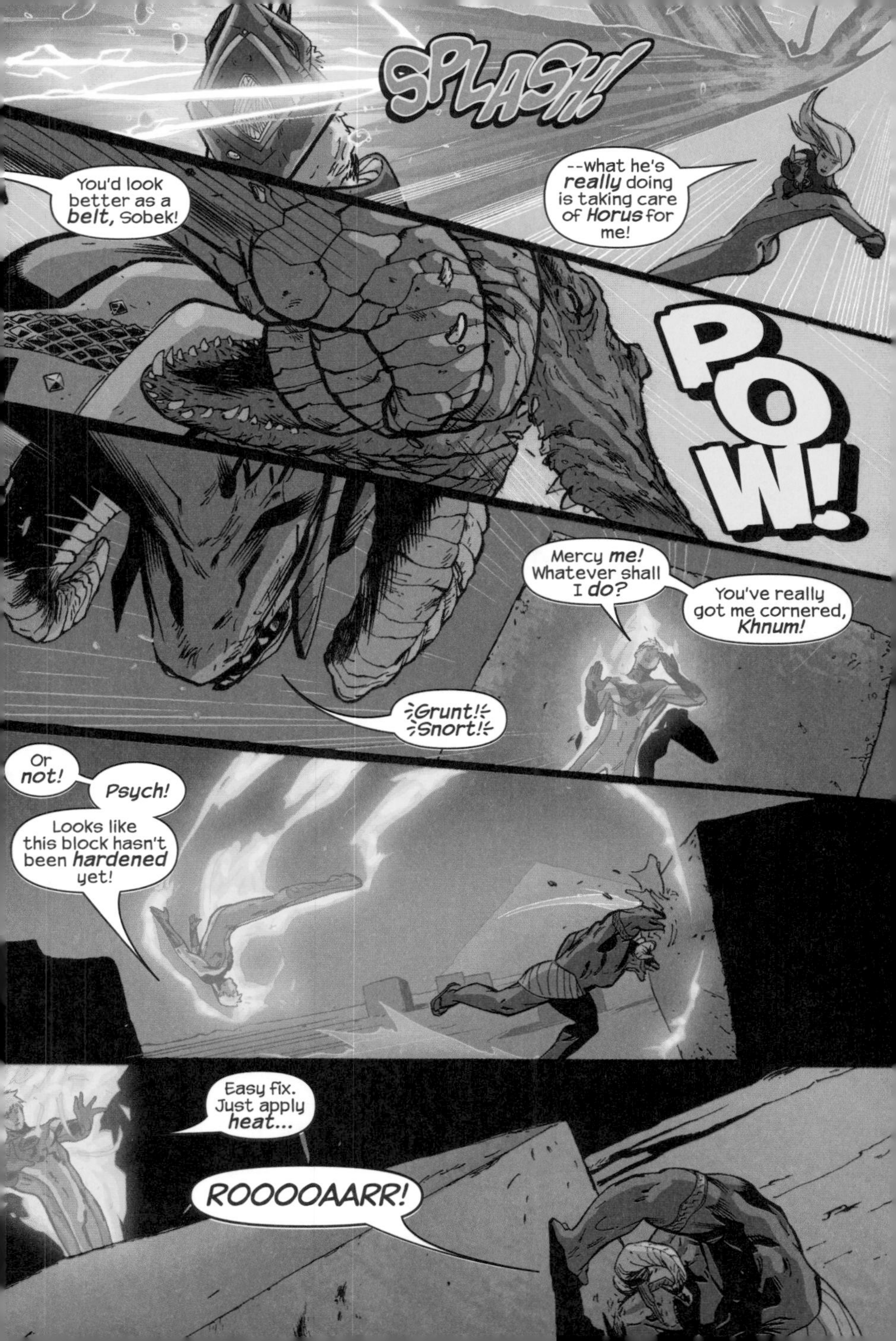
SPLASH!
You'd look better as a belt, Sobek!
--what he's really doing is taking care of Horus for me!
POW!
Mercy me! Whatever shall I do?
You've really got me cornered, Khnum!
Grunt! Snort!
Or not!
Psych!
Looks like this block hasn't been hardened yet!
Easy fix. Just apply heat...
ROOOOAARR!

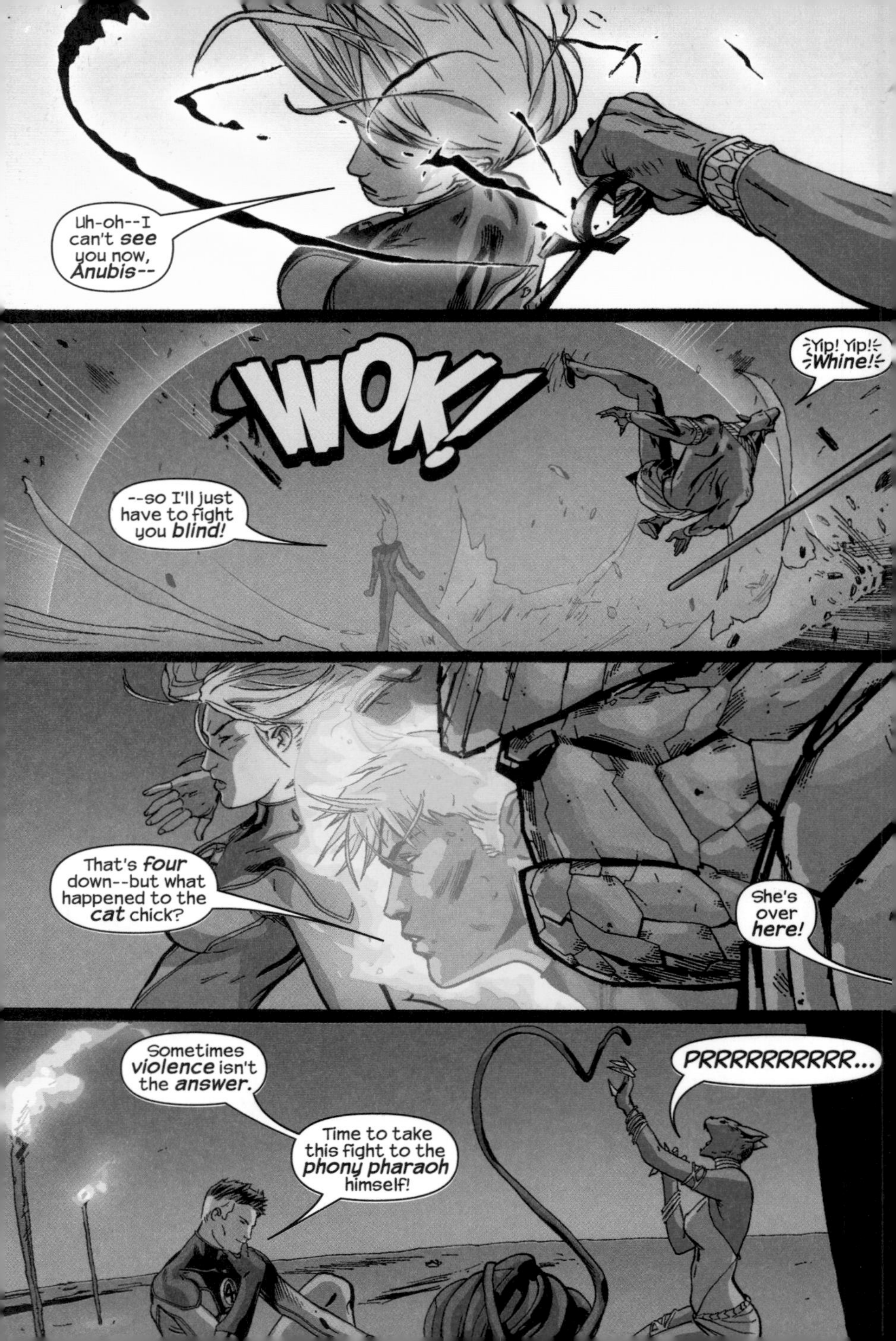
Uh-oh--I can't see you now, Anubis--
WOK!
Yip! Yip! Whine!
--so I'll just have to fight you blind!
That's four down--but what happened to the cat chick?
She's over here!
Sometimes violence isn't the answer.
PRRRRRRRRR...
Time to take this fight to the phony pharaoh himself!

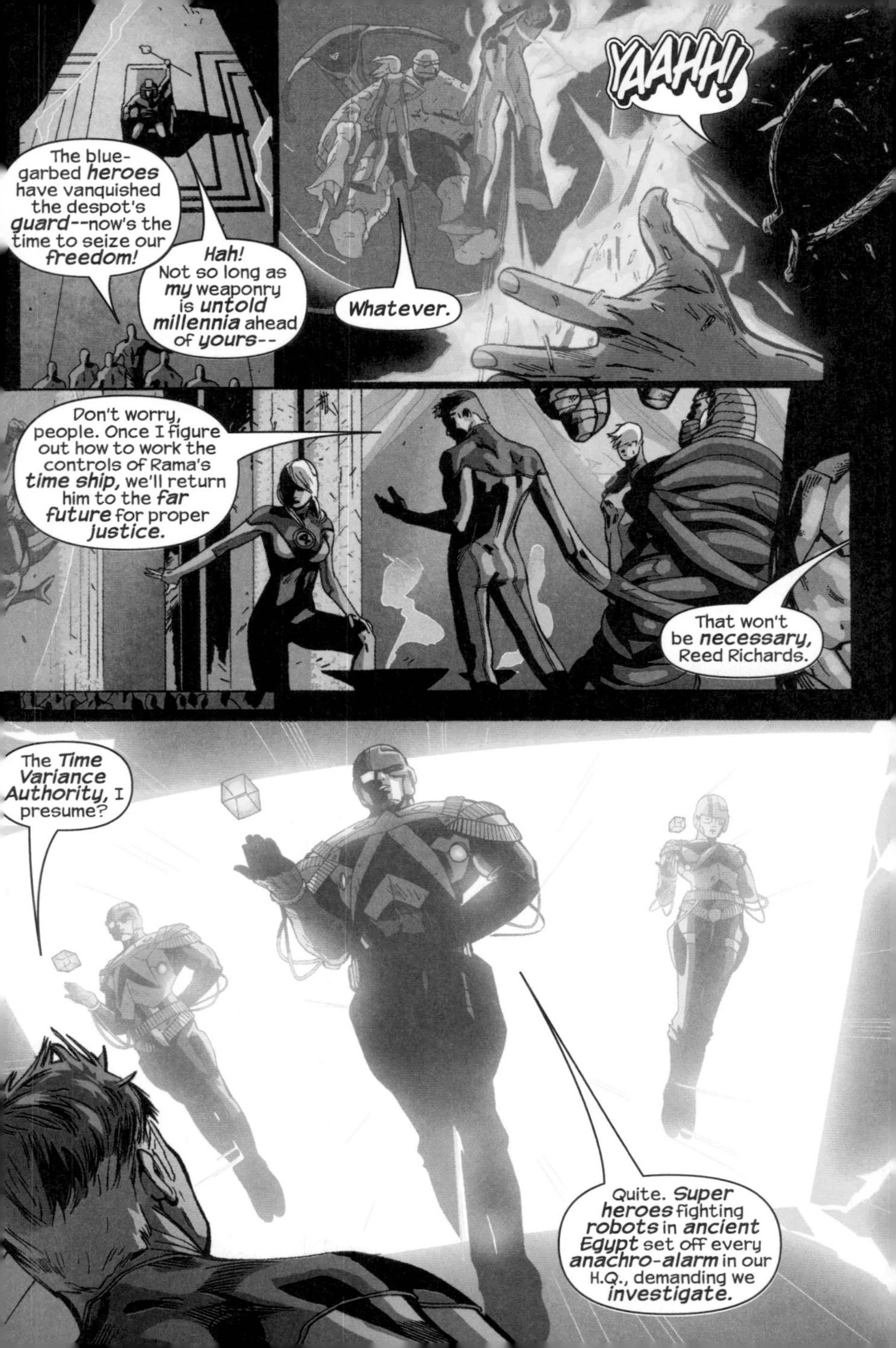
YAAHH!
The blue-garbed heroes have vanquished the despot's guard--now's the time to seize our freedom!
Hah! Not so long as my weaponry is untold millennia ahead of yours--
Whatever.
Don't worry, people. Once I figure out how to work the controls of Rama's time ship, we'll return him to the far future for proper justice.
That won't be necessary, Reed Richards.
The Time Variance Authority, I presume?
Quite. Super heroes fighting robots in ancient Egypt set off every anachro-alarm in our H.Q., demanding we investigate.

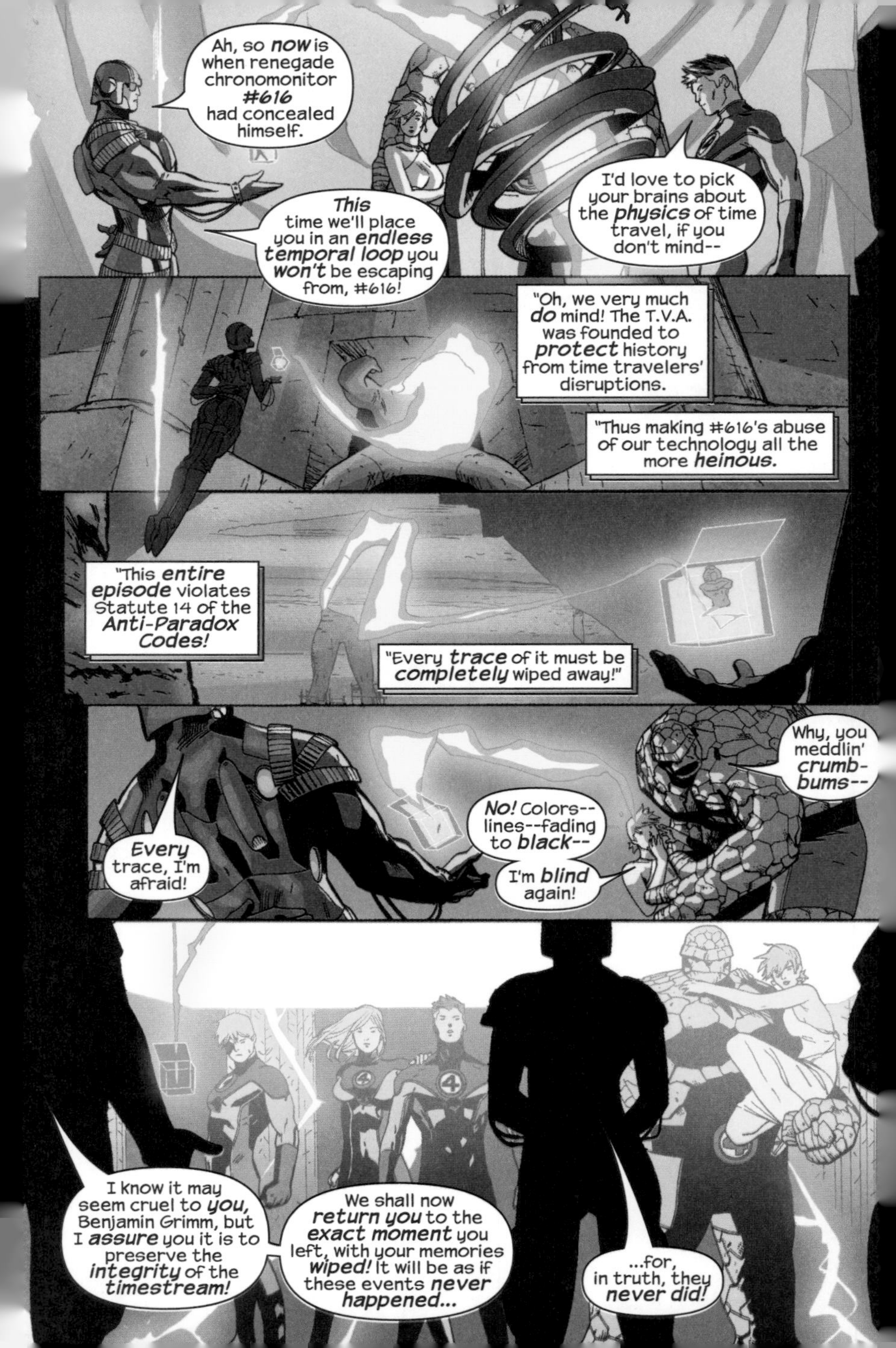
Ah, so now is when renegade chronomonitor #616 had concealed himself.
I'd love to pick your brains about the physics of time travel, if you don't mind--
This time we'll place you in an endless temporal loop you won't be escaping from, #616!
"Oh, we very much do mind! The T.V.A. was founded to protect history from time travelers' disruptions.
"Thus making #616's abuse of our technology all the more heinous.
"This entire episode violates Statute 14 of the Anti-Paradox Codes!
"Every trace of it must be completely wiped away!"
Why, you meddlin' crumb-bums--
No! Colors--lines--fading to black--
I'm blind again!
Every trace, I'm afraid!
I know it may seem cruel to you, Benjamin Grimm, but I assure you it is to preserve the integrity of the timestream!
We shall now return you to the exact moment you left, with your memories wiped! It will be as if these events never happened...
...for, in truth, they never did!

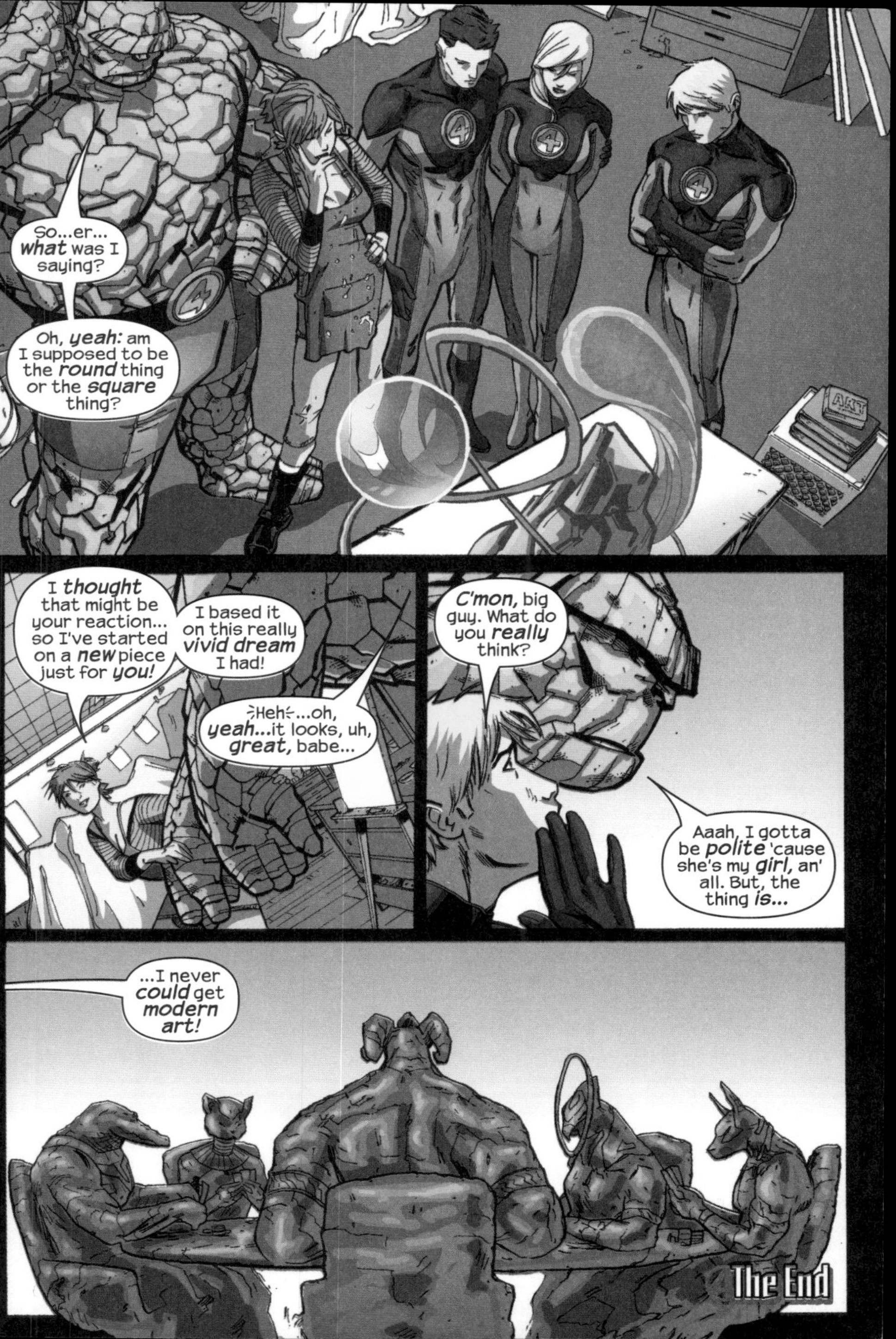

So...er... what was I saying?
Oh, yeah: am I supposed to be the round thing or the square thing?
I thought that might be your reaction... so I've started on a new piece just for you!
I based it on this really vivid dream I had!
Heh...oh, yeah...it looks, uh, great, babe...
C'mon, big guy. What do you really think?
Aaah, I gotta be polite 'cause she's my girl, an' all. But, the thing is...
...I never could get modern art!
The End

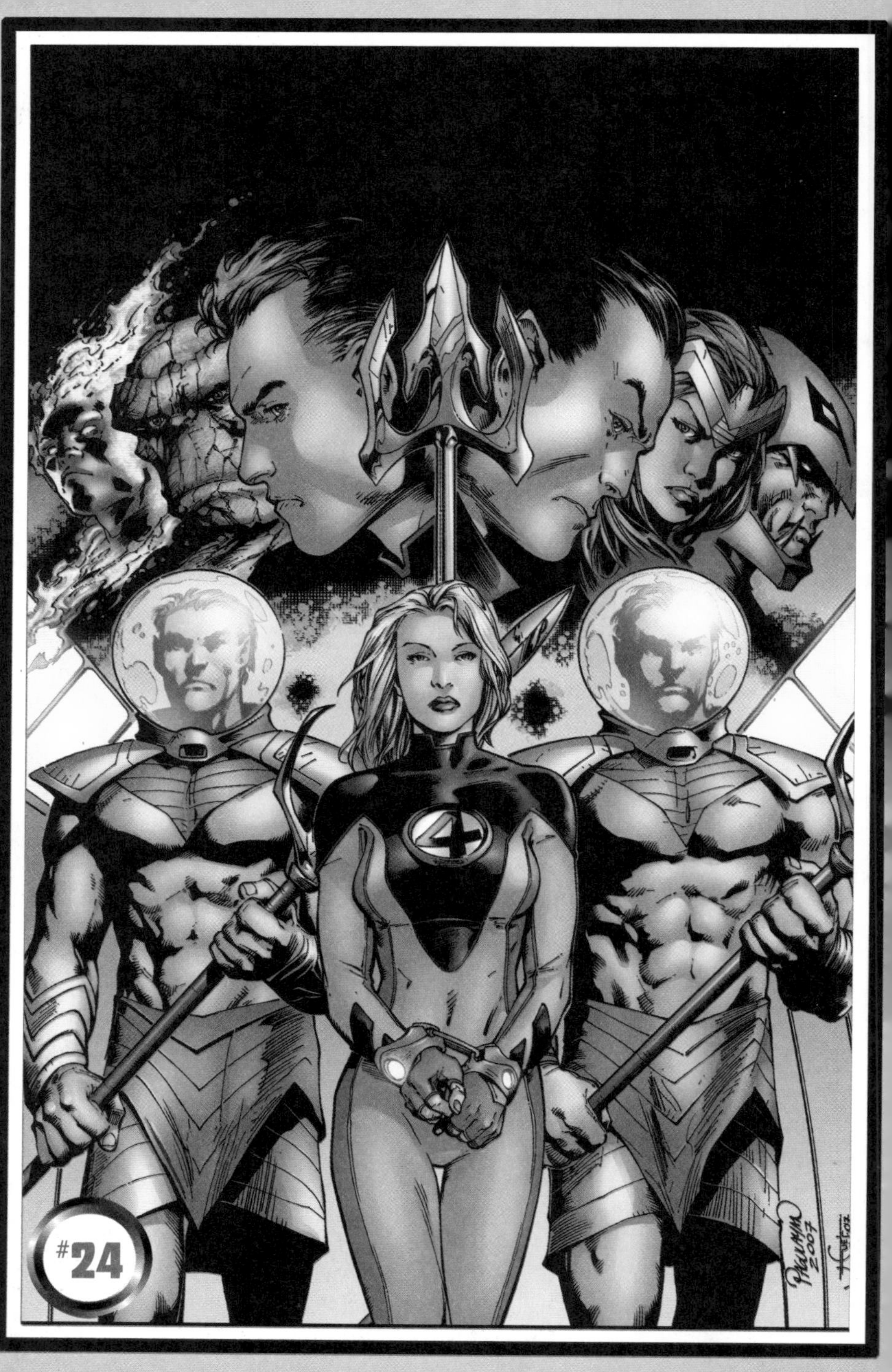
#24

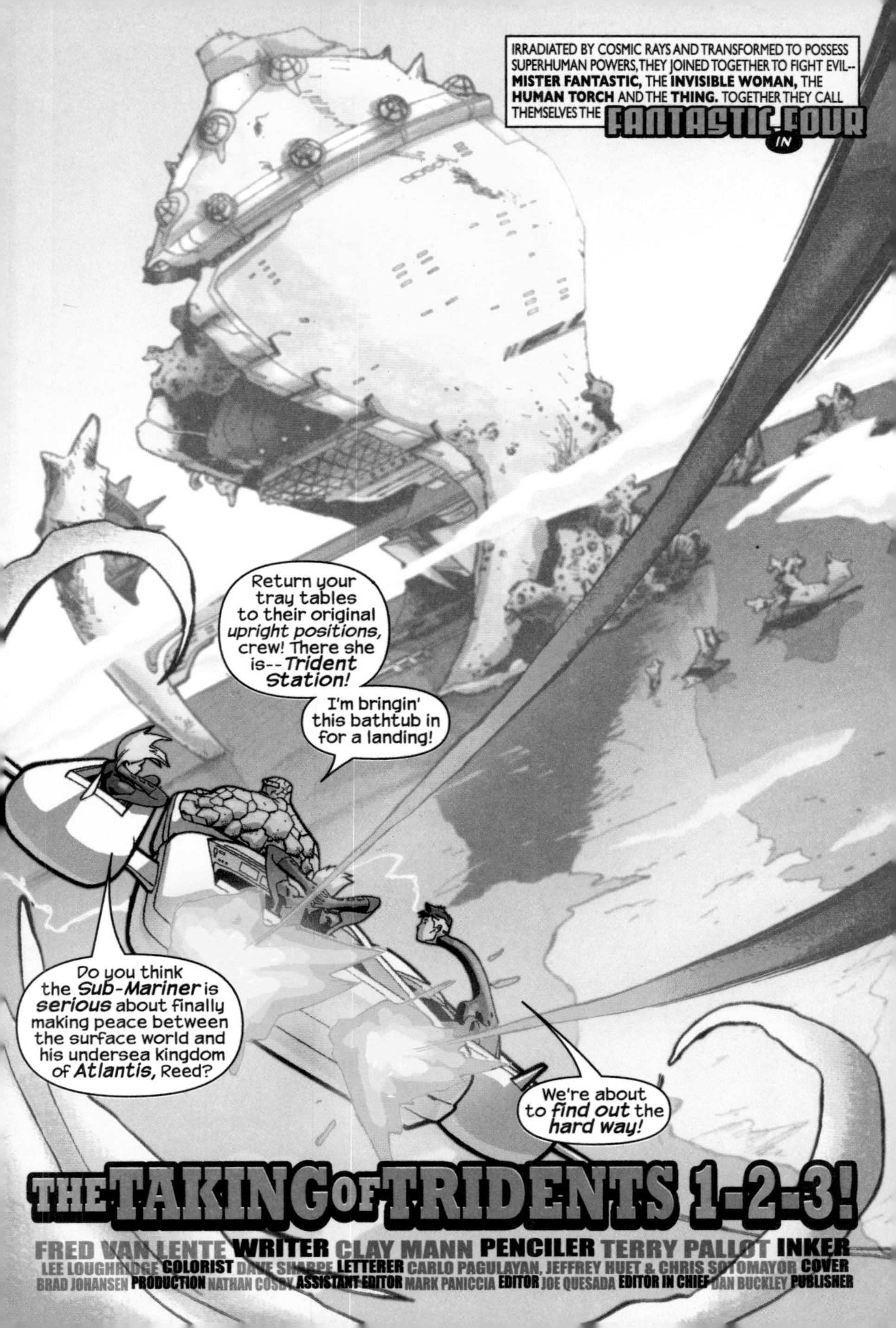

IRRADIATED BY COSMIC RAYS AND TRANSFORMED TO POSSESS SUPERHUMAN POWERS, THEY JOINED TOGETHER TO FIGHT EVIL-- MISTER FANTASTIC, THE INVISIBLE WOMAN, THE HUMAN TORCH AND THE THING. TOGETHER THEY CALL THEMSELVES THE FANTASTIC FOUR IN
Return your tray tables to their original upright positions, crew! There she is--Trident Station!
I'm bringin' this bathtub in for a landing!
Do you think the Sub-Mariner is serious about finally making peace between the surface world and his undersea kingdom of Atlantis, Reed?
We're about to find out the hard way!
THE TAKING OF TRIDENTS 1-2-3!
FRED VAN LENTE WRITER CLAY MANN PENCILER TERRY PALLOT INKER
LEE LOUGHRIDGE COLORIST DAVE SHARPE LETTERER CARLO PAGULAYAN, JEFFREY HUET & CHRIS SOTOMAYOR COVER
BRAD JOHANSEN PRODUCTION NATHAN COSBY ASSISTANT EDITOR MARK PANICCIA EDITOR JOE QUESADA EDITOR IN CHIEF DAN BUCKLEY PUBLISHER

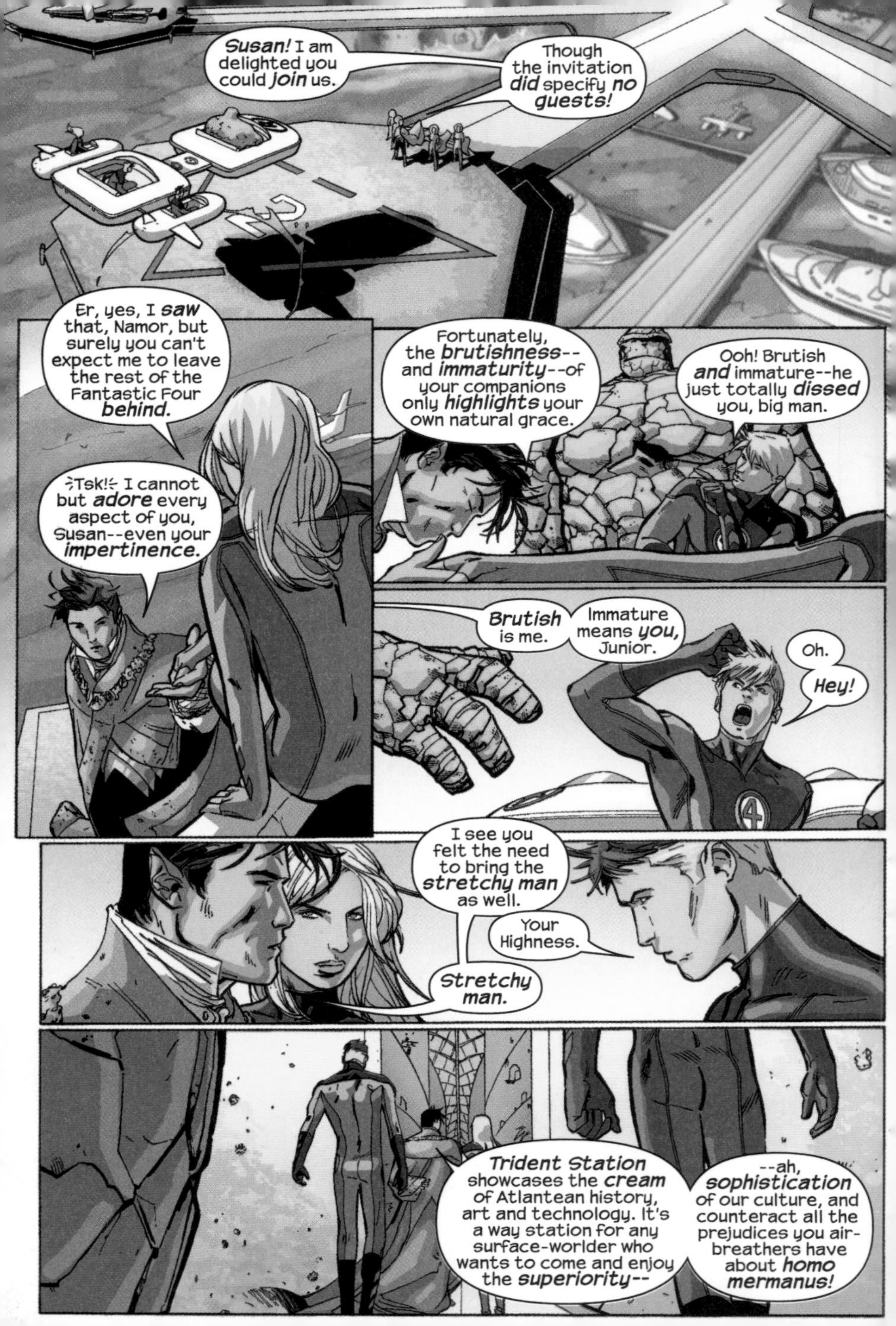
Susan! I am delighted you could join us.
Though the invitation did specify no guests!
Er, yes, I saw that, Namor, but surely you can't expect me to leave the rest of the Fantastic Four behind.
Tsk! I cannot but adore every aspect of you, Susan--even your impertinence.
Fortunately, the brutishness--and immaturity--of your companions only highlights your own natural grace.
Ooh! Brutish and immature--he just totally dissed you, big man.
Brutish is me.
Immature means you, Junior.
Oh.
Hey!
I see you felt the need to bring the stretchy man as well.
Your Highness.
Stretchy man.
Trident Station showcases the cream of Atlantean history, art and technology. It's a way station for any surface-worlder who wants to come and enjoy the superiority--
--ah, sophistication of our culture, and counteract all the prejudices you air-breathers have about homo mermanus!

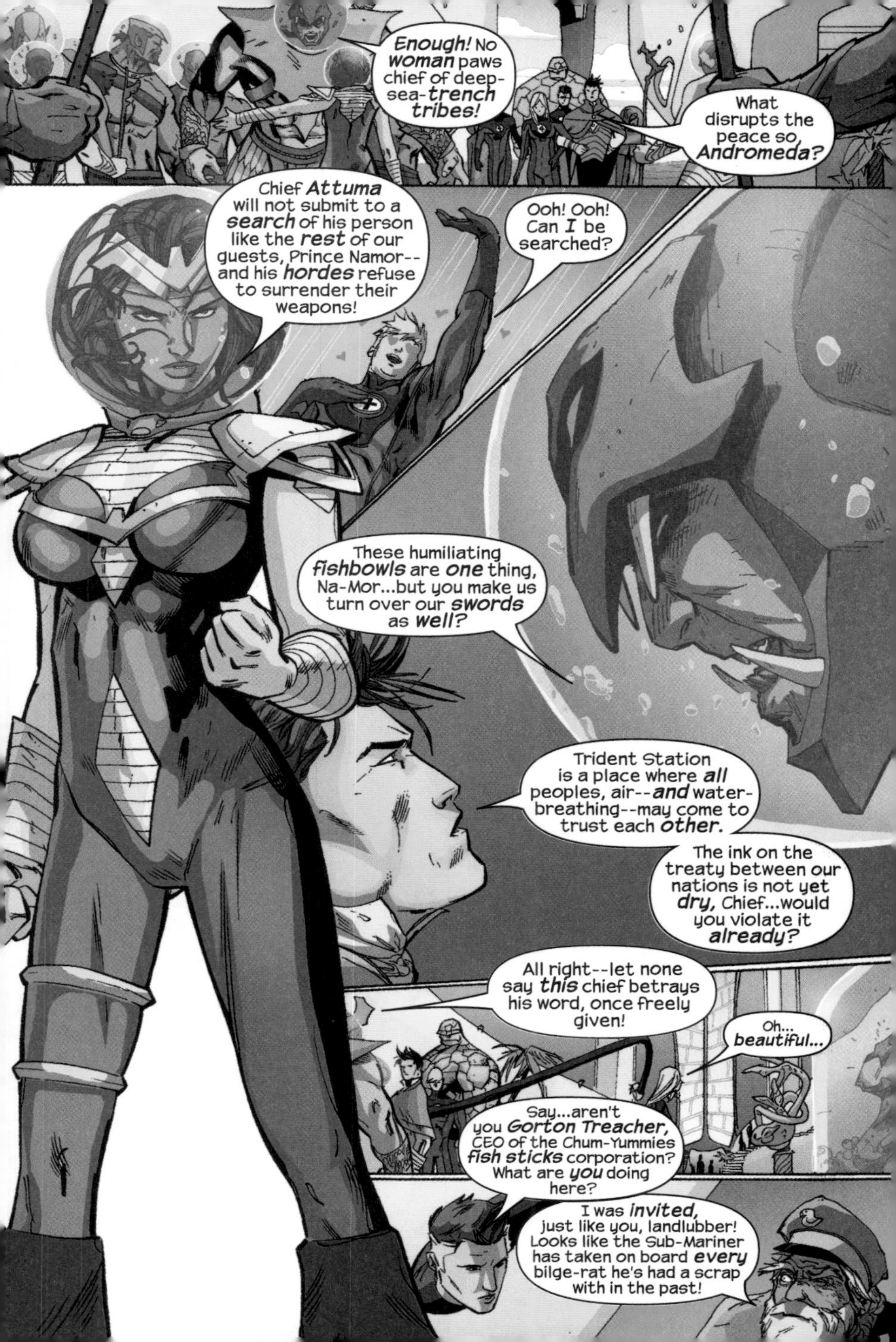

Enough! No woman paws chief of deep-sea-trench tribes!
What disrupts the peace so, Andromeda?
Chief Attuma will not submit to a search of his person like the rest of our guests, Prince Namor--and his hordes refuse to surrender their weapons!
Ooh! Ooh! Can I be searched?
These humiliating fishbowls are one thing, Na-Mor...but you make us turn over our swords as well?
Trident Station is a place where all peoples, air--and water-breathing--may come to trust each other.
The ink on the treaty between our nations is not yet dry, Chief...would you violate it already?
All right--let none say this chief betrays his word, once freely given!
Oh... beautiful...
Say...aren't you Gorton Treacher, CEO of the Chum-Yummies fish sticks corporation? What are you doing here?
I was invited, just like you, landlubber! Looks like the Sub-Mariner has taken on board every bilge-rat he's had a scrap with in the past!

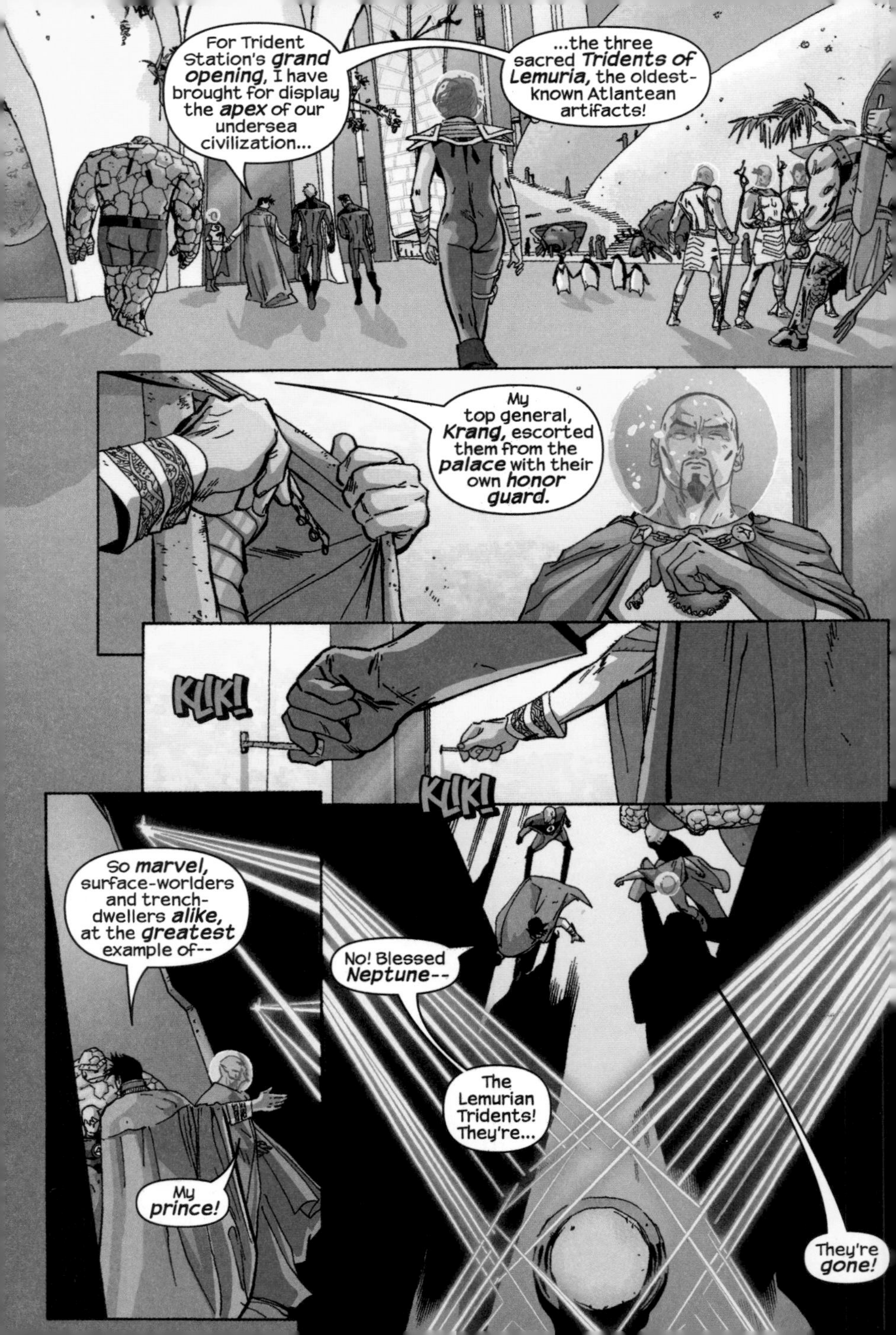
For Trident Station's grand opening, I have brought for display the apex of our undersea civilization...
...the three sacred Tridents of Lemuria, the oldest-known Atlantean artifacts!
My top general, Krang, escorted them from the palace with their own honor guard.
KLIK!
KLIK!
So marvel, surface-worlders and trench-dwellers alike, at the greatest example of--
My prince!
No! Blessed Neptune--
The Lemurian Tridents! They're...
They're gone!

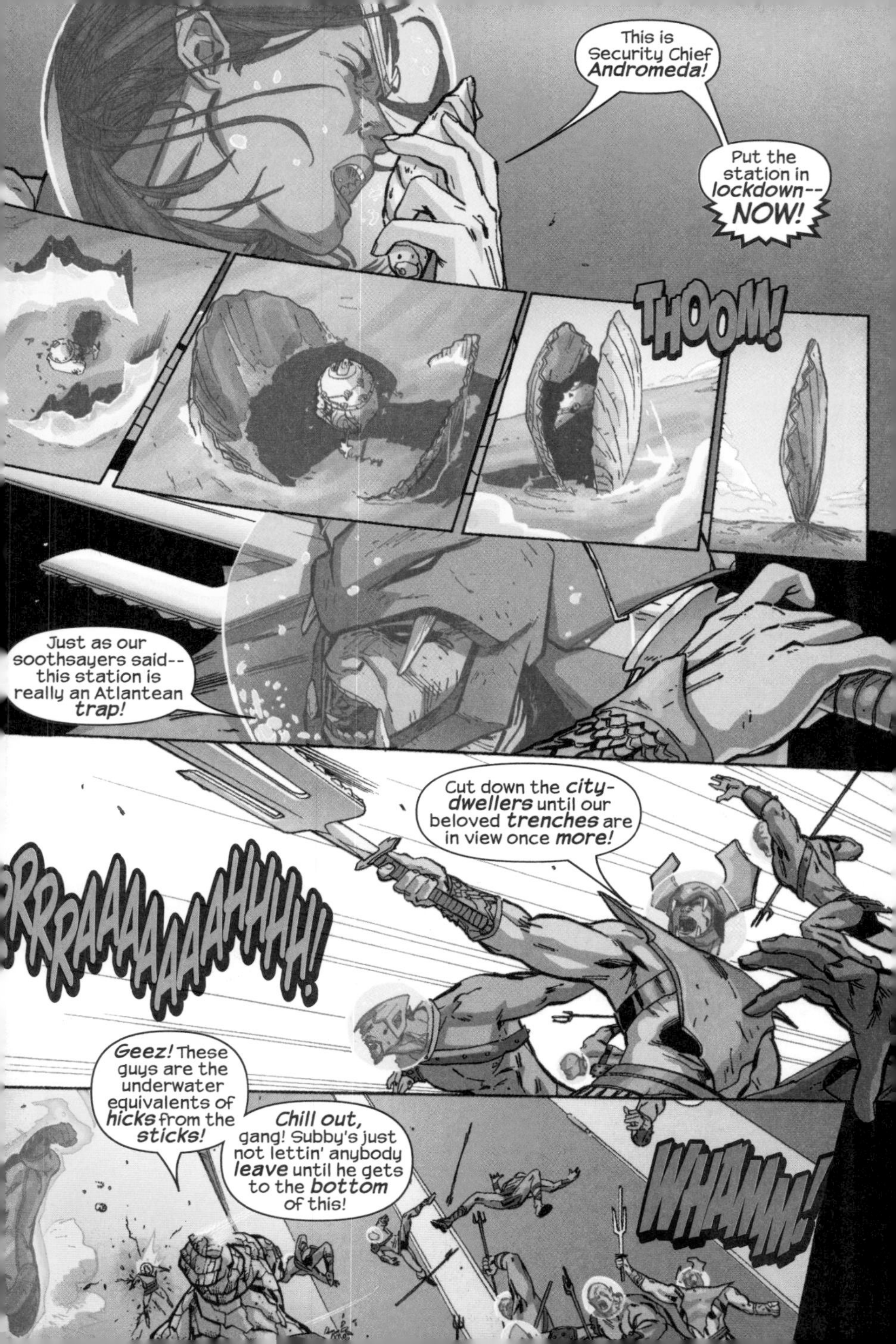

This is Security Chief Andromeda!
Put the station in lockdown-- NOW!
THOOM!
Just as our soothsayers said-- this station is really an Atlantean trap!
Cut down the city-dwellers until our beloved trenches are in view once more!
RRRAAAAAAAAHHHH!
Geez! These guys are the underwater equivalents of hicks from the sticks!
Chill out, gang! Subby's just not lettin' anybody leave until he gets to the bottom of this!
WHAMM!

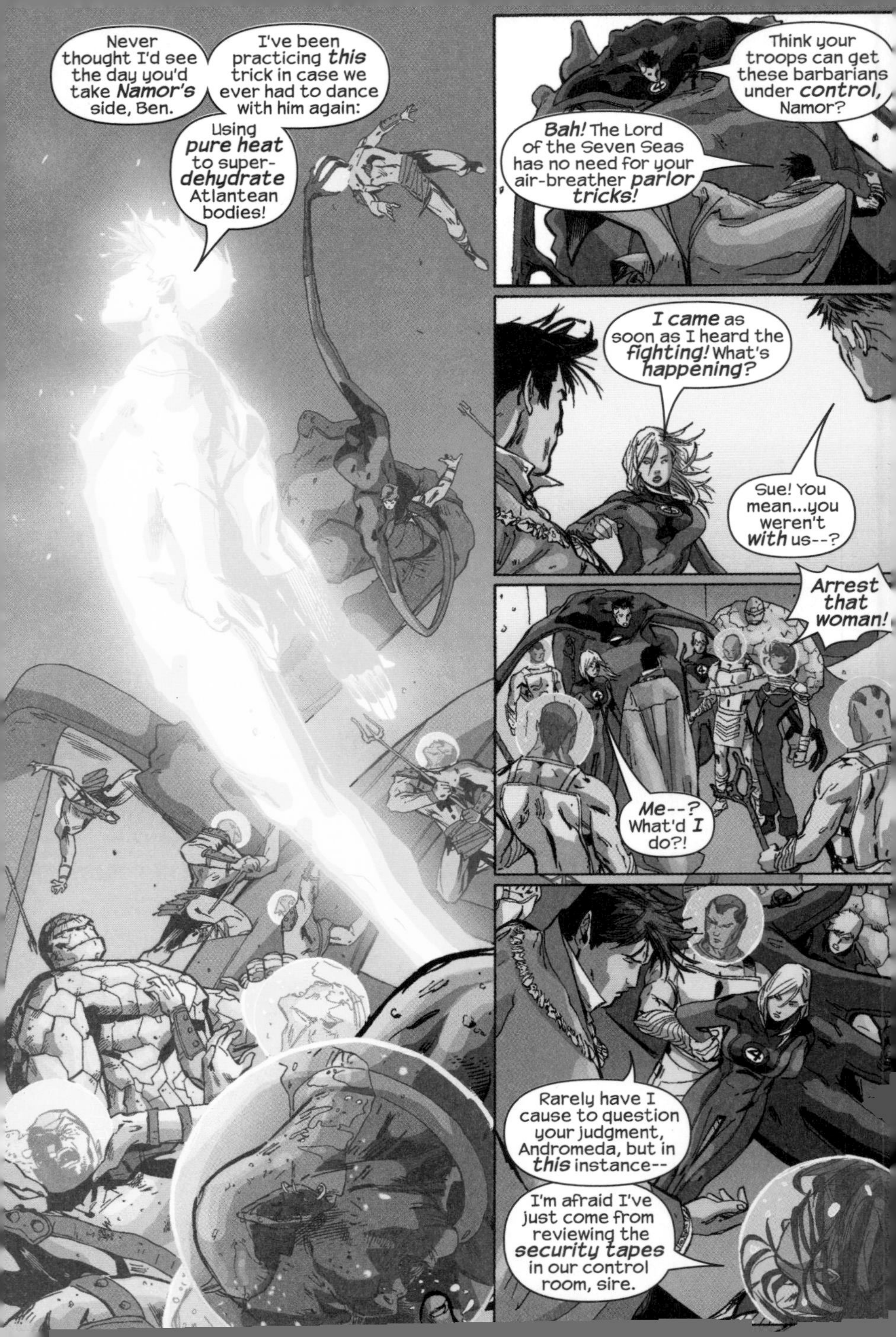

Never thought I'd see the day you'd take Namor's side, Ben.
I've been practicing this trick in case we ever had to dance with him again:
Using pure heat to super-dehydrate Atlantean bodies!
Think your troops can get these barbarians under control, Namor?
Bah! The Lord of the Seven Seas has no need for your air-breather parlor tricks!
I came as soon as I heard the fighting! What's happening?
Sue! You mean...you weren't with us--?
Arrest that woman!
Me--? What'd I do?!
Rarely have I cause to question your judgment, Andromeda, but in this instance--
I'm afraid I've just come from reviewing the security tapes in our control room, sire.

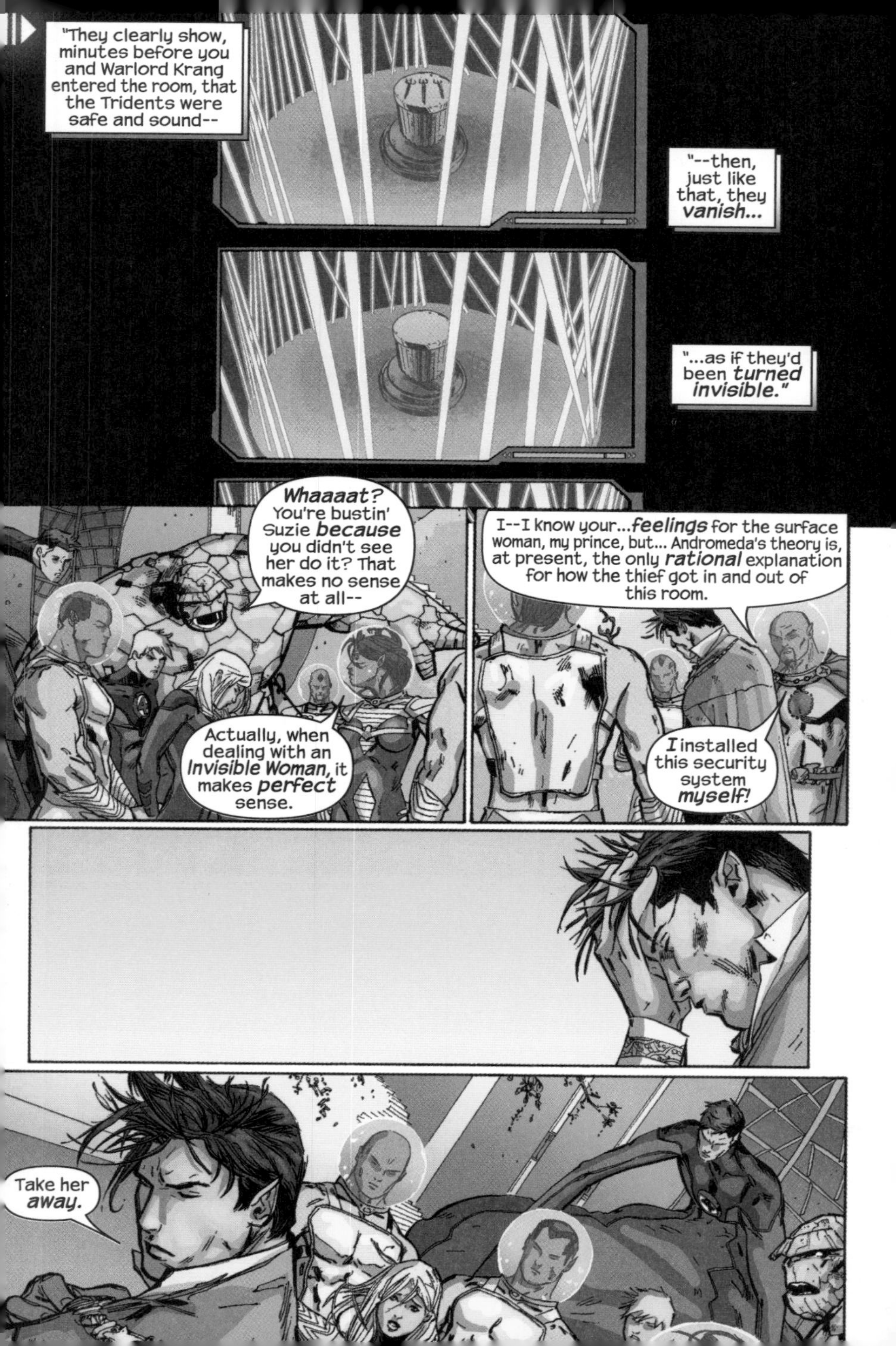
"They clearly show, minutes before you and Warlord Krang entered the room, that the Tridents were safe and sound--
"--then, just like that, they vanish...
"...as if they'd been turned invisible."
Whaaaat? You're bustin' Suzie because you didn't see her do it? That makes no sense at all--
Actually, when dealing with an Invisible Woman, it makes perfect sense.
I--I know your...feelings for the surface woman, my prince, but... Andromeda's theory is, at present, the only rational explanation for how the thief got in and out of this room.
I installed this security system myself!
Take her away.

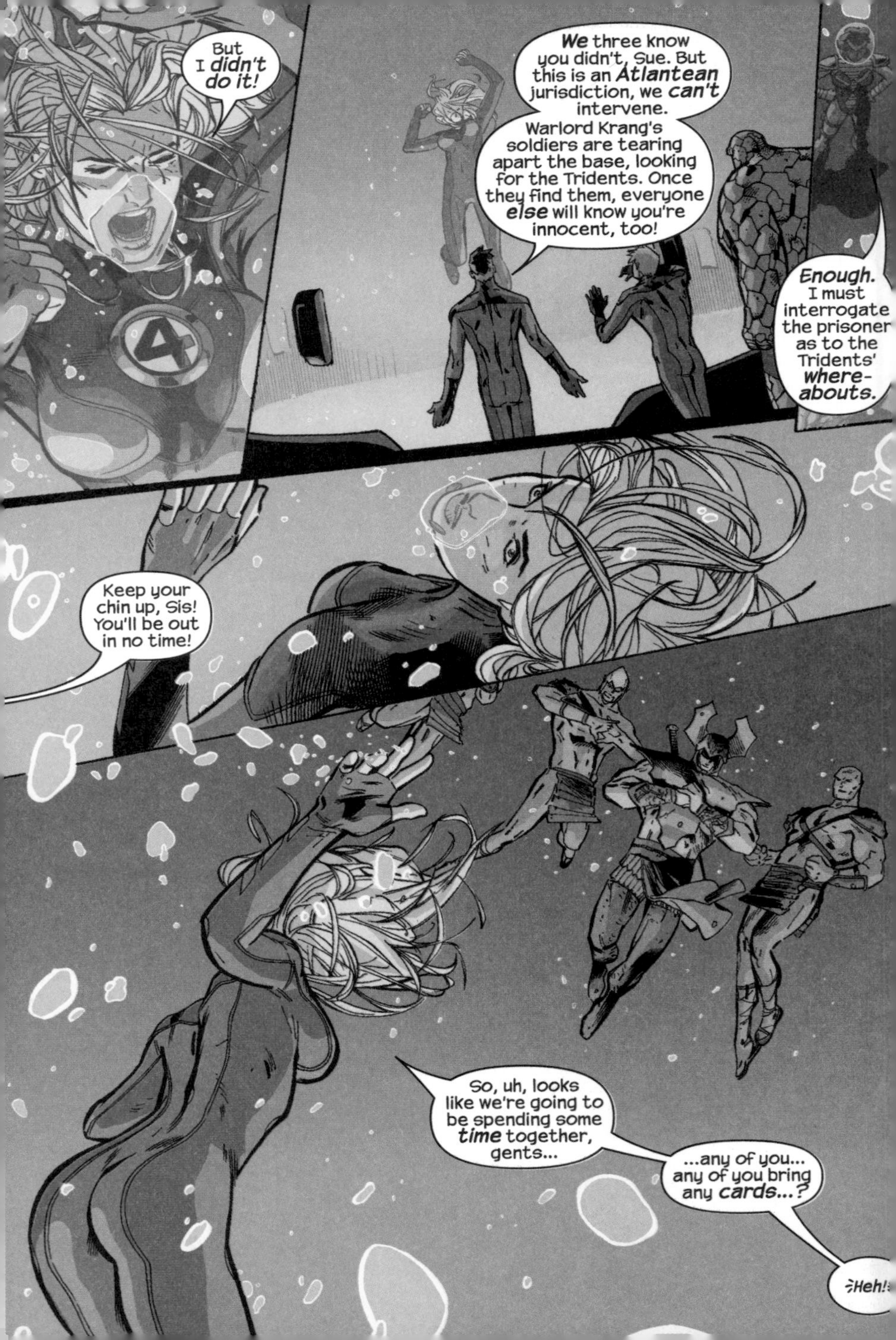

But I didn't do it!
We three know you didn't, Sue. But this is an Atlantean jurisdiction, we can't intervene.
Warlord Krang's soldiers are tearing apart the base, looking for the Tridents. Once they find them, everyone else will know you're innocent, too!
Enough. I must interrogate the prisoner as to the Tridents' whereabouts.
Keep your chin up, Sis! You'll be out in no time!
So, uh, looks like we're going to be spending some time together, gents...
...any of you... any of you bring any cards...?
Heh!

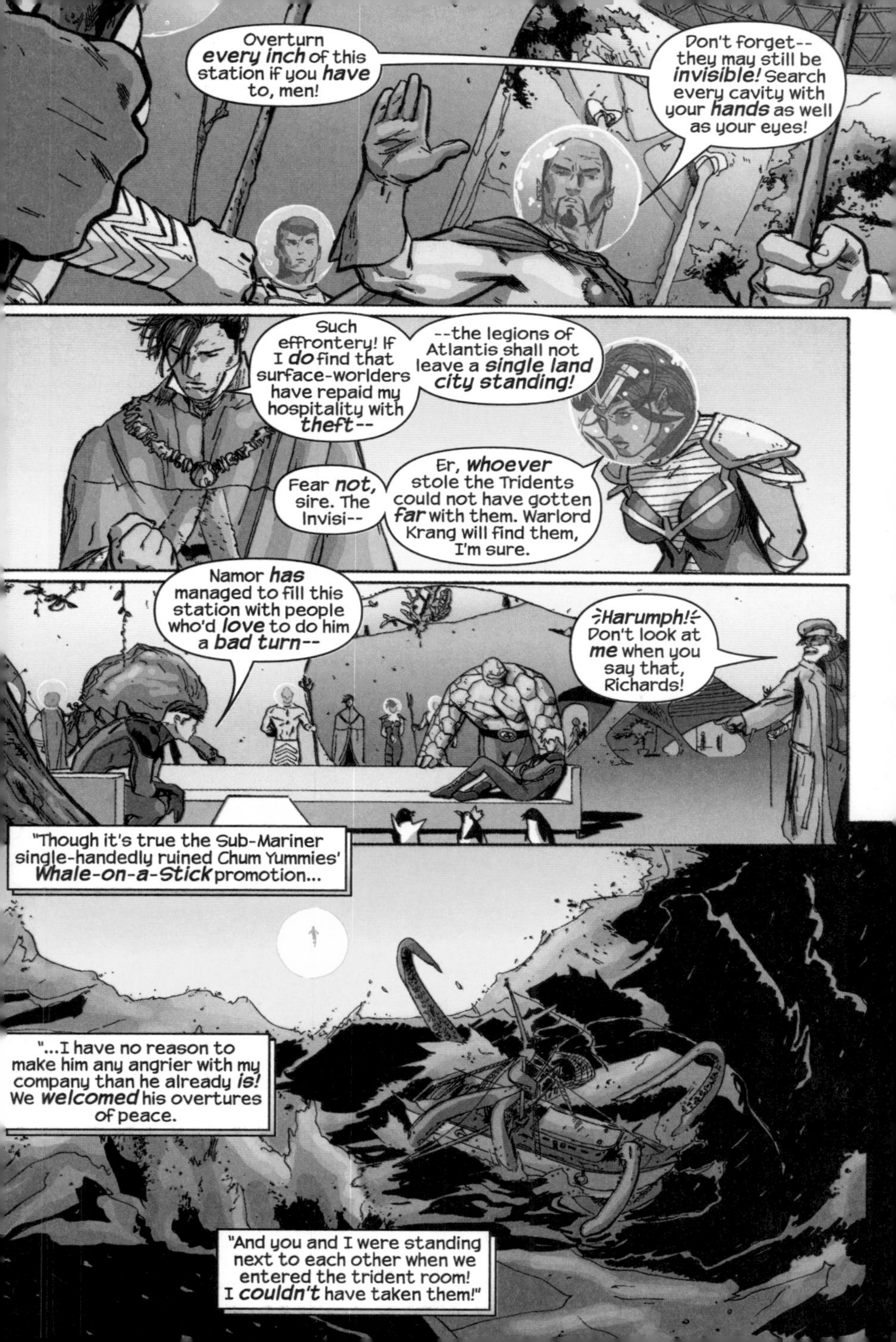

Overturn every inch of this station if you have to, men!
Don't forget-- they may still be invisible! Search every cavity with your hands as well as your eyes!
Such effrontery! If I do find that surface-worlders have repaid my hospitality with theft--
--the legions of Atlantis shall not leave a single land city standing!
Fear not, sire. The Invisi--
Er, whoever stole the Tridents could not have gotten far with them. Warlord Krang will find them, I'm sure.
Namor has managed to fill this station with people who'd love to do him a bad turn--
Harumph! Don't look at me when you say that, Richards!
"Though it's true the Sub-Mariner single-handedly ruined Chum Yummies' Whale-on-a-Stick promotion...
"...I have no reason to make him any angrier with my company than he already is! We welcomed his overtures of peace.
"And you and I were standing next to each other when we entered the trident room! I couldn't have taken them!"

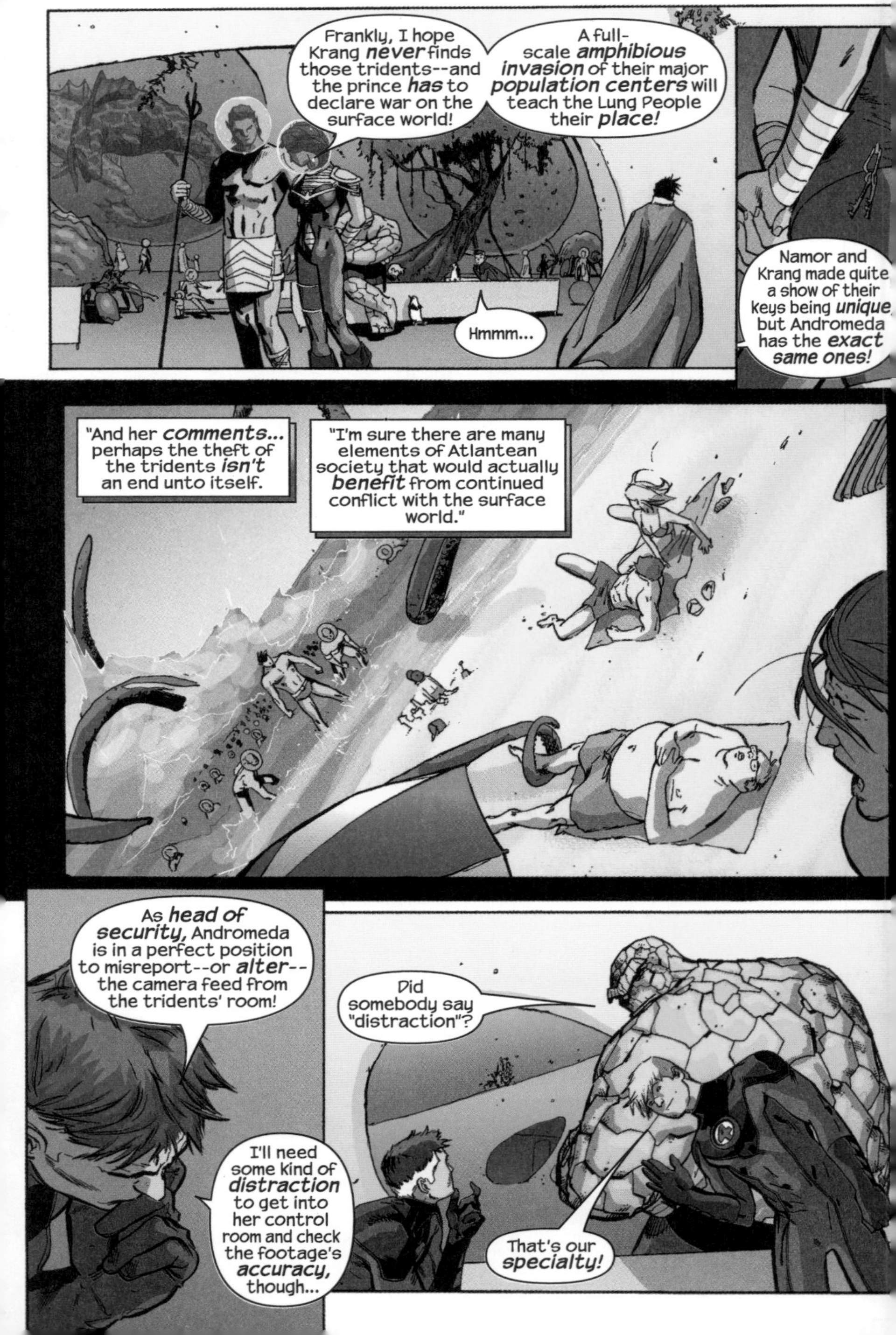
Frankly, I hope Krang *never* finds those tridents--and the prince *has* to declare war on the surface world!
A full-scale *amphibious invasion* of their major *population centers* will teach the Lung People their *place!*
Hmmm...
Namor and Krang made quite a show of their keys being *unique*, but Andromeda has the *exact same ones!*
"And her *comments...* perhaps the theft of the tridents *isn't* an end unto itself.
"I'm sure there are many elements of Atlantean society that would actually *benefit* from continued conflict with the surface world."
As *head of security,* Andromeda is in a perfect position to misreport--or *alter*-- the camera feed from the tridents' room!
I'll need some kind of *distraction* to get into her control room and check the footage's *accuracy,* though...
Did somebody say "distraction"?
That's our *specialty!*

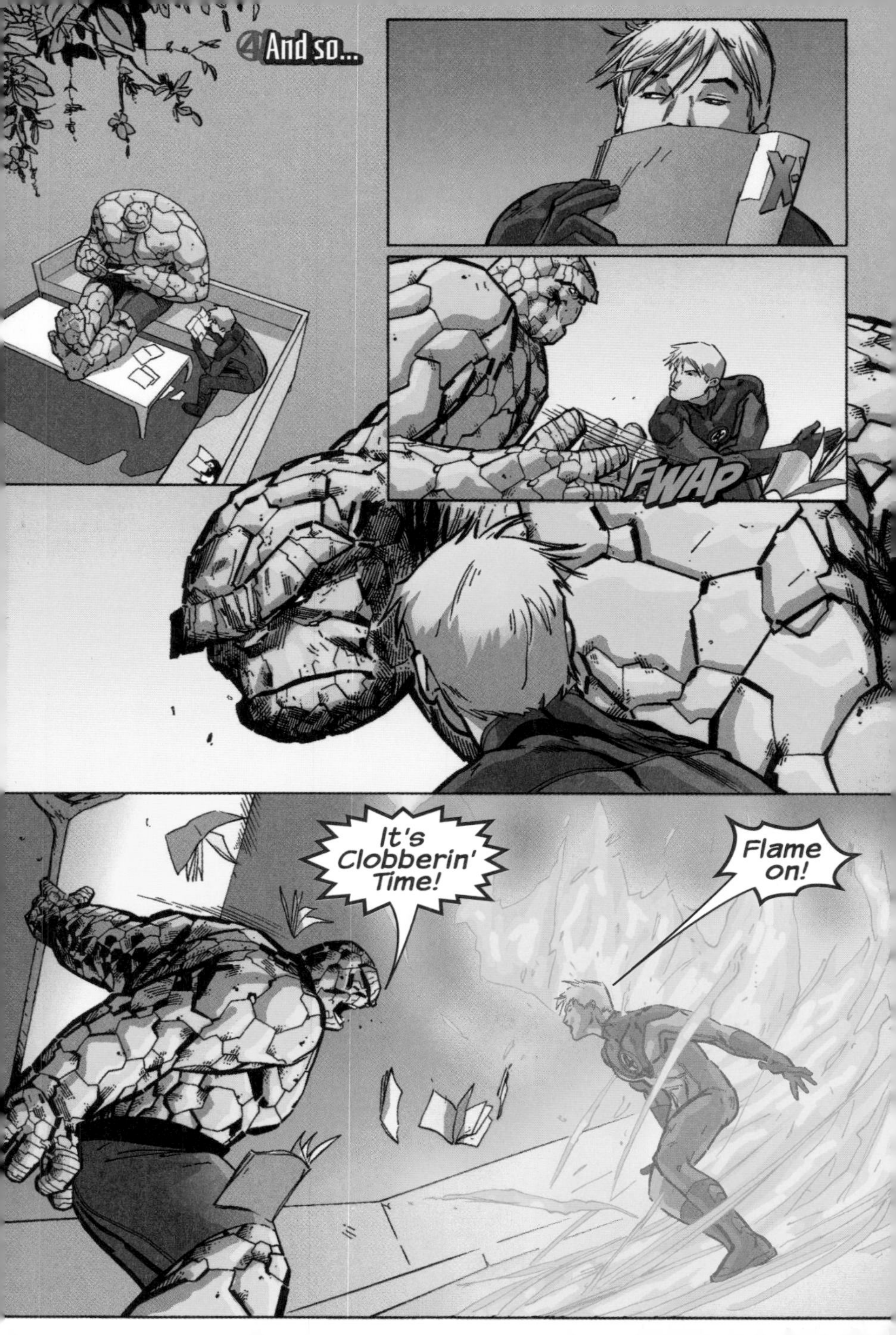
And so...
FWAP
It's Clobberin' Time!
Flame on!

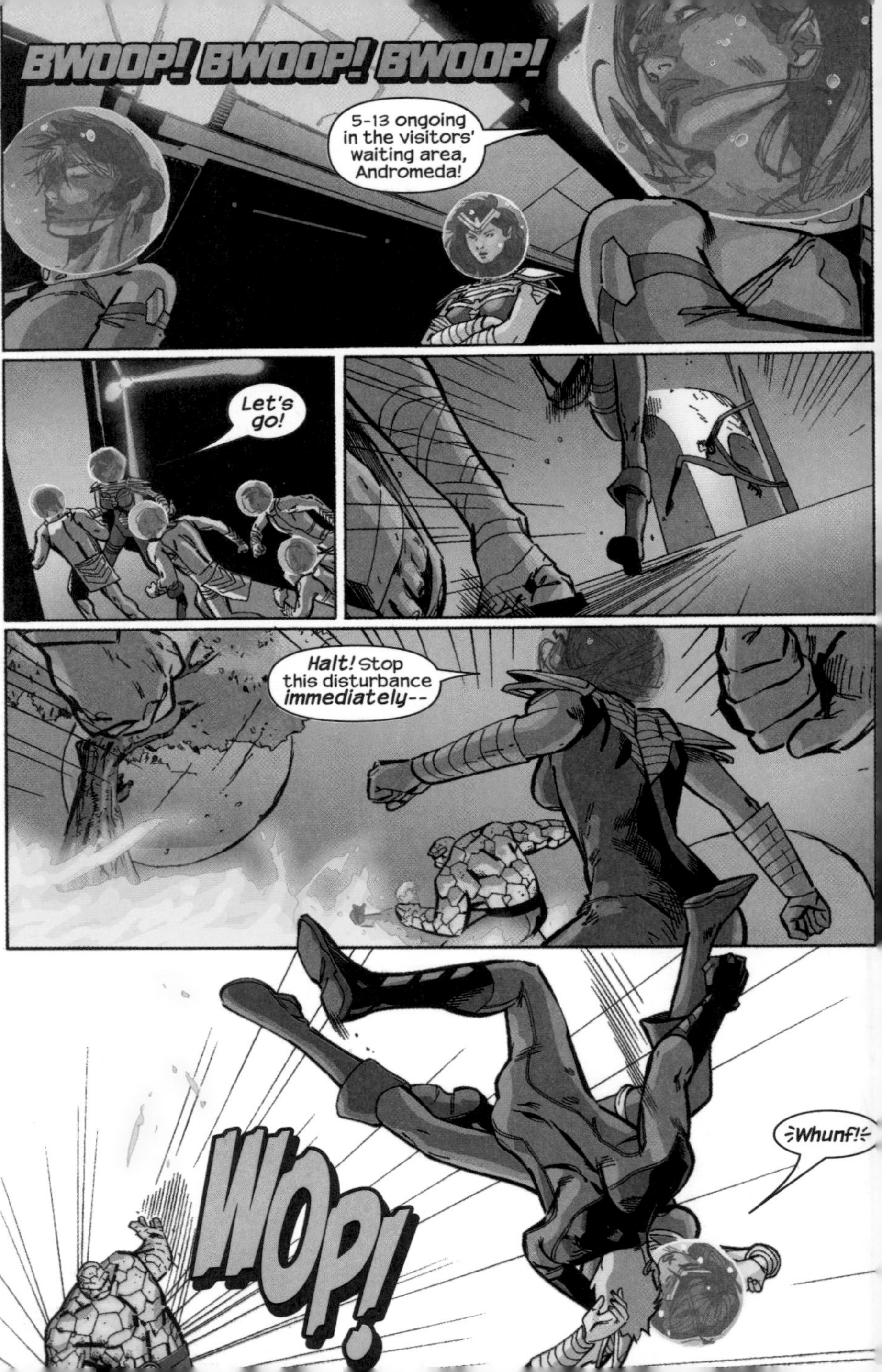
BWOOP! BWOOP! BWOOP!
5-13 ongoing in the visitors' waiting area, Andromeda!
Let's go!
Halt! Stop this disturbance immediately--
WOP!
Whunf!

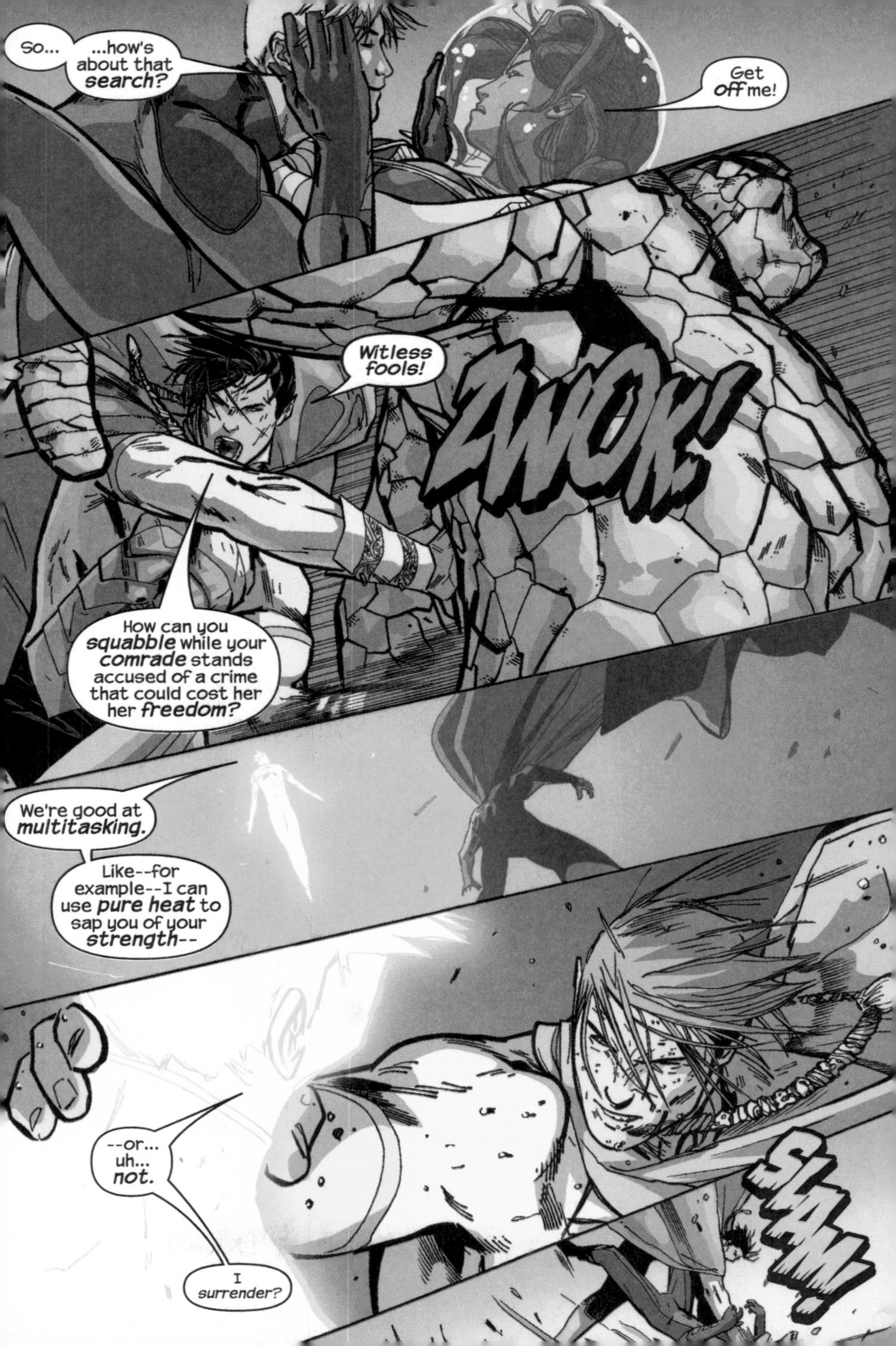
So...
...how's about that search?
Get off me!
Witless fools!
ZWOK!
How can you squabble while your comrade stands accused of a crime that could cost her her freedom?
We're good at multitasking.
Like--for example--I can use pure heat to sap you of your strength--
--or... uh... not.
I surrender?
SLAM!

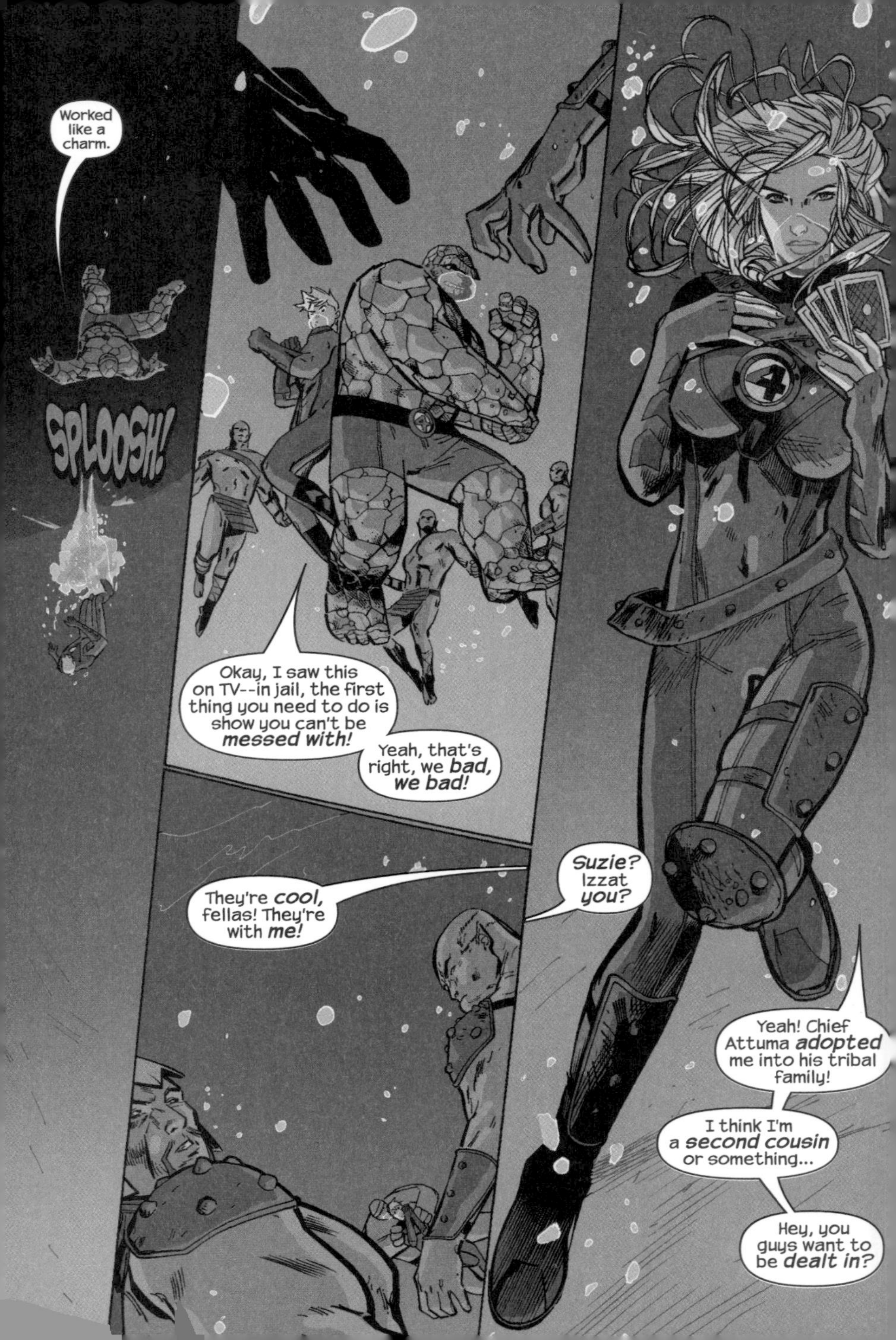

Worked like a charm.
SPLOOSH!
Okay, I saw this on TV--in jail, the first thing you need to do is show you can't be messed with!
Yeah, that's right, we bad, we bad!
They're cool, fellas! They're with me!
Suzie? Izzat you?
Yeah! Chief Attuma adopted me into his tribal family!
I think I'm a second cousin or something...
Hey, you guys want to be dealt in?

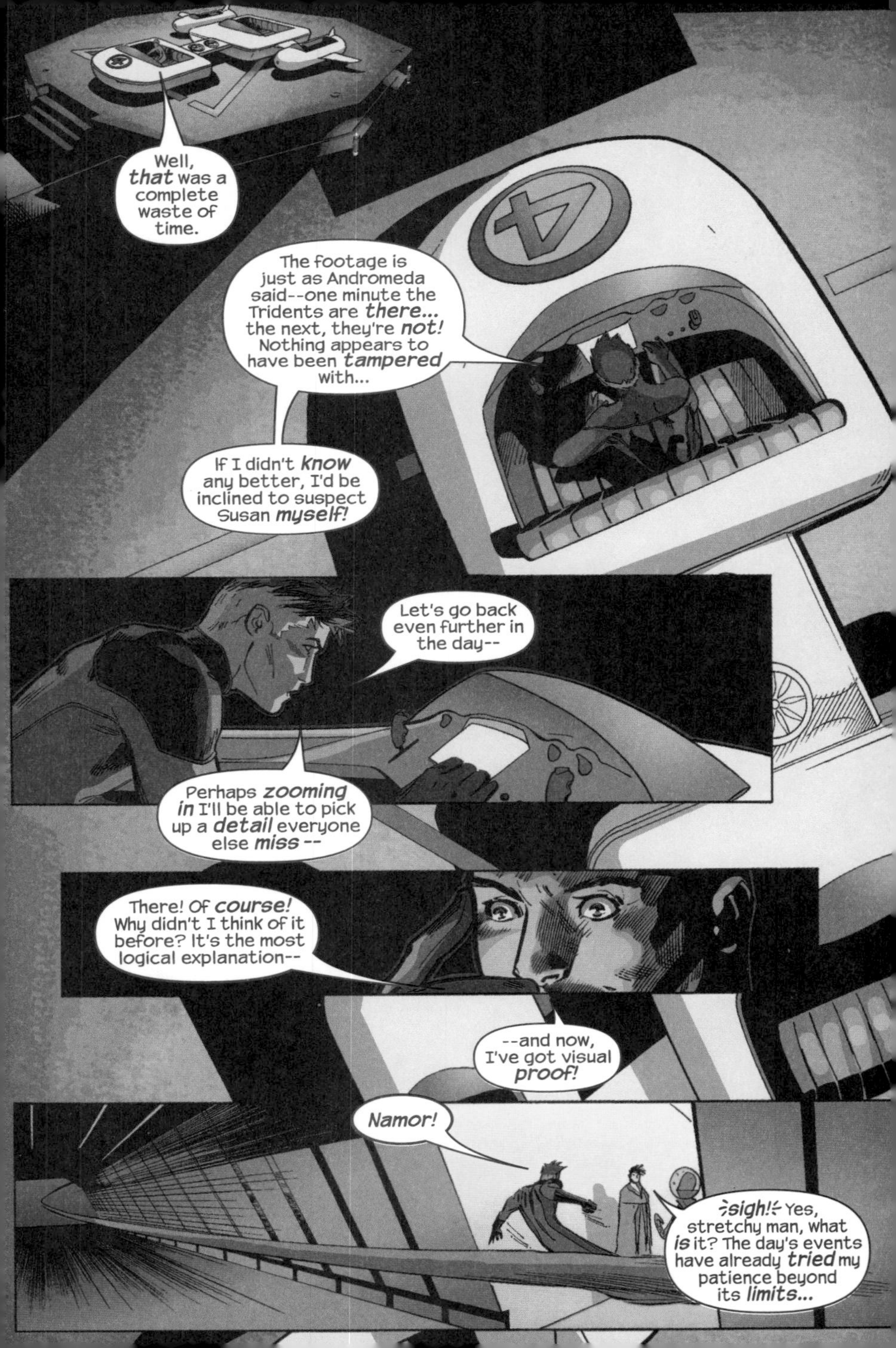
Well, *that* was a complete waste of time.
The footage is just as Andromeda said--one minute the Tridents are *there...* the next, they're *not!* Nothing appears to have been *tampered* with...
If I didn't *know* any better, I'd be inclined to suspect Susan *myself!*
Let's go back even further in the day--
Perhaps *zooming in* I'll be able to pick up a *detail* everyone else *miss --*
There! Of *course!* Why didn't I think of it before? It's the most logical explanation--
--and now, I've got visual *proof!*
Namor!
sigh! Yes, stretchy man, what *is* it? The day's events have already *tried* my patience beyond its *limits...*

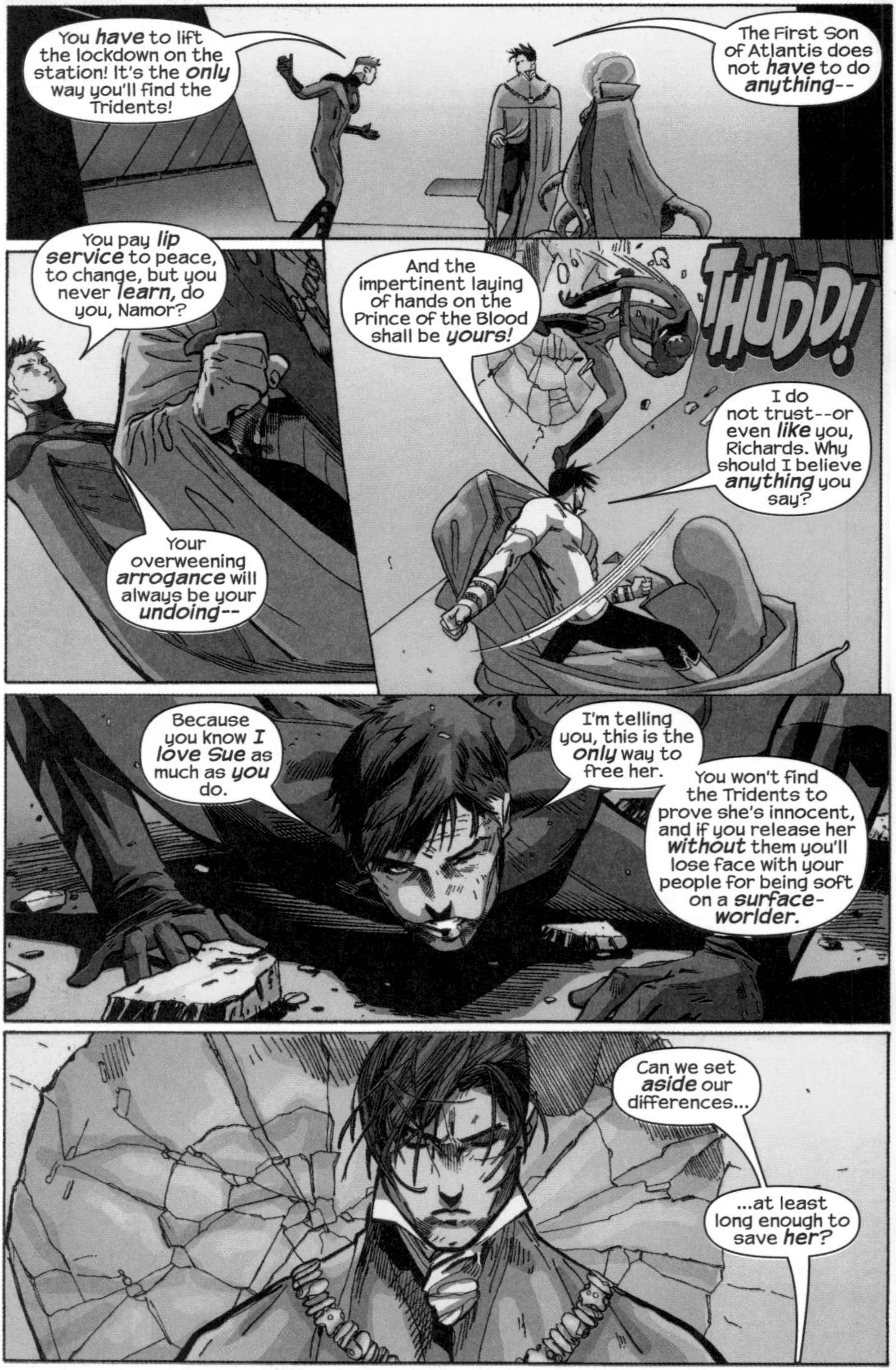
You have to lift the lockdown on the station! It's the only way you'll find the Tridents!
The First Son of Atlantis does not have to do anything--
You pay lip service to peace, to change, but you never learn, do you, Namor?
Your overweening arrogance will always be your undoing--
And the impertinent laying of hands on the Prince of the Blood shall be yours!
THUDD!
I do not trust--or even like you, Richards. Why should I believe anything you say?
Because you know I love Sue as much as you do.
I'm telling you, this is the only way to free her.
You won't find the Tridents to prove she's innocent, and if you release her without them you'll lose face with your people for being soft on a surface-worlder.
Can we set aside our differences...
...at least long enough to save her?

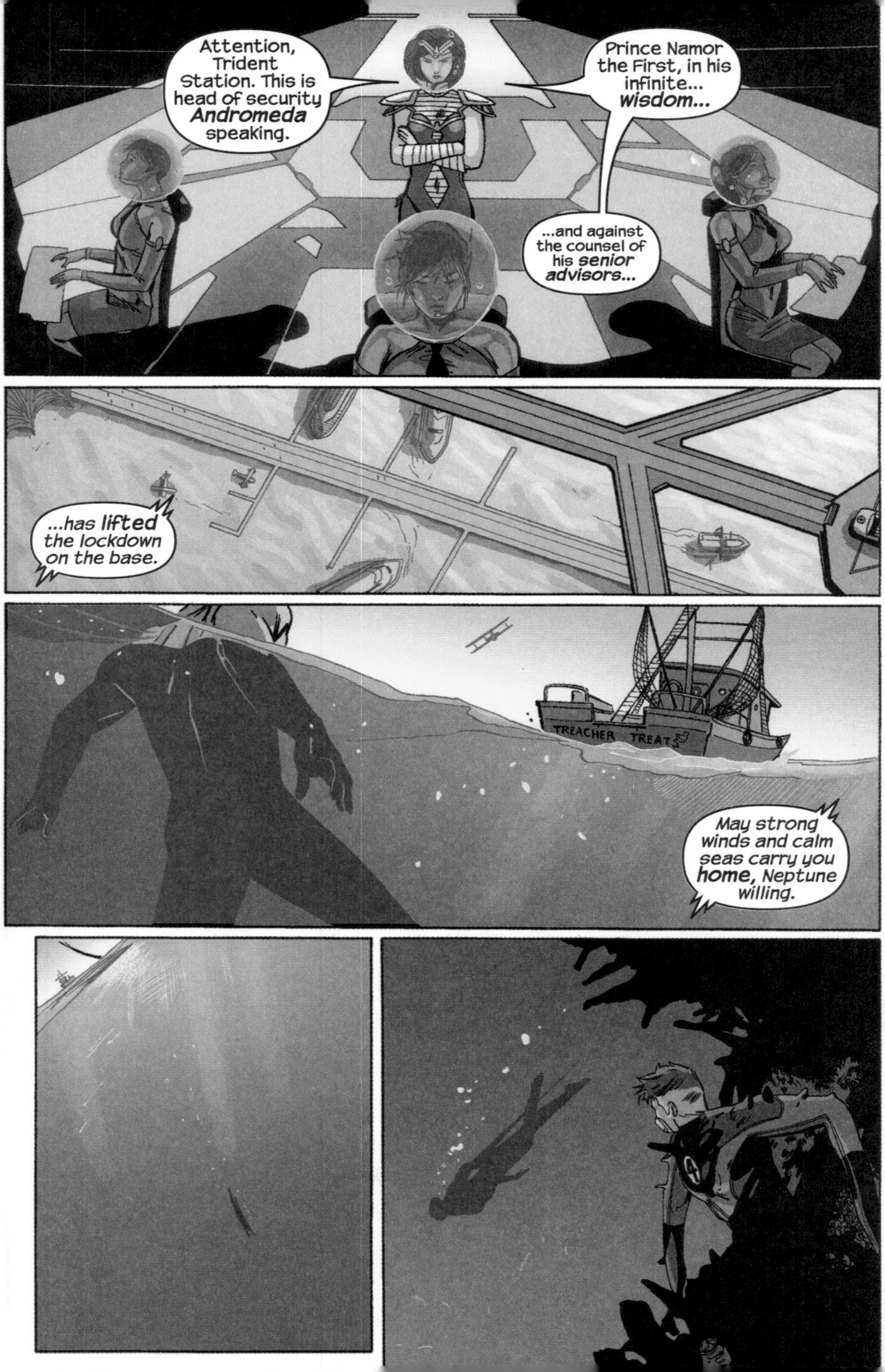
Attention, Trident Station. This is head of security Andromeda speaking.
Prince Namor the First, in his infinite... wisdom...
...and against the counsel of his senior advisors...
...has lifted the lockdown on the base.
TREACHER TREATS
May strong winds and calm seas carry you home, Neptune willing.

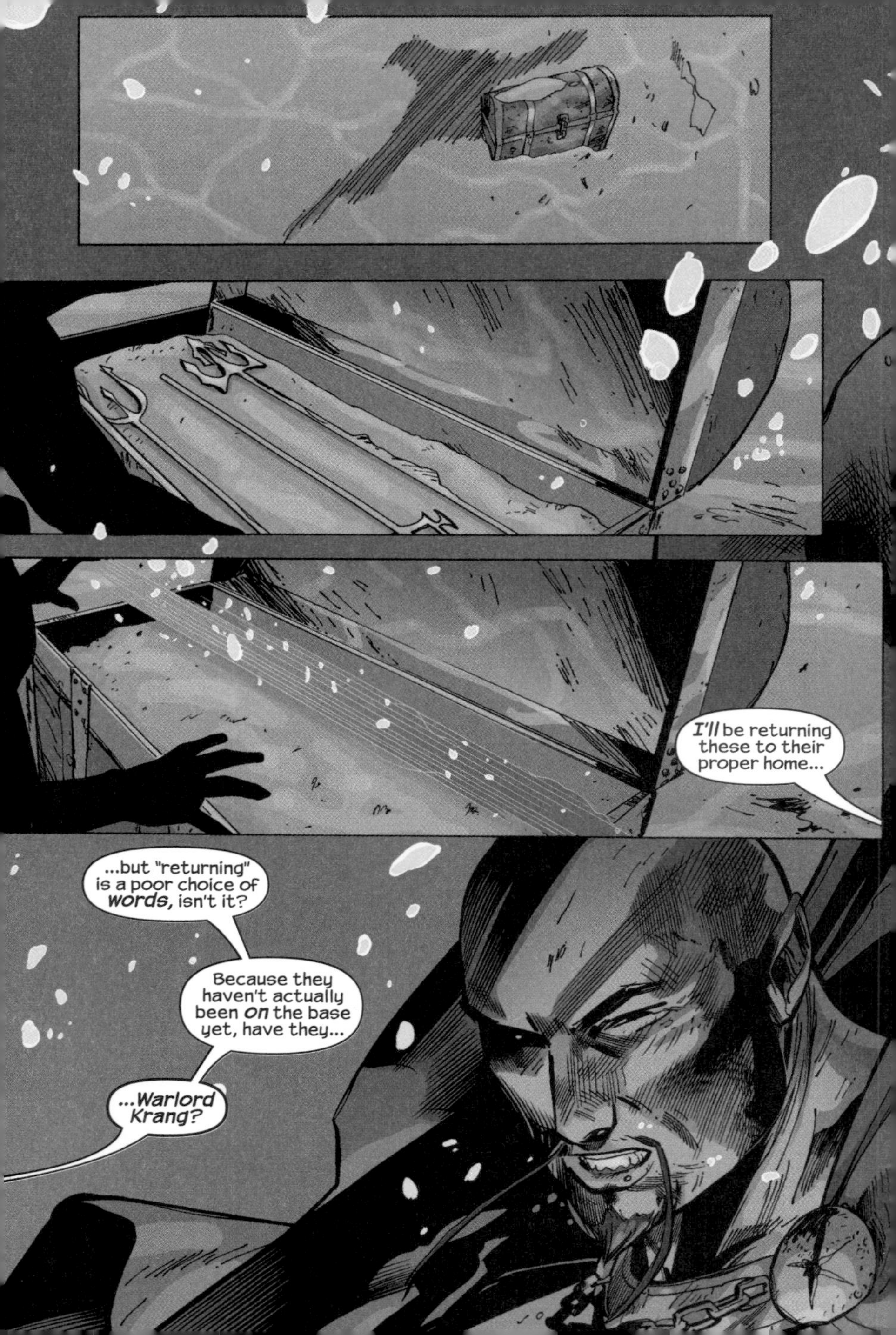
I'll be returning these to their proper home...
...but "returning" is a poor choice of words, isn't it?
Because they haven't actually been on the base yet, have they...
...Warlord Krang?

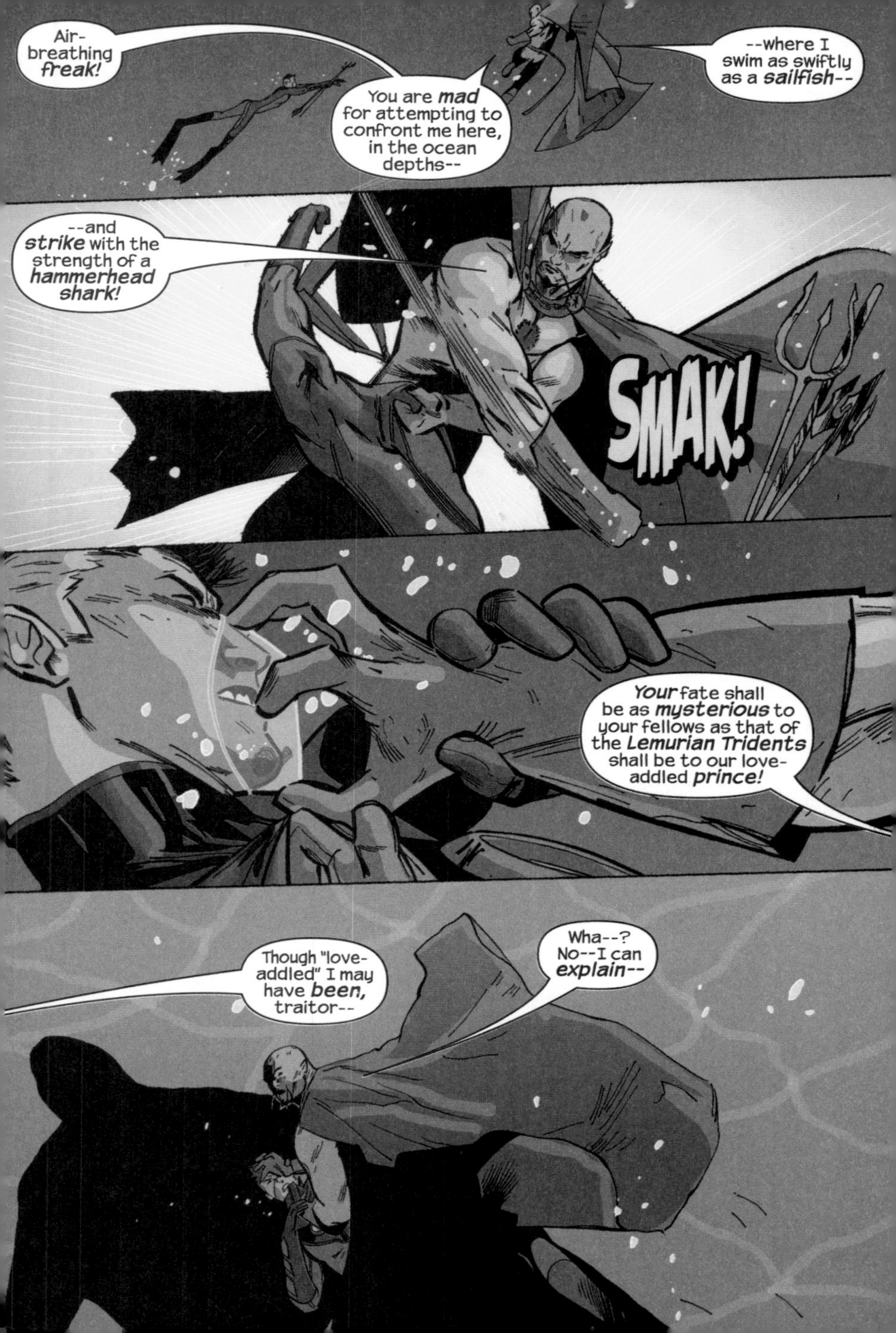
Air-breathing freak!
You are mad for attempting to confront me here, in the ocean depths--
--where I swim as swiftly as a sailfish--
--and strike with the strength of a hammerhead shark!
SMAK!
Your fate shall be as mysterious to your fellows as that of the Lemurian Tridents shall be to our love-addled prince!
Though "love-addled" I may have been, traitor--
Wha--? No--I can explain--

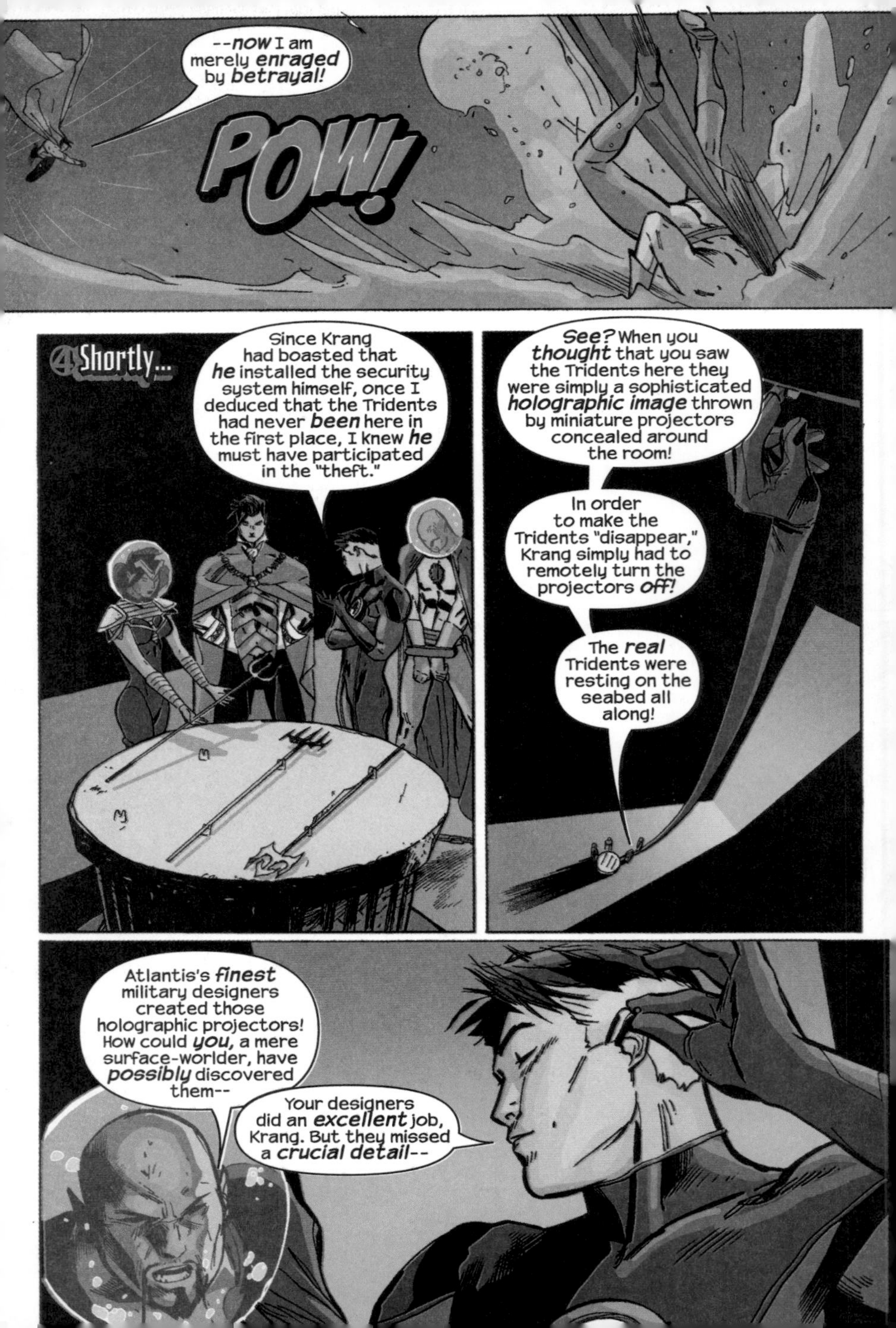
--now I am merely enraged by betrayal!
POW!
Shortly...
Since Krang had boasted that he installed the security system himself, once I deduced that the Tridents had never been here in the first place, I knew he must have participated in the "theft."
See? When you thought that you saw the Tridents here they were simply a sophisticated holographic image thrown by miniature projectors concealed around the room!
In order to make the Tridents "disappear," Krang simply had to remotely turn the projectors off!
The real Tridents were resting on the seabed all along!
Atlantis's finest military designers created those holographic projectors! How could you, a mere surface-worlder, have possibly discovered them--
Your designers did an excellent job, Krang. But they missed a crucial detail--

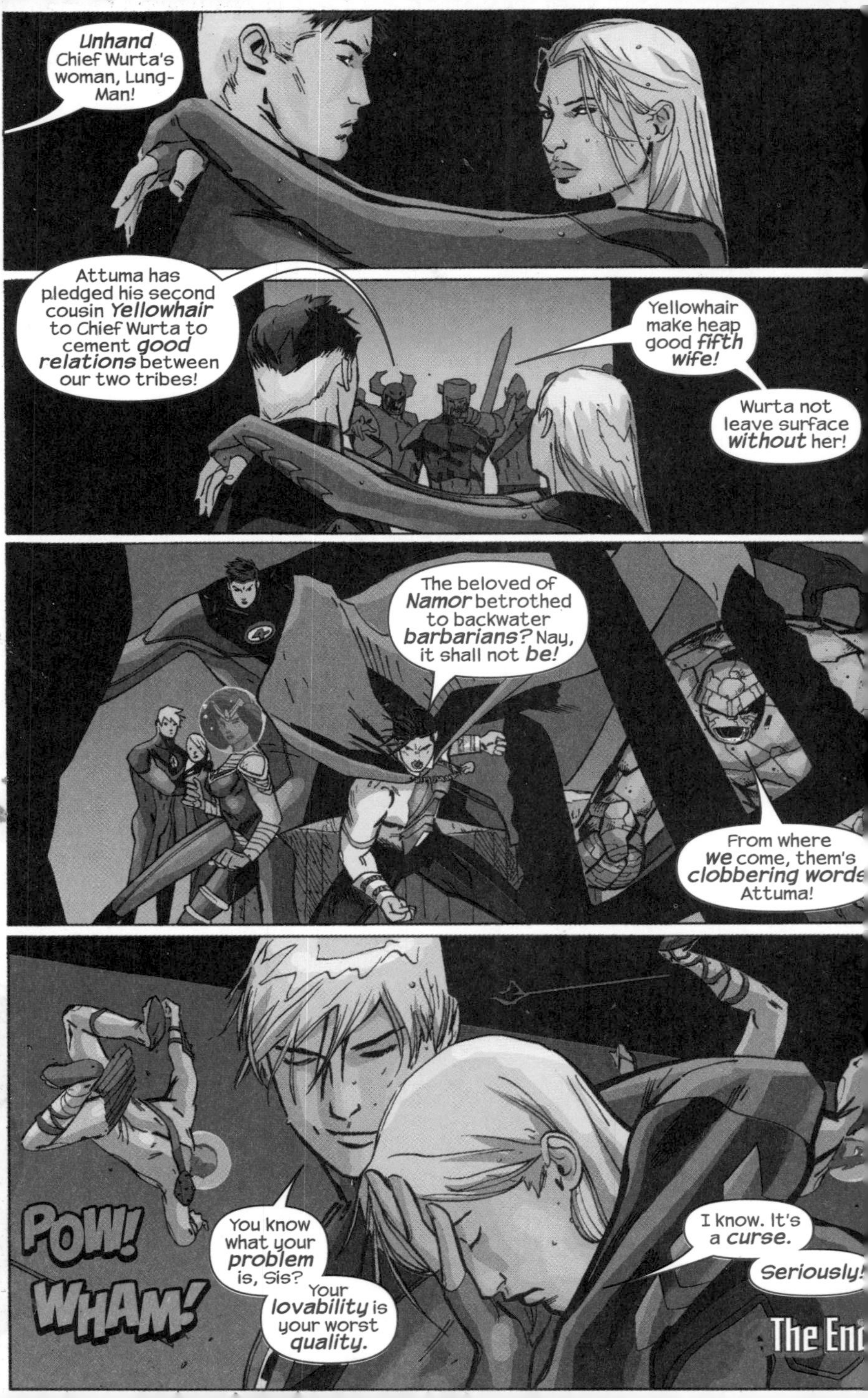
Unhand Chief Wurta's woman, Lung-Man!
Attuma has pledged his second cousin Yellowhair to Chief Wurta to cement good relations between our two tribes!
Yellowhair make heap good fifth wife!
Wurta not leave surface without her!
The beloved of Namor betrothed to backwater barbarians? Nay, it shall not be!
From where we come, them's clobbering words
Attuma!
POW!
WHAM!
You know what your problem is, Sis?
Your lovability is your worst quality.
I know. It's a curse.
Seriously!
The En

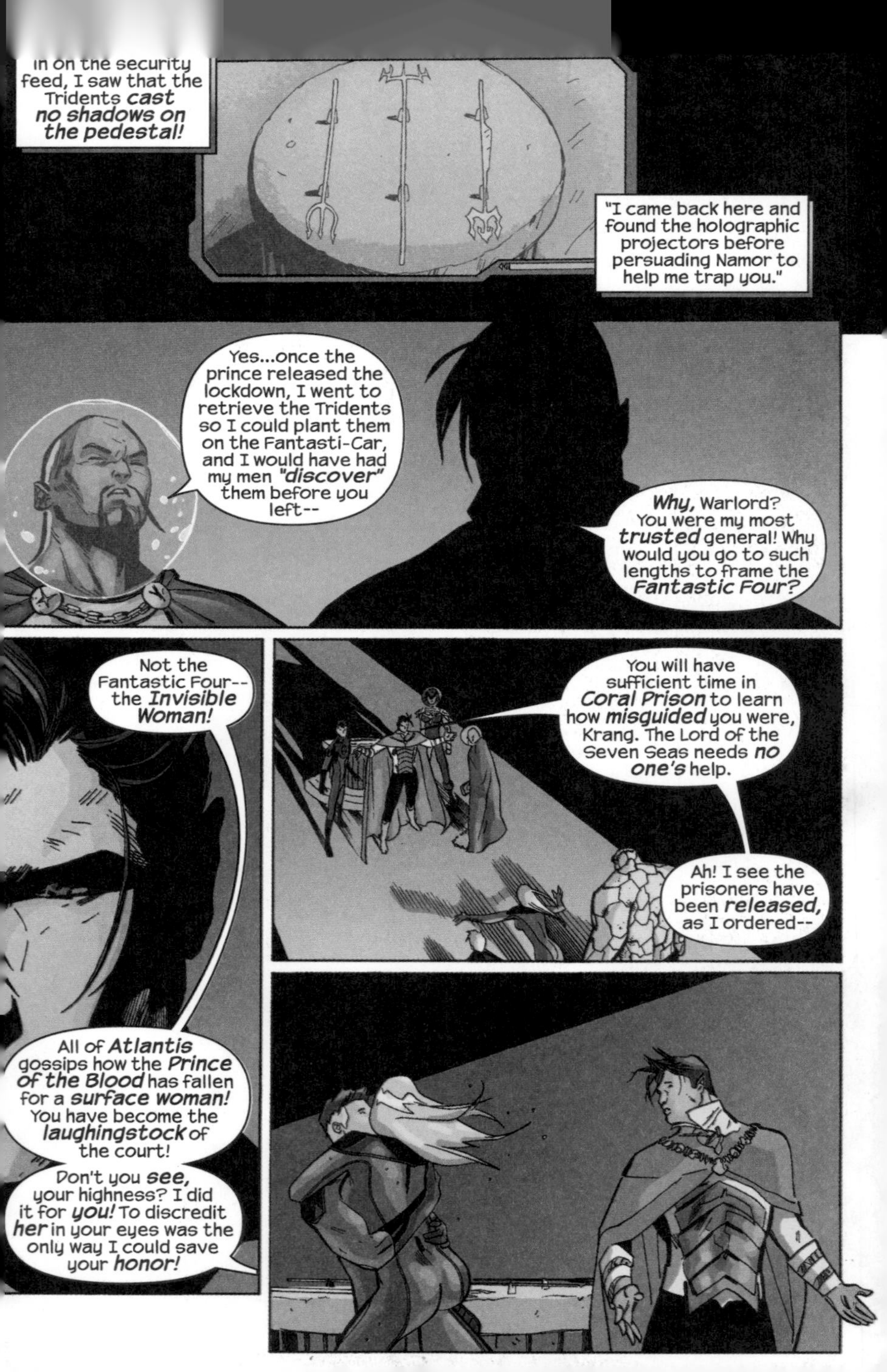
in on the security feed, I saw that the Tridents cast no shadows on the pedestal!
"I came back here and found the holographic projectors before persuading Namor to help me trap you."
Yes...once the prince released the lockdown, I went to retrieve the Tridents so I could plant them on the Fantasti-Car, and I would have had my men "discover" them before you left--
Why, Warlord? You were my most trusted general! Why would you go to such lengths to frame the Fantastic Four?
Not the Fantastic Four-- the Invisible Woman!
You will have sufficient time in Coral Prison to learn how misguided you were, Krang. The Lord of the Seven Seas needs no one's help.
Ah! I see the prisoners have been released, as I ordered--
All of Atlantis gossips how the Prince of the Blood has fallen for a surface woman! You have become the laughingstock of the court!
Don't you see, your highness? I did it for you! To discredit her in your eyes was the only way I could save your honor!